The River

A Spiritually Transforming Journey

The River

A Spiritually Transforming Journey

BETTY A. RODGERS-KULICH

XULON PRESS

Xulon Press
2301 Lucien Way #415
Maitland, FL 32751
407.339.4217
www.xulonpress.com

Unless otherwise indicated, Scripture quotations taken from the Word English Bible (WEB)—*public domain*.

Printed in the United States of America.

ISBN-13: 978-1-6305-0538-7

Table of Contents

Introduction

God will go to any length to set up an encounter with us. He will use natural and supernatural means of His choosing. Our responsibility is to recognize His hand at work, then choose to cooperate with the steps He lays in front of us in order to connect us to His intended destiny.

This book, "The River" is a step of obedience to cooperate with my destiny that God has been laying out for over twenty years. Since 2001, God has given me prophetic words about writing. In 2018 after a prompting from the Lord that it was time to dust off those words, I began asking God and listening for clear direction in how to cooperate with those words. The Lord led me to revisit some old journal entries. I had learned about journaling through a class taught by Dr. Mark Virkler (www.cwg-ministries.org) on "How to Hear God's Voice" and I have continued the practice for two decades. The genesis of the book came from three different journal entries written in different years. These journal entries became the foundational story line of the book.

During my review of the specific entries, the Lord quickened me to type them out using a fictional character I called Melissa. Melissa took on a life of her own and God continued where my journal entries left off, crafting this fictional novel. As I yielded to the story line that Holy Spirit continued to give me, I found many of my own past experiences played out through Melissa's character. As the Lord give me spiritual pictures that would appear like a movie upon my mind, I would type what I saw and heard. God would pull out of my memories past fears, failures and disappointments, as well as deep desires to be used of God as He played out the story line of this book. I was transformed in areas of my inner walk with the Lord and I know that Holy Spirit will do the same for you as you read Melissa's spiritual journey.

May you encounter God through this book, so that your spiritual walk is transformed, and the Kingdom of God is advanced.

Blessings as you read,
Betty

Acknowledgements

Writing a book is seldom an entirely solitary endeavor regardless of the solitary hours the writer spends committing words to paper. I consider myself supremely blessed and fortunate that during my days and weeks alone in my office, I was not alone. I have a support team that was continually encouraging me to finish strong, because they believe in me but more importantly, they believe in the God who called me to write this book.

First of all, I am grateful to Father God, Jesus and Holy Spirit, who always desire to speak to us and to me. When I heard the words of the Father, "write this book, now", I knew His voice yet at the same time, I struggled with the concept of a fictional book. Thankfully I continued to listen, and He continued to speak and guide me through to the final word in the final chapter.

Thanks also to Dr. Mark Virkler, Author of the teaching book and seminar; "How to Hear God's Voice" (www.cwgministries.org). Your seminar set me on the pathway to train my ears to hear the voice of God more than twenty years ago.

To Rick Kulich, my loving husband of 47 years, I'm grateful for your encouragement, support and your tireless editing. You are always willing to be my unseen assistant at the ready, helping me find a word or key words and open my thoughts with phrasing suggestions to improve the manuscript. You added color to the book and my life.

To Millie Jarvis and Lynda Shults, Thank-you for being the first readers/ editors of the unedited version of the manuscript, all 400 pages! I'm sure it was a long slog and I'm grateful for your encouraging thoughts and the invaluable edits each of you submitted. You helped me improve as a writer.

To Dr. Rob McCorkle & Dr. Don Richter. I appreciate both of you for always taking the time to answer my pleas for help with how to get started in publishing. I am so glad you both subscribe to the idea that there are no stupid questions.

To Pastor Dwight & Pastor Tammy Bennett, my church family and friends who always encouraged me that I could write this book.

Thanks to my technical typing expert Deanna Ralph who tried to help me fix glitches in the manuscript document that I could not fix. You never tell me no because you are always ready to help!

To Michelle Gehrt for being a forerunner & encourager for me with your 52-week devotional – *Behold! God is Speaking to Us*. I'm glad you went first!

And finally, to Rocio Cancino for always telling me "Vamos, puedes hacer esto" and translating this book into Spanish.

Dedications

To all my family members who encouraged me to always take a risk with Jesus.

To my daughter Carrie, Son-in-law Sam, grandchildren Isaiah, Cailey, Jacob & Adelynn. May you always choose to follow after Jesus with all your heart and to find your own spiritual and transformational journey with Jesus.

To everyone who desires to know Jesus more intimately, experience the love of the Father, hear the voice of Holy Spirit and to one day join me at the Marriage Feast in the *City*!

Chapter 1

The Cathedral
A Day Like No Other
The Journey Begins

"Blessed are those whose strength is in You,
who have set their hearts on a pilgrimage." (1)
Psalm 84:5

"Through the gate and go out" Micah 2:13

It was a day that would radically change my life. A day like no other, brought me to an incredible journey. It was an adventure that transformed who I was into who I would become. It was a day that began changing me from the inside out and set me on a wonderfully different pathway. My life took a new direction that day and I would never be the same. It was the day I found the River.

A journey must begin somewhere, so let me tell you how I got to the River. Looking back, my journey was birthed from God orchestrated events in my life. I had not asked for these events, nor was I seeking. But God, the Father, knew what I needed to become fulfilled. As my creator, He knew what I needed to achieve purpose in my life.

I'm a school teacher and I had just ended a year from hell. My class room had been full of emotionally troubled kids. Kids raising themselves, mouthy and in your face. They were disrespectful and forced to attend but cut class on a whim. Despite this environment, I really wanted to help make a difference but grappled unsuccessfully with the power to do so. I felt frustrated and defeated. I just needed a summer break that was uneventful, stress-free and predictable. But even as I considered this, part of me wanted more. I was restless but didn't understand why. Deep down, I yearned for more than the daily grind, yet I was too fearful to go looking for it. Risk taking had not turned out well. Failures always seemed to follow, so security became my best option. I decided getting a little sun at the pool while reading a good spy novel would be enough.

I told myself that my life was good. But as soon as I had determined to enjoy the summer with a good book, an irritating restless flutter started to rise from deep inside. I shoved it back down.

Stepping out, doing something different, was too scary, to different, and to unpredictable. It would involve risk. The thought of change and risk stirred up fear. Fear was a familiar intimidator that I had come to know. I learned how to live with it and keep it in the closet most of the time. Keeping it locked up, I could live life safe, managed and controlled.

But if I was honest, I was torn between two opposites. It was like I had twins living inside of me. A safe twin and an adventurous twin. They spared for who would ultimately win control. My safe twin lectured the adventurous twin about risks. Although the adventurous twin had fascinating come backs, I would usually side with the safe and controlled twin. I told myself risks could lead to unplanned events. Unplanned events meant no control. No control was too scary. So, a quiet summer with a spy novel was the direction I would take.

That resolved, I decided to read emails and catch up on some long overdue communication with my adventurous best friend Jenny. Unlike me, Jenny had taken her wild and crazy inner twin's leading and had gone right from college to become a missionary in Germany. She had no real financial backers and no real established missionary connections. She followed what she felt was a direction from Holy Spirit.

I never understood why she wasted her education major and a sure retirement fund to leave everything behind and move to Germany. Now she worked in a coffee shop sharing Jesus and the Good News of His Gospel. I thought she was crazy. Logic said she should have waited until she had retired to become a missionary. But, every time we talked, she sounded happy and fulfilled. There never appeared to be a hint of regret that she worked in a coffee shop, made only enough money to meet her needs and had no plans for retirement. That meant no control over her financial future. I couldn't handle even the thought of that.

While I pondered this, my adventurous twin said, *See what you could be doing if you were not so afraid?*

My logical twin said, *Right, and who is going to be there to look after her, pay her medical bills or support her in old age? You took the right path.*

Agreeing with the logical twin, I hit the return key with gusto and opened my email. To my surprise I found one from Jenny with the subject line: "Exciting News & A Question". I quickly jumped to the message to see what the exciting news could be.

"God has been so good!" Jenny's email started out. "Got a bigger apartment. I now have two bedrooms. There is no excuse, you simply must come and visit! You are on summer break, so I want you to come as soon as possible for three weeks. I know you are not big on traveling alone, but listen girlfriend, I'm not taking 'No' for an answer! Email me when you have your dates and I mean three weeks! Buy your ticket and I'll take care of the rest. Love Ya! Jenny"

In that moment I knew that somehow my adventurous twin had set me up. My fingers wanted to type in an immediate response such as, "I don't think I can make it ...". My adventurous twin was leaping for joy. My safe twin was running "What if" scenarios. My emotions voted with my safe twin. But my spirit was doing cartwheels with my adventurous twin. Now it was up to my will. *What should I do? Should I flip a coin?* My will was emotionless and wasn't taking sides. It came down to my choice.

"Jesus, what should I do?"

It was out of my lips before I could pull it back in. *Why did I ask that?* Deep down I felt "Go!". I sighed and gave up. The struggle was over, and my adventurous twin was grinning from ear to ear. My safe twin was pouting and whining.

4

"Ok God. I will be adventurous and go visit Jenny. I hope you know what You are doing!" Speaking that out seemed the appropriate response in spite of my inner turmoil.

The Frankfurt touchdown was soft and without a bump. It was a perfect landing for what had been a perfect trip so far. Everything was going as planned, uneventful and safe. My safe twin was happy. My adventurous twin was happy too. That combination was a little scary because they never seemed to agree. The weeks leading up to the trip had been an emotional roller coaster as I forced myself to honor my word to Jenny and ignore my safe twin's warnings.

I easily found the airport tram to the train station and purchased the ticket for Stuttgart. It was uncannily easy. This entire trip made me think forces beyond my control were at work. It was alarming and uncomfortable to think God may be involved in my life more than I had realized. *Did I want that?*

The train came right on time and my luggage was stowed. I made my way toward my seat without a problem and I bent over to grab my carryon bag. I was about to man-handle it up to the carry-on storage, when a man's hand grabbed the bag for me.

"Here, let me help you with that." His voice was pleasant and soothing.

I turned to thank him and saw that he was about my age and nice looking. Although I had never met him before, he felt familiar. My logical mind pushed that thought down, but my heart said, *You know him. He is safe.* The thought although illogical, brought peace and security.

"Thank you! That was nice of you." I said with honest joy.

"No problem." He replied with equal joy.

I didn't recognize his accent, but he spoke flawless English. I sat down in the window seat and he sat down next to me in the aisle seat.

"Where are you going?" he asked as he showed me his ticket stub. My surprised look must have confirmed my doubts about the coincidence that his seat was next to mine and he was headed to Stuttgart.

"Oh, to Stuttgart also to meet up with my best friend".

"Going on an adventurous journey, are you?"

Why would he ask that? I wondered. If only he knew the irony of his question and my consistent internal debate about this trip.

"Well I don't know what fits your definition of an 'adventure' but yes, it's a journey that has held quite enough adventure for one day. You see, I'm not one to take risks. I like knowing that my steps are planned and controlled." *Now why had I shared an intimate detail like that?*

"Ah, but where is the fun in safe?"

"Well, don't get me wrong. I like fun. For example, fun at an amusement park is stretching enough. There I can choose to skip a ride if I think it's too risky."

"I see. Well, I'm sure that you will love your adventure here." He said it with such certainty.

"Oh?" I had a question in my voice. *Why was he so certain my time in Germany would be adventurous?* Changing the subject, I quickly said, "I am looking forward to meeting my friend soon. We haven't seen each other for over two years, so we've got a lot of catching up to do."

Before I knew it, I had told Him my entire college life, how Jenny and I met, teaching and probably every daunting experience that I had ever faced. When I finally paused, I'd realized I'd told him my life story, warts and all and I still didn't know his name.

"Wow! I'm sorry for talking your ear off. I don't know why I was so talkative. I guess I'm tired. By the way, I'm Melissa." I held out my hand for the formal handshake attempting to get out of this embarrassing hole I had dug for myself.

"David." Smiling, he gripped my hand firmly.

"So, David, I've talked to much, where are you headed?"

"Oh, you could say I'm on an adventure or journey myself. You see I work for a large enterprise. My boss has sent me to Stuttgart to meet with a client. This client is beginning the process of embracing a new and rather big life reorientation. It's going to change their future. I'm like the person that lends help, support and connection as they move forward."

My puzzled, "tell me more" look must have caught his attention. He continued.

"The organization I work for specializes in helping people and groups reach their fullest potential. You could say we are in the people business."

"That sounds amazing and fulfilling. Sounds like you and your organization must have lots of experience and contacts to be able to help people reach their full potential. There are many ways that could go!" I was genuinely impressed.

"Yes, the organization has been around a long time, with millions of hours of experience, interaction, wisdom and resources."

A voice came over the speakers in German then English. "We will be approaching the Stuttgart station in a few minutes. Please gather all your belongings. Please do not stand or walk until the train has come to a complete stop."

I couldn't believe it! The hour and thirty-minute trip seemed like just a few minutes. The train pulled into the station and slowly came to a stop. A part of me was sad to see David go because he was easy to be with and intriguing. The opposite of myself! As we exited the train, he helped with my carry on and followed me off the train. Part of me wished he would stay with me. *Where was my adventurous twin now?*

As we stepped down onto the platform, David spoke. "Try your phone for wi-fi. You may want to see about letting your friend know that you've arrived."

"Great idea!" We stepped aside as I searched my phone for a wi-fi signal. Sure enough, it popped up and connected, delivering a text from Jenny. It read. "Good news, bad news! Car trouble. I'm running two or so hours behind. Wait for me at the coffee shop in the station. I'll text when I'm almost there."

My safe twin was awakened and in full anxiety. My face must have shown my inner panic.

"What's wrong?" David picked up on my mood change immediately.

"Jenny is running two or more hours late. This wasn't part of the plan! She wants me to wait for her in the coffee shop."

Suddenly the fatigue of the travel hit me. I was uncomfortable that the plan had changed and had no strength to deal with my rising anxiety.

David again was in tune with my feelings. "Hey, I got the perfect thing for you. It will take your mind off waiting and keep you occupied. In fact, I guarantee you will feel invigorated and forget all about the time."

I smiled at how comfortable I felt with David and especially how his presence made me feel calm.

"Oh, what great idea do you have?" I laughed as he took my arm and we walked to pick up my luggage. His touch brought even more peace to my anxious thoughts.

"We are going to store your luggage, then I'm going to walk you over to the local historic cathedral."

"Why the local cathedral?"

"It's has beautiful architecture and it survived WWII. The view from the top is amazing."

"I do love seeing old historical buildings."

"I thought you would but make sure you catch the view from the tower. It is captivating."

"You make it sound almost enchanted, like I'll be entranced or enraptured by it all."

"Well, some have said that would be an understatement."

I laughed at the thought that a view, no matter how spectacular could captivate so fully.

"Another curious feature they recently discovered in the basement renovations was a running stream built into the foundation."

"Well, that is something I've never heard of. Why would any architect build a stream into the foundation? Now you're really doing a sales pitch." I laughed incredulously.

"No, it's true, really!"

David was so sincere, I had to ease his shock at my questioning his word. "Ok, I'm sold."

David relaxed and smiled. "You'll have plenty of time to see it and there isn't an entrance fee."

My safe twin was pushing for the safety of the coffee shop, but my adventurous twin had jumped out in front, effectively silencing my safe twin's plea.

The stream did intrigue me. A good walk and climbing some stairs seemed wise after sitting so much. I could use the cardio exercise before the long car ride with Jenny. My safe twin was quiet leaving my adventurous twin in charge, yet my inner spirit was peaceful. Like before, I wondered if God was intervening in my life.

"Thank you, David. I don't need that much convincing, plus it's a great solution while I wait for Jenny."

"No problem, it fits into some of my job descriptions, you might say." He laughed deeply.

We made our way to the lockers to stow my stuff. The cathedral was an easy walk, and felt safe to navigate back alone. The cathedral came into view as we rounded the corner of a building. I stopped in my tracks. It was massive and towered over everything. It was intimidating yet welcoming. I felt drawn to explore it.

"Like it?" David asked.

"It takes my breath away. Do you think I can see most of it before I need to leave to meet Jenny?"

"Sure! That won't be a problem. Look around inside and explore. Just go with what pulls your attention and time will fly. Before you know it, you will be on your adventurous journey."

"Wow, are you sure you're not with the visitor's bureau?" I laughed.

Although we'd only met, I enjoyed his company. I wished he didn't need to leave for work.

"Go ahead now and get started. I'm going to take off and let you get going."

Before I thought better of it, I impulsively hugged David and thanked him again for all his help. He had come along exactly when I needed the support. I felt a connection with him.

"David, I can't thank you enough. In this short time, it seems like we have been friends forever. Hopefully, one day our paths will cross again."

"I'm sure that's possible. I look forward to it. Now get going on your journey. Discover the adventure that you are meant to have." With that, he turned and so did I.

I walked a couple of steps and turned to ask David for an email or phone number, but he was nowhere to be found. It was like he had vanished.

The cathedral was magnificent. It was built in the Neo-Gothic design with vaulted ceilings, arches, flying buttresses, and beautiful stained-glass windows. It had 3 towers. The central tower stood many feet higher than the others. That had to be the tower with the view.

Checking my time and feeling safe, I went in search of a map. Smiling at the door keeper as I entered, he nodded, smiled back and handed me a map. I opened the map and quickly glanced at the cathedral's layout. I saw nothing to keep me from venturing out and exploring. In fact, the map was user-friendly.

I explored the ground floor, viewing the religious imagery, sculptures, architecture and especially the stained-glass windows which sent rainbow shafts of ethereal light all over causing many people to sit and bask in their surroundings. I found everything rich with beauty and history. Mindful of the time, I kept glancing at my watch. Amazingly, hardly any time had passed though I had covered the first floor.

Next, I wanted to see the city view from the tower that David had made sound so beautiful. On the map, I saw a spot marked "Tower." The door was located right at the back of the main sanctuary. With plenty of time to see the city view, onward and upward I went. The tower pulled me to come and explore.

Strangely, the door to the tower was small, plain and without signage. I tried the handle. It opened with ease exposing a spiral staircase that only went up. Several turns on the tower stairs, I came to a landing with a well-worn bench. I sat for a minute, caught my breath and then continued. Up and up. First, I noticed the freshness of the air, then a slight breeze, indicating that I was close to the top. With great expectation, I muscled up the last steps, seeing the parapet through an open door.

I stepped through the portal's opening and saw the parapet wall continued like a crown around the entire top of the tower. It allowed a 360-degree view. I was higher than I imagined; so high, I could see over the city to the horizon. The sun appeared brilliant, like it was being magnified from an unseen source.

It illuminated everything and enthralled me. I felt captivated and pulled to the light. Everything glowed with the haze of a rainbow. It mesmerized me. I stared out at the brilliance and my mind filled with fantastic images. *What lay hidden over the horizon?* For me it was a strange thought. Suddenly conscious of time, I knew I needed to move on. I wanted to see that stream! The thought of the stream was just as captivating. *Why would an architect allow a stream to run through the foundation?* It didn't make sense, but I wanted to see it.

I made my way back to the tower door and began my decent. I quickened my pace. I wanted to see that stream. On and on, I wound my way down. Certain, I should be back at the main floor by now, I looked at my watch. I was shocked at how little time had passed. I pushed back all concerns and continued down. After a few more spirals, I felt anxiety bubble up. The safe twin had taken notice. *Had I taken a wrong set of stairs?* No, there had only been one access. As panic from my safe twin surfaced, the steps opened to a dimly lit hall. Now that was strange. *Where was I?* How had the spiral steps brought me to the basement rather than the main floor? Pushing the safe twin's concerns down, I determined to find that stream. I looked at my watch. I still had plenty of time. *Now where was that stream and why was I compelled to find it?*

I could only proceed to the right. The need to find the safety of the first floor faded as I walked on. With every step, all I could focus on was finding that stream. David's voice of "adventure" sounded in my inner ear and quieted my safe twin's whining to find an exit, get directions or get back upstairs to other people. Ignoring the safe twin, I held onto David's word of "adventure". I walked down the dimly lit corridor with more confidence, renewed strength and an excitement to find that stream. The more I walked the corridor, the darker the area became. Yet, I was not afraid. There was enough illumination to proceed. That's all that mattered!

"There is a River" Psalm 46:4

When I approached the end of the corridor at the back wall, the floor abruptly ended. I all most stepped off into the water. The urgency calmed and peace came over me. I gazed at the stream in wonder. It was small and moving along slowly from left to right. The corridor had become a dead end at the edge of the stream. The stream crossed the end of the corridor making the shape of a "T". The architect who had built the church had apparently purposed to have the stream accessible by his intentional design. *But why?* The floor and walls contained and channeled the flow of the stream and I saw three steps leading down to allow access. The water was dark. I couldn't ascertain its depth.

I was filled with curiosity about what this unique place had been used for. *Was it a baptismal? Was it an escape in times of war?* As I was pondering, a small row boat came through the opening in the wall on my left and drifted toward the steps. I was intrigued at the sudden appearance of the empty little boat. The boat's years of use were apparent by its well-worn condition *Where had it come from? Why was it appearing in this moment?* As I watched, the boat came up to the steps and nestled its nose right where the steps and channel wall formed a corner. Although the stream kept moving, the little boat rested. The boat was empty except for two oars.

My eyes followed the stream. In the right-side wall, was a large beautiful gated arch. It was open, permitting the stream and anything else to flow out. It was high enough to allow even a tall person to sit in the boat and pass through. The opposite was true on the left-side wall. Here the opening only allowed the height and width of the boat to pass. A person would have to lay down to make it through.

From the left side, I could hear faint sounds of bubbling water . It reminded me of a bubbling fountain full of life. I looked back at the right opening and saw that the gate could be closed preventing anyone from going through the portal. But right now, it was wide open, allowing passage.

Should I get into the boat and see where the stream goes? What a strange thought. Something inside of me was jumping at the chance to get in and see where it would take me. My safe twin was screaming *NO!* My adventurous twin was even more vocal with *YES!* My logic said, *Obviously, the builders of this place built the access. A boat is here. Go! Where did it lead? Where would I end up? How would I get back?*

The safe twin argued, *What if there is another short opening that only allowed the boat to get through? You could be hurt and injured or worse, dead! You have no map. The tunnel is dark. You can't see where it goes once you go through the gate. Don't risk it! You've seen enough. Leave! Now!* My heart was beating fast, I could feel it in my throat.

The adventurous twin calmly spoke up in what sounded like David's voice. It caught me off guard. "Certainly, if it was dangerous, the builders would not have built the steps for access. A boat wouldn't be floating around. I would have warned you if there was danger."

In that moment, I didn't care that the voice sounded like David's. I knew to think through the pros and cons would abort this adventure.

I glanced at my watch and there was amazingly plenty of time. In that moment, my heart was set. I would step out and do this. Pushing the safe twin down, I quickly walked down the steps and got into the boat. The little boat didn't rock or tip. That was strange. I stepped onto the solid bottom and sat on the first seat facing forward. I was about to lean over and push off the wall when the little row boat moved out on its own and started slowly moving toward the large arch. The safe twin pointed out the oars in the boat. I could always row back if I needed to.

As I settled in for the ride, I felt the boat begin to pick up a little speed. No worry. It was not fast enough to prevent me from rowing back. I felt restful and decided to let the stream take me where it had been designed to go and see where this journey took me. The boat approached the arch. The speed of the stream's current was steady. Through the portal the boat glided. As I got farther away from the arch, the area grew darker until I was in utter darkness. Everything was quiet and hushed. Remarkedly, I was not afraid. A voice sounding like David inside my head said, "Trust and see."

I felt the boat drift against something, and I could sense a shift in direction. *Where was this journey going to take me?* After a few more bumps, the boat turned. Then I saw light, faint but sure. As my eyes adjusted, I could tell that the stream was still making its way through the solid stone tunnel. Ahead, I could see the tunnel's end. I needed to squint my eyes the closer I came to the light. It was so intense! I was excited to see where my little journey was taking me. I turned back around expecting to see the city or at least the cathedral tower. I saw only mountains. My safe twin clamored, *How will you make it back to meet Jenny?* My adventurous twin spoke right back and said with certainty, *Trust the experience. David would not put you in harm's way.*

The stream opened into a narrow canyon with high mountainous walls. The boat continued to meander through the canyon walls, the stream now forming a River. The River picked up speed and the canyon widened with the current carrying me in the middle. I felt safe which was not my usual mode. The colors and sights in the canyon were breathtaking. Abundant life was everywhere around me covered in the same rainbow glow I'd seen on the tower. Trees and shrubs appeared in hues beyond the usual color palette. Rocky outcroppings looked like clusters of variegated ruby roses or turquoise gemstones set in backgrounds of ochre.

Soon the walls of the canyon were far from me. The River filled the area, giving the appearance of a lake. The current kept moving me forward and centered.

The sun was warm, yet not too hot. *A perfect day to be on an adventure.* Another unusual thought for me to have. All I could see were mountains. Pine trees were scattered on the sides of the mountains, giving the air a fresh, clean smell. I was enraptured, with no fear of being in the uncontrolled unknown. It felt right. I was at peace.

Where was here? Suddenly, I had a reality check. I had no clue where I was. *How would I ever get back? What time was it? Jenny!* I looked at my watch horrified to discover that it had disappeared. *How could that be?* I began to have the bizarre feeling that I had crossed over into another reality or dimension. Everything around me looked familiar yet was different. It was surreal.

Extreme fatigue abruptly fell over me. Fighting sleep, I felt there was no way to stop this adventure and get back to Stuttgart and meeting up with Jenny.

Just then, David's voice gently floated through my mind. "Trust the adventure. It is your journey to take this River where it leads."

Everything seemed super charged; the air, my emotions, and the view. Yet my eyes drifted shut. I felt like I could sleep forever. Not wanting to fall overboard, I figured I should lay down for a quick nap. That made sense. With logic directing me to nap, the fact that I wasn't likely to crash on this wide river-lake, I curled up on the seat, feeling safe, while hearing David's voice faintly on the breeze.

"Welcome to your journey!"

I drifted off in deep sleep.

Chapter 2

The River
They Shall Know Me

**"I shall see Your face; I shall be satisfied when I
awake with seeing Your form" Psalm 17:15**

I awakened to the sound of water lapping and the rhythmic sound of rowing. When I opened my eyes and sat up, something fell against my neck startling me. My focus shifted. I touched the area thinking a bug was crawling on me, instead my fingers found a smooth chain. *Where had it come from?* I was curious, but more about my current location. I looked around and saw I was still on the River. It had narrowed down to about 30-40 feet; still calm, meandering like a resort lazy river. The walled canyon had disappeared. Instead what I saw was a flat plain spreading out as far as I could see on either side. Once again hearing the rhythmic sounds of rowing, I turned to see what was making the sounds. A man was rowing, and I immediately knew He was Jesus. How I knew I don't know. I just did. The real, in the flesh Jesus. I could see the thorn scars on His forehead as the breeze moved His hair. I was astounded, delighted and intrigued.

My safe twin was gasping out, *This can't be real!*

My adventurous twin was large, in charge, and said, *Go with this.*

Jesus looked at me and smiled the biggest and most loving smile. One that said, "I've been waiting for you!" I had a thousand questions. *Why? How? Where? When? Was this a dream?* In that moment, I knew.

It was like Jesus had spoken to me with answers to all those questions and more. I knew that I was on the adventure of my life. Inside my safe twin was shrinking and my adventurous twin was growing stronger. With clarity I heard a voice in my inner most being, *No turning back.* Somehow, I was okay with that.

I didn't have a worry about others missing me. I didn't have any cares at all. I was not hungry. I wasn't tired. I was at peace. I knew that Jesus was going to take me places and show me things that would forever change my life; beginning now! I was ready. My life as I knew it had all changed in those few seconds.

I turned my gaze over the bow of the boat toward the horizon, pondering what lie ahead. My eyes caught again the brilliance on the horizon. Now, I wanted to know what waited for me beyond what I could see. The little stream in the church was now far behind me.

"Focus again on the horizon and the brilliant light." Jesus spoke sweetly from behind me. "What can you see? Let your eyes see with new perception and perspective."

What I saw now was a magnificent sparkling structure. It was massive. It rose higher than I could imagine any structure could possibly be built. As it rose up toward the heavens, the clouds prevented seeing just how high it went. It was equally as massive horizontally as it was in height. The structure projected beams of light, diffusing in every direction across the land. The structure was beyond description and anything I had ever seen. But the most captivating aspect was its brilliance. It resembled a multifaceted star. I wanted to stare but the brilliance was almost blinding. Every angle had features that caught my eye as it sent out rays of light. The light was brilliant white, yet somehow created the glow of a thousand rainbows. It was incomprehensible and indescribably beautiful.

After a few minutes of gazing, the Lord spoke, drawing my attention away and back to Him. "It is the most beautiful thing you have ever seen, correct?"

"Yes!"

"It is the *Eternal City* and your final destination."

I turned to look again, blinded by its radiance and fascinated by how the beams of light emanating from it illuminated everything they touched. There were no shadows even from the clouds above. Everything was touched by the light.

Jesus spoke again. "The *City* will become your eternal home! It's where the River ends. You will be forever in its light. Your experiences within its walls will bring you great joy and peace. But there are still many things for you to see and do before you live there".

Jesus stopped rowing. We sat for some time, on the still River not needing to speak. Sleepiness overcame me once again.

Knowingly Jesus said, "Go ahead and take a nap. I'll take care of things." Without a thought or care, I curled up on the seat and fell asleep.

It could have been two minutes, two hours, or two days. I don't know, but I awakened to nothing. There was no noise, no movement nor sounds of the water lapping on the sides of the boat. No breeze touched my face. Nothing! I opened my eyes with a start, fearing somehow that Jesus had left me in the boat alone in the middle of who knows where. But as soon as I opened my eyes, I saw Him sitting at the back of the boat. I was still on the first seat and He had moved to the last seat leaving the middle rowing seat free. *Why had He stopped rowing?* Even as I had the thought, Jesus spoke.

"No, I'm not tired."

The thought occurred to me that He might want me to row the boat and share the experience.

"Do you want me to row?"

"Yes"

I cautiously made my way to the center seat. As I got up, I felt the chain move around my neck. "Jesus, why do I have this chain around my neck?"

"It is a gift from the Father and Me. It is a tangible reminder of our love for you and symbolizes your choice to take this journey on the River. Don't lose it!"

I took hold of each oar. They felt way too big for my hands. Could I actually do it? Could I move us forward? How was I to steer the boat? I was facing toward the back of the boat, looking at Jesus and His beautiful, smiling face. His face was full of assurance and delight that I could apparently do this.

"If I do all the work, then we will get there too fast. Timing is always important on the journey," Jesus said.

By "there", I knew He must mean the sparkling *City* on the horizon. I took slow and deliberate strokes. With some practice, I was able to coordinate both hands to do the work, moving us along at a slow and steady pace. I couldn't see where I was going on the River, so I kept my eyes on His face, looking for a clue or sign that I was about to run into something. Keeping the two shore lines equal distance, I kept rowing; amazed that watching Jesus would keep me on course.

"Again, He measured, waters that were to the knees" Ezekiel 47:4

After some time, I began to notice that the banks of the River were higher. There were signs on the banks that the River had been deeper at some point. Here the River level was low and appeared to be at the lowest level it had ever been based on the high-water marks on the banks. I glanced over the side of the boat and could see that the water was shallow. In fact, this small row boat was barely clearing the bottom. If we were carrying a couple of more people, we would not have had enough water draw to clear the bottom.

He noticed my glance, my study. "Do you want to know why the water level of the River is low?"

"Yes."

"It is because the number of churches who practice My Presence and allow the River to flow in their midst has declined. Many churches were once like the cathedral where you got into the boat. They had the River flowing. The church and the people were full of power and life. This life created a great volume of water for the River. But the number of these churches has diminished. Many have totally shut off access to the River. People have despised it because it is messy, and everything gets wet from the mist that rises from it. Some churches restrict it. Few seek it. Others do not know that it exists in their church's foundation."

"Wait. Are you saying all churches once had a River?"

" Yes, if they were birthed by Holy Spirit rather than a man."

Now I was pondering all the churches I had attended. *Had there been a River in their foundation?* If so, it was not talked about.

Jesus continued. "Some have turned their focus from the River to other things. Their stream has either dried up from neglect or has become a trickle. Only someone searching for more will find The River."

Had I been searching for more? Was that the source of my restlessness? Is that why God had intervened in my life? I was about to ask Jesus these questions when He continued.

"As a result, the River's volume is down. Only a few places around the globe keep their streams running full. Some are trying to return to the stream but it is difficult to revive what is dying or already dried up. Few have levels that would even get your feet wet, let alone come up to your thigh. River depths that would allow many people to travel the River are few. I long for the River to be full and powerful once again, allowing many to make their journey to the *City*."

I was saddened by this new awareness. *Why would people turn from this opportunity to experience more of Jesus? Why had I for so long?* I began to see my safe twin in a new light. No risk. No reward. It took on new meaning.

Jesus answered my pondering. "Times of the later rains will bring a new season and a new volume. People will find that their thirst for the Water of Life can only be satisfied by the Creator's River."

I shifted my focus to the high banks on the River and realized that I couldn't see the lay of the land anymore. I was curious about what I was missing as we passed. Jesus, took note of my curiosity and commented.

"Lost opportunities and experiences lie beyond what you can see. Here the shallow depth of the River hinders people from reaching them. Therefore, the rich experiences provided on their journey are never embarked upon. The transforming attributes for their lives are missed."

"Jesus, are there things along the way that I should be experiencing? I don't want to miss anything you have for me."

"Yes, but do not worry, the Father will make sure you have the opportunities needed. Everything will come in the right season. Every experience along this River will bring you life. You may not always understand it. It may look like death and not life, but all things are designed to bring you to a better place as you make the journey. I have purposed that you will experience everything necessary for your transformation on your journey. Right now, I have another experience for you. Let Me take over rowing and let's move on."

"They will mount up with wings like eagles"
Isaiah 40:31

We moved down stream quicker with Jesus rowing. I continued to enjoy His company and words were not necessary. I was content to be in His presence. I glanced around noticing the scenery had not changed. The weather was perfect. It was sunny but not hot or humid and there was still a slight breeze to keep it refreshing.

I noticed there were still no shadows from the clouds. As I looked at the clouds and their shapes, I saw a small speck, high up in the sky. I purposed to focus my eyes on it. I could hear high pitched piping notes as I focused on it and it sent chills up my spine. It was an eagle! I was fascinated with His soaring dives. It was effortless. He glided on the unseen. A part of me yearned to be an eagle too and fly alongside Him. What wonders I could see! What views I would have! It would be a life-changing perspective, I was sure.

In that moment, I felt the boat hit shore and realized that Jesus had brought us to an area of the bank over which the eagle was circling. Here the bank's edge allowed access up to the flat plain. Beautiful grass was rippling with the breeze. The boat steadied itself on the shore and Jesus motioned for me to climb out. He followed me up to the grassy plain, but I could not keep my eyes from this magnificent bird. I had to put my hand over my eyes to see at times as He soared into the sun.

"I see the eagle has caught your attention. Ever wonder what it would be like to fly like an eagle?"

Apparently, Jesus had read my thoughts. Thoughts that especially contradicted my safe twins' safety standards. What was going on inside of me?

"This is no ordinary eagle. He is God's Holy Spirit that hovers. Notice how He hovers over us even now, always present and always near. I want you to lie down in the grass and watch."

Now the eagle had even more of my attention. I wanted to learn everything about Him. So, I laid down. The grass was tall enough that when I laid down, it surrounded me like undulating green curtains. I caught the sweet smell of the grass as the warm sun shone down. I put my hand up shielding my eyes allowing me once again to find Holy Spirit soaring above. He swooped lower in the sky. I could clearly see His beautiful plumes spread out and ripple on the edges of his wings. I was amazed at how good my eyesight was to see at that distance since I was nearsighted and didn't have my glasses with me. Holy Spirit looked down at me and let out a piercing eagle call. It sent chills throughout my body and suddenly I was filled with such a longing to soar with Him.

"All things are possible." Jesus's voice startled me.

I sat up to look at Jesus. *Had He read my mind? How did He know that inside I wanted to be up there, free and flying alongside Holy Spirit?* He nodded.

I must have had an incredulous look on my face because He said, "Take off running and flap your arms."

How many times as a kid had I done that? Suddenly, a memory from my past popped into my mind. I was jumping from a silo ladder and the extreme consequences of that action came flooding back to me. For a moment in time, I was pulled one direction by my safe twin reminding me of the consequences, memories and scars of that adventure. On the heels of that came another flood of emotions filled with incredible excitement and possibilities. Then a voice inside my head feeling like my adventurous twin and sounding more like David said, *Take the risk. Step out and fly.*

The inner turmoil vanished. Now it was up to my decision. I got up from my grassy bed and stood up. Imitating the start of this adventure, I didn't let my reasoning stop me. I raised my arms and began to flap as a bird does and took off running as fast as I could through the knee-high grass laughing like a child. A part of me was glad that no one was around but Jesus in case my actions didn't produce the results that I was hoping for. Within seconds of flapping my arms, a supernatural sensation came over me.

I was transformed into an eagle. I looked down at my feet as I began to lift off the ground and they were no longer feet but talons. I glanced out of the corner of my eye and saw not an arm but a feathered wing. I knew that if I looked at the rest of my body, I would look like an eagle. I flapped my wings effortlessly and mounted up to circle Holy Spirit. Off we flew. I followed a little behind to perceive His slightest movements and copy them.

As we flew, I caught sight of fields far below with trees scattered here and there. I don't know how I knew, but I felt these fields were the boundaries of different earthly church influences. We flew around some more and came down to land in a large tree in the heart of a large field. It had been a monumental oak with a massive trunk and limbs that spread out in every direction. The tree appeared dead. We landed high up on one of the bare limbs.

Not thinking I asked. "What does all this mean? Why is this tree bare? Is it dormant? Why all the sizes and separation of fields and scattered trees?" My words came out as eagle sounds. It was somehow freakier to me than having the eagle body.

Holy Spirit gave me explanations to all my questions and more, but the answers came directly into my mind and spirit. It was like I had read an entire file on the subject. I knew all of it in an instant. This was a new learning experience. The supernatural ability to impart or transmit knowledge without words was really possible and not science fiction.

"The massive oak is dead. It has run its season of life."

I felt sad because I could see the massive limbs going out in all directions and knew that in its prime, it had provided a habitation for many. *Had the view of the City been blocked by its once massive canopy?* A strange thought? I looked all around the base of the tree for any sprouts from acorns. Nothing! No signs of life or reproduction anywhere.

What was the lesson of this tree and field? My internal communication kicked in.

"The tree represents a large church from a long time ago. It didn't reproduce because it had put all its strength and energy into getting a bigger outreach to draw as many people as possible to its self. It had dominated this area of the plain for many seasons and so its field boundaries also enlarged. Instead of helping people on their River journey, it kept them to its self. It has run its season of life and its influence is gone. Now, other churches can spring up and have opportunity to become influential in this part of the plain. Their field boundaries will change the landscape."

29

As we sat, I pondered on this information. There had been such potential in this tree to reproduce itself and feed multitudes. It could have been an example to others. It should have helped refresh and send others on their journey. Instead it had hindered, stunted or prevented growth around it. Had it not turned its energy to itself, it could have left a great legacy. Now its chance for life was over. Another would take its place. I wondered about its choices.

> **"Blessed be the Lord, my Rock, Who teaches**
> **my hands to war, and my fingers to battle."**
> **Psalm 144:1**

Holy Spirit rose up and was off. Although I had many other questions, I took off after Him. We soared so high I could clearly see that the *City* appeared to ascend through the clouds, up into the heavens. We came down and began to circle, coasting down on the air currents. As I looked down, I saw a huge rock, more like a grand boulder below. I don't know why but, I was immediately glad to see it and wanted a closer look. Holy Spirit continued to circle down until we landed on the grassy plain right beside it. Up close I could see that the rock was a deep clear red like the color of blood drawn out in a test tube. The grass here was short and allowed us to walk along the enormous boulder. The rock seemed out of place and curiosity drew me. There were no other rocks or mountains near. I noticed small chips of the rock lying on the ground around the base of the boulder. As I examined the chips more closely–my eyesight was amazing–I had this knowing that this was no ordinary rock, but it was The Rock–Jesus! On each chip letters were engraved. They appeared as all types of languages. Holy Spirit spoke to my spirit.

"Yes, this is the Rock of Salvation–Jesus Christ. There are more rocks like this scattered throughout the plains. They are extensions of His Essence. No one is ever far from one. He has His Presence everywhere and anyone can come take comfort, shelter or gain protection. They are "touch" stones. They allow a traveler on the River to connect with Jesus when they have a need."

Amazing! My spirit replied. *That knowledge brings me comfort.*

"These chips or touchstones at the base of the rock are foundational truths. They are His words that travelers can pick up and take with them to strengthen themselves with a portion of the rock. It is a measure of the Living Word that they can carry. Over time, travelers encounter another rock and take more of His foundation, more of His truth, more of His Essence. The chips and stones can be gathered and given to others who have needs. They are like "flint". They can be used as an arrowhead to pierce and take out the enemy. They can be struck to create a spark that will catch fire and burn bright, bringing light and warmth."

As we walked around the rock, I noticed that it was long and large but not too tall like the oak tree had been. It did not hinder anyone looking for the *City*. It never dominated the landscape but was low enough to always allow a view of the *City*. It could provide shelter from the elements because a part of it had an overhang. It was long enough to hide behind from an enemy, yet it was shaped in such a way that someone could climb upon it for better sight and direction.

Holy Spirit hopped up steps that took us to the top of the rock. I felt connected as if I were one with it. A part of me didn't want to ever leave this place. As we reached the top and I looked toward the *City*, I was blinded by the brilliance of the reflecting light beams. The rays covered the entirety of plains with spectacular beams of glorious light and rainbows.

Without warning, Holy Spirit took off in flight and I followed. Shortly we were flying back over the dead oak and approaching the River. Holy Spirit came down to land on the grassy plain. As I followed my talons turned back to feet and my whole body transformed into my human appearance. But Holy Spirit remained an eagle. He nodded at me and flew off going higher in the sky until He was out of sight.

"A memorial forever" Joshua 4:3-9

I walked over to the River's edge and found Jesus sitting there with His familiar smile. I could tell that He was pleased that I had stepped out and taken this adventure. I loved looking upon Him and feeling that same connection to Him as I had at the rock. Seeing Him made me think about the chain around by neck. Had I lost it while flying with Holy Spirit? I reached up to see if it was still around my neck. Yes! As I touched it, I felt a new object hanging from the chain. Whatever it was it warmed against my skin.

"Yes, I've given you a touchstone from the rock. It will become a 'Stone of Remembrance' for you. It is a polished piece engraved with My name, Alpha and Omega. A symbol to you that I AM is always with you. It will connect you to all that you experienced on that flight."

The stone continued to warm my skin as He talked. "There are many more adventures that lie ahead for you, but we must move on down the River. There is a place of refreshing for you to experience since you had your Holy Spirit flight."

"There is a River, the streams of which make the City of God glad" Psalm 46:4

We were not traveling in the boat long before we pulled over to the embankment. I saw a small clear stream was running across the flat plain that had cut its way over time in a gradual descent to the River. I remembered I had caught a glimpse of it from above while I had been soaring with Holy Spirit. It had looked like a beautiful tiny greenish-blue ribbon lying on top of the ground. I had not noticed where it came from or where it went. But, I observed how it had greened up the area wherever it flowed. I was pondering why Jesus had stopped, when He began to speak.

"This is one of several 'streams of refreshing' that flow into the River. They help to keep the River's volume up, as well as supply necessary nutrients to the makeup of the River. But these streams are now few. The streams come from deep deposits of water that have been tapped into. They are artesian. Someone paid a great price to open up and bring forth this water. You would know some of them through history as great outpourings of My Spirit, Great Revivals or Renewals. I am sad that what man paid a great price to find and release can also by the hand of man be shut down. These streams of refreshing can have a short life. But where there is a thirst for more of My Refreshing, in time, someone will pay the price again and a new stream opens up."

As He was speaking about this, I looked closer and could see and hear bubbles in the clear small stream as it poured into the River. The bubbling sound reminded me of the cathedral stream where it had entered through the smaller opening in the left side wall. As it emptied into the River, there was a little swirl to the water that moved the back of the row boat to and fro.

"You need to get out now and experience this refreshing for yourself. You have many adventures to take before you reach the *City*. This refreshing time will take you far and help sustain you until you can enter another place of refreshing. Along your journey you will have places of refreshing where "watering" for your soul is provided. Sometimes it will be a light refreshing mist. Other times it will be full immersion. But each time, whether you are aware of it or not, I will be taking responsibility to set up times of refreshing so you are renewed body, soul and spirit. It's a key for your journey."

I got out of the boat. Jesus held on to the edge of the embankment because the back of the boat wanted to pivot with the eddy of the stream's flow. The River's level was knee deep so I was able to walk from the River into the refreshing stream. The bed of the stream was full of tiny smooth rocks of every color. Some glistened like gold, emeralds or diamonds. The stream's level was only about ankle deep.

I stood wondering how to receive the refreshing of this water when Jesus gently spoke. "Just lie down."

Remembering that He had mentioned immersion, I laid down on the small pebbles, putting my head upstream. They shifted around my body like a soft mattress. As I settled down, the water flowed around my head and body; warm and comfortable. It brought immediate relaxation to my body. My skin felt plump, my bones felt strong, my joints lost all stiffness and aches. The water covered my ears, yet it didn't create any pressure or discomfort. Instead the sounds of everything around me– birds, wind, water lapping against the row boat–went away, and a great peace settled over me. I could hear the sound of my own breath. As I listened, my breathing slowed to a peaceful state of rest. I was carried away with thoughts and visions of the goodness of God; His glory and His power. I saw visions of saints gone on before that were now a great cloud of witnesses encouraging me to go for all this journey had to offer. I don't know how long I laid there. It seemed like time stood still as I was caught up in all my mind was experiencing. My body was at total rest. Everything felt right.

At some point, I realized we were back on the River in the row boat and moving down stream. Jesus was rowing, and I was curled up on a seat. I was relaxed and didn't have a care in the world. I sat up wondering how I had gone from lying in the stream bed to lying in the rowboat. It was another of the many curious happenings that I was coming to accept on this new journey. Trying to make sense of all I was experiencing, wasn't going to happen. I did look down at my hand and fingers to see if they were all wrinkled from the time of soaking in the stream or if my clothes were wet. Everything was normal. I heard Jesus chuckle. As I looked at Him, He smiled a smile that told me all was well. Time was unimportant. Talk was not necessary. Being together was enough.

I sat up and moved toward the side of the row boat to let my hand dangle in the water as we moved down the River. The water was a deeper shade of blue and as I looked down through it, I realized that I could not see bottom. I was about to ask Jesus about this when I noticed that we were at a place on the River where the two parallel embankments began channeling the River into a circular cove. Trees circled the cove except for one small area where it made a beach. The beach was covered with glistening pure white sand reminding me of rainbow glitter. Jesus stopped rowing and I noticed that we were stopped dead in the water in the center of the cove. No current was moving us even at a snail's pace. No air was moving, yet it was not uncomfortable.

Jesus said, "The current here is deep and flows fast right through this cove, yet you would not know it with the natural eye. Many things like the current are hidden deep in our lives that we can be unaware of and yet they affect the flow of our life. There is an opportunity here for you to encounter something in your life you are unaware of that affects you."

I don't know why, but in that moment, fear tried to grip me. Had my safe twin been stronger, she would have spoken up with a quick reason about why I should be afraid. *What was lurking deep in my life that I was not aware of? How was it influencing my life?* I didn't have a clue and I wasn't sure I wanted to know.

"Don't go there!" Holy Spirit's voice spoke to my spirit.

Is it a bad thing? My mind shouted back.

"Don't go there!" Holy Spirit spoke more emphatically.

Is it going to be ugly, big and scary when I see it? My mind reeled.

"Don't go there!" Again, Holy Spirit's voice spoke stronger.

My mind was still working, *Will this bring back memories that I have buried because they were too painful?*

"Don't go there!"

The more I wondered, the more anxious I became. I quickly lost all the peace I had known moments ago.

Jesus's voice was calm, clear and firm. "Stop! Take control of your thoughts! Every thought trying to raise itself up in your mind that is not bringing peace or is big and frightful, is from the enemy. The devil does not want you to advance on this journey. If he can't stop your journey, then he will try to stop it in this place so you never move on. Take those thoughts captive and make them obey you. Do not obey them. Do not give him an advantage to hinder your journey. Command the thoughts to be silent. Bind them up! If they will not obey you, then punish them by using a piece of the touchstones as a sword and bring them into submission. The weapons that I have given you are able to pull down and silence the thoughts."

Touchstone? I remembered it at the rock, but I had been an eagle. Eagles do not have pockets! So how was I to have any other than the piece attached to the chain? A warm feeling, like warm water poured into my pocket suddenly got my attention. I automatically put my hand into my pocket to see what was making the sensation. What I felt were several pieces of the rock chips. *How had they gotten there?* I had only looked at and picked up a few pieces with my talons to see what was written on them back then. *How did they get in my pocket?*

"When you made the connection and touched the Living Word of the rock, they became a part of you and Holy Spirit placed them in your pocket. They will always be with you. Now stop those thoughts!"

I looked closely at the flint pieces and one illuminated more than the others. I perceived it was the one to use. Somehow, I realized I needed to lay it against my forehead and as I did so, I knew immediately what was written on the chip. I spoke the words out with power. Immediately, all the powerful negative thoughts retreated.

I said "You will be silent. I take authority over you and nothing will hurt me. (36) In the name of Jesus, the Living Word!" (37)

"Good. Now remember this lesson well. Do not let the enemy of your River journey take advantage of you again. Now that you have your mind under the control of your spirit, I want you to get out of the boat and walk over to that beautiful sandy beach."

"Stepped down from the boat, and walked on the waters" Matthew 14:29

"What?! Did you say to get out of the boat and walk, as in walk on the water?"

"Yes." He said it with such a smile of delight on His face that I wanted to snatch it off. "If you can fly with Holy Spirit, you can surely walk on water."

"Walk on water?" I couldn't see bottom. I knew how to swim but to step out expecting to walk as if the water wasn't water, was crazy. As I was processing this, another part of my mind said, *He's right you know. Both are equally supernatural.*

Jesus had not failed me yet. I decided to be obedient. I took off my shoes and swung the leg closest to the edge of the boat over and let my foot touch the water. My foot got wet and the water felt cool as it slid over the top of my foot and between my toes. I felt around for anything solid to step onto and found nothing. Minutes went by as I slowly felt for the solid surface that would let me get a leg up and stand up. NOTHING! I edged closer and got both feet out over the edge, touching the water in hopes that when both feet touched, a supernatural event would take place. I wanted the water to become a solid surface as if there were some clear hard plastic runway rising from the depths to give me solid footing. But nothing happened except that both feet were now wet.

I turned to look at Jesus. He was not there! He was not in the boat at all. I quickly looked around for Him, frantic emotions rushing through me. The water began to taunt me. Loud voices came at me from all the surrounding water. It was as if the water was demonically mocking me for not having the faith to step out in obedience. I was full of fear, anxiety, and disgust for not being able to step out and trust. Why was this so hard when flying had been so easy? It didn't make sense and, in this moment I couldn't find a solution.

"Stop! Take control of your thoughts! Every thought that is trying to raise itself up in your mind that is not bringing peace, or is big and scary, is from the enemy who wants you to fail. He wants you to stop here and never move on." His passionate words flooded my mind.

His voice and words came crashing in over the sound of the water's voice. The call of Holy Spirit caught my attention from high overhead. I turned my gaze upward and heard Him call again. My ears heard an eagle sound, but my spirit heard "The Lord on high is mightier than the noise of many waters!" (38) Immediately, the mocking waters quieted. They were not gone but the volume was subdued and I could now hear the wind had picked up in the rustle of the trees.

Again, I clearly heard the Holy Spirit call out. My ears heard the eagle, but my spirit heard "Good. Now remember this lesson well. Do not let the enemy of your journey ever take advantage of you again."

"Counsel in the heart is like deep water"
Proverbs 20:5

Holy Spirit continued, "Many things are hidden deep in your life that you are unaware of. They affect how you live. There is something here for you to encounter and confront." With His words I knew that I was in a battle with the enemy to face hidden fears. I had a choice to make.

"Jesus, where are you?" As I repeatedly yelled, a movement caught my attention and I scanned the shore by the beach. Jesus came out from the trees and was now standing on the white sand. Immediately a peace came as I located His presence. Although He was some distance from the boat, I felt Him right there with me.

I looked at Him looking at me. I raised my voice so that it would carry across the water to Him. "Jesus, I know that you want me to confront things that are hidden deep in me that obviously want to control my actions. I don't want them to control me. I want You to always control me. What is within me that I need to confront and bring to the surface? Please help me deal with all of this."

As if He was right beside me in the boat, my mind heard, "Although I am always with you, your focus can shift from Me to what is taking place around you. In this case, you became focused on the water and the lack of firmness that you thought you needed. The more you searched for what you thought you needed, the more your natural senses confirmed that it was going to be impossible. Every natural confirmation canceled out more of your focus and trust in Me." His voice in my thoughts continued.

"I diminished in your focus and the power of the natural circumstance grew. You were looking at the created rather than on the Creator. You lost touch with Me and therefore I could not strengthen your inner spirit to overcome the natural. When you desired to fly, and I told you that all things were possible, you never lost your focus on Holy Spirit. Your desire was to fly and you did so supernaturally. But when I asked you to walk on the water and do another supernatural thing, your focus immediately became you and how you were going to do what I was asking of you."

"What I asked you to do was not your heart's desire. You wanted to fly, and it rose up as a passion within you. It was My passion for you to experience walking on water, but it wasn't yours. It was only your desire to please Me that got you to the point you took off your shoes and sat on the edge of the boat. That was a start. If you had kept your focus on My Face, you would have been transformed by the love and passion coming from Me to you. My eyes and your eyes would have locked. What was in Me would have passed to you. You could have done anything supernatural. Your power to do the supernatural would have sprung up from the subjugation of your fear and the transformation of our connection. You would have been stretched in your faith by your faith. Now, what are you going to do? What will be your choice?"

"I want to choose to do it and to be stretched. I want to make Your desires my desires. I want this supernatural step of faith to be as it was with Holy Spirit and flying. I want to experience all that you have for me." The words rushed out of me. No safe twin spoke up to argue with my inner spirit. Rather a little bubble of excitement started to surface from my adventurous twin.

"Ok, step out and walk to Me."

I was not quick to jump out of the boat. Rather, I looked into the depths of the dark waters and immediately saw into the expanse of my own soul. I saw that I was terrified. I could feel the panic first. But as I focused on the source of the panic, I saw what held me captive. It was fear! The fear took on the forms of dark specters and ghostly apparitions floating and undulating deep in me. I decided to grab hold of them and bring them to the surface.

"I'm scared and I'm afraid." I spoke out the words loudly and with force. They needed to be brought into the light.

"Now we are getting closer to the truth. What are you afraid of? What brings fear to you?" His words carried to me from the shore.

I took another look into my soul. It was dark, not wanting to give up its secrets. But I wouldn't quit. I kept focused, looking at them and asking Holy Spirit to give me eyes of understanding. Suddenly, a multitude of childhood memories came rising to the surface like a geyser. Memories of when I was three; accidently walking off the boat dock and falling into the water between the boat and the dock. The screams of my mother, the frantic efforts of my father trying to push the boat away from the side of the dock so that he could get to me; the shouts of onlookers. The memory of cold dark water just like this River going over my head and up my nose overwhelmed me. I felt the burn up my noise and darkness pulling me downward as if it was happening all over again. I shuddered.

On top of that buried memory came another memory floating into my consciousness. I had crafted a homemade sliding board from the barn hayloft. I had used a thin piece of molding and pushed it up from the barn floor through the hayloft opening. I climbed up the hayloft ladder, stepped onto the landing and sat down on the molding expecting a wonderful slide. My next memory was hitting the cement floor face first, then waking up in the hospital; eyes swollen shut and a broken nose.

Before I could remember more of that past accident, another childhood memory undulated into view. I had thrown my doll, with an umbrella duct-taped to its body, out a high silo opening and followed with my own umbrella like Mary Poppins. The resulting pain of that past broken arm now shot through me again and I grabbed my arm.

Memory after childhood memory of bad experiences added their weight upon my chest. My mind's eye saw memories of displeasing people I had wanted to make happy. Other fears and apprehensions that had attached themselves to my soul made their ghostly appearances too. The buried feelings of not measuring up, the fear of failure, disappointments, near-death experiences and being powerless over them all surfaced. On and on they flooded over me. Once buried these past ghosts now loomed up with an enormous weight. I gasped for a breath as my chest constricted with it all.

Then His loving voice from the shore carried over all the tumult like a soft gentle breeze. "Your past does not have to define who you are today. Your past is just that – past. Today, in this moment, My power and provision is available to step out of your past. I am the God of the moment. One of my names is 'I AM'." At the mention of His name, the touchstone on my chain warmed and all suffocating and distracting emotions vanished.

"This moment holds all of your future. This moment contains all of my power and provision for that future. Step out and take a risk. What is the worst that could happen? You sink? I knew a man once who did that very thing and I was right there to take hold of his hand. I will be there for you too! Focus on Me. Keep Me as your only thought and as your only focus. Look into My eyes. They will reach into your inner person and strengthen you to do the supernatural. My power can break the power of anything that comes upon you and the chains to your past. Step out onto the water or fly as an eagle. It is all the same."

Without letting my mind go back to the ghosts of the past, I sat on the boat's edge, both feet feeling only water, and pushed off the boats edge. I could feel my feet going down hitting nothing solid. I was sinking.

You're sinking! My mind screamed. *You're not going to succeed just like those memories proved before. You are a failure.*

But the next thing I knew, I was not in the water but on the white sandy shore standing beside Jesus, His warm hand holding my wet one.

"Ok, let's try that again." Jesus said with what sounded like a chuckle in His voice.

He started off for the water pulling me along and His grip on my hand was firm. He wasn't letting go. I was glad He was holding my hand because I knew that the supernatural that was within Him would transfer to me and I could walk where He would lead me, even on water. I could feel the warm sand on my feet as we walked toward the water's edge. As we approached the water, I looked down to see if my feet would sink or someway be on top of the water.

As I was about to find out, He squeezed my hand firmly and said almost sternly "Keep your eyes on Me!"

I looked up immediately, and we kept on walking. His hold on my hand was firm, not waiting around for my scientific investigation. I never took my eyes from Him as He walked a couple of paces ahead of me keeping a steady pull on my hand. I had missed the moment of seeing how the natural and supernatural co-existed. I wanted to look down at my feet. I couldn't feel if they were wet. I couldn't feel the water at all. I wanted to peek but knew that was not an option for this moment. From my peripheral vision, I knew that we were moving away from the beach toward the boat. But to glance down would be an open door for looking to the natural, letting the other deep things within me come to the surface. I didn't want to allow the enemy of my River journey to bring defeat.

"Distractions and looking to the natural can bring a shift in focus that allows your enemy to get you to question the supernatural, even for a second. A second would be all it takes to sink." Jesus was aware of every thought running through my mind, even before I was.

Another choice came to my mind in that instant. I could follow behind Him as now or walk beside Him. I chose to walk beside Him. I stepped up my pace and the pull on my hand lessened. Jesus looked at me and I at Him. We both smiled. My faith switch had been flipped by Holy Spirit because I had received His thought as an action and then took the steps to obey it. I was moving forward with the purpose of reaching the boat and getting back to the next phase of the journey. *Where would the River take me next?* I was eager now to move forward.

We reached the boat and climbed in. I put my shoes back on, amazed that my feet were perfectly dry and without sand. I looked at Jesus and He just smiled.

"It is all in the revelation. You have now had two supernatural experiences that will help you on your journey. Remember it's not just desire to please me but feeling my passion that connects to the supernatural. Remember the need for focus and keeping your eyes on Me. Walking with Me, not after Me. It is about revelation and perceptions of your connection to Me. It's all about destination. You could have walked by yourself from the boat to Me if you had had the revelation that I was the destination. But you focused only on the task of walking on water. That was your focus, not Me."

"For Peter, when he walked on water, I was his destination. His focus was to come and be where I was and do what I was doing. He stepped out and walked. But along the way, Peter shifted his focus from Me to the supernatural event taking place. He wanted to observe how the supernatural was becoming natural. Understanding with the natural mind, will never be enough to keep your position in the supernatural."

"The natural realm yields to the supernatural realm because it is the Father's desire and I always do what He desires. He and I are one in passion and purpose. When you connect to our passion and purpose, you will flow in the supernatural too! Now let's move on. Take up the oars again."

As I got up to climb over to the rowing seat, I felt the chain and the stone of remembrance nestle down against my skin, but it felt heavier. Before I took hold of the oars, I touched the chain and realized that now there were two items hanging from it. My eyes darted to Jesus and as usual He was smiling.

"It's another reminder gift, but it is only half of a whole." Jesus said.

As I fingered it, I could tell it was not a full circle but a partial circle with an extension off one end. On the other end there appeared to be some kind of indentation or hole.

I was curious to see it and how it was attached to the chain, but Jesus drew my attention to Him saying, "There will be another time to take a closer look. Now we need to move ahead."

As much as I was curious, I also knew to let it drop. I took the oars and began moving on down the River. With the sounds of the oars slicing into the water, I forgot about the new piece on the chain. I was quickly lulled into daydreams of what possible new things I might see on the River ahead with Jesus.

Time passed. Time was so different here. Jesus was now at the oars, but we sat motionless. I don't know if I had been relaxing or napping. I wasn't sure. I couldn't remember, but the effects I was feeling were wonderful. I felt energized. Jesus looked at me with that all knowing smile, and all was well.

Faintly, my ears picked up the high-pitched sound of Holy Spirit far above my head. I looked up and couldn't see Him, yet I could hear His sounds more distinctly. He must have been soaring high on the wind currents circling overhead. I was focused on His calls high above but became more curious about what He was doing. *Where was He?* I focused and searched the sky, while shielding my eyes from the light, looking for a tiny speck. His calls became more distinct and loud. I focused on the sounds as a beacon to His Presence.

I finally spotted Him. As my eyes picked up His tiny speck of body, I knew in my spirit that He knew we were connected. Slowly and purposely, He began to circle downward. His body was getting more visible as he descended. He circled us one last time and landed on the bank near us. Holy Spirit looked at Jesus and Jesus at Him. In an instant, Holy Spirit flew over to the row boat and landed on the empty seat. He was big. His plumage was almost iridescent gold. Jesus motioned to the space beside Him and Holy Spirit hoped over to it. They communicated. I don't know how I knew this, but I did. Not a word or sound was spoken. Then Holy Spirit took off and quickly soared into the sky out of sight.

My curious expression about their interaction must have caused Jesus to answer. "Holy Spirit, Father and I, are in continual communication with each other. We know what the other is thinking, saying or needing. When there is no communication going on, Holy Spirit hovers, waiting for the next connection. You experienced this when He and you made connection. We flow as one. I hear from the Father and do His bidding. Holy Spirit hears and does our bidding. He hovers, circles, watches, waits. He is ever near. He is ever ready to perform the Father's will. We serve one another. Together We support the weightiness of the Glory. Oneness of mind, connects Us."

"Holy Spirit felt your desire to connect as you looked up for Him. In the second that you desired and looked up, He was connected to you and came to you as He comes to Me. You watched Him. He watched you. Both of you were aware of the other. Both of you were communicating, Spirit to Spirit. We become as one flow of knowledge and wisdom. This is unity."

We continued on down the River. The plains were still with us, but the current had quickened. The current now moved the boat steadily centered on the River, eliminating the need to row. Time passed yet it felt endless. At some point, I curled up on the seat for another nap. I awakened to the breeze blowing across my face and hair. I had no idea how long I had been sleeping and discovered a little wet drool running down the side of my cheek. The boat was stopped again.

I sat up looking for Jesus and our present location. The boat had drifted from the center of the River closer to one bank. *Where was Jesus? Had I lost Him?* I felt some anxious feelings wanting to arise. His past words about taking my thoughts captive came tumbling clearly into the midst of my anxious thoughts. I immediately put them down like closing the curtain on a stage. I refused to give them any audience on the stage of my mind.

Although a breeze had awakened me, there was not any breeze noticeable as I sat up. Curious! *Was the wind from Holy Spirit? Was it a nudge to awaken me?* I turned to look around again in all directions and this time I saw Jesus walking on the far side of the River. He was walking toward the River and the boat. He knew that I had seen Him, and He waved a wave of greeting, then pivoted His wrist making the gesture of "come here".

I had a knowing that He had been coming and going. I was curious about what He had been up to, wondering too, if I had missed anything important. I felt a little bit ashamed for not being more aware of His Presence and His movements. Holy Spirit's voice resonated in my heart "There is no condemnation to those who are in Christ." (12) I was at peace instantly. As usual, Jesus was aware of my thoughts and motioned more emphatically for me to come join Him. I waved back and took the oars.

As I placed my hands on the oars, I instantly knew that He had been preparing something new and important for me and my journey. For a moment, I wondered if I should walk on the water over to Him. As I checked that thought in my spirit, I knew I had permission, but I continued to wait and see if Holy Spirit had more to impress upon my inner spirit. A stronger impression came to my spirit to row the boat to the shore.

I grabbed the oars and maneuvered the boat easily. I nudged the front of the boat upon the shore. Jesus grabbed the front of the boat and pulled it, securing it. I got out and we climbed up the embankment onto the grassy plain. It was flat with knee high blades of grass that were going to seed. There was also shorter grass scattered throughout, making it an easy walk. As we walked from the shore, I noticed there was nothing that broke the horizon. Everywhere I looked I saw the plain. *Where are we going?* my mind was asking. I wasn't expecting an answer but, Jesus replied anyway.

"You'll see in time, for now don't focus on the destination. Instead, enjoy the walk with Me."

"Consider the lilies" Matthew 6:28

I pulled my thoughts back from the possibilities to watch Jesus as He walked a few paces ahead of me. I focused on His back and noticed how strong and tall He was. I knew that His legs were capable of taking longer strides, but He apparently adjusted His gait to match mine. As we walked on for a while, a butterfly with brilliant colors flitting and dipping occasionally into the grass captured my attention. It moved along in the same direction with us. Gradually, it came closer as we continued to walk away from the River. I had a thought that it was monitoring our progress. The butterfly came along parallel, getting closer after each dip. Soon it would be within touching distance. I watched to see what was attracting its attention.

At that point I noticed that all around us were small clumps of white flowers. Some looked like miniature daisies and others looked like miniature lilies. As I took in the beauty of the flowers, I lost sight of the butterfly. It had disappeared. I wondered if the butterfly's job had been to direct my attention to the beautiful miniature flowers. I was suddenly filled with remorse thinking I might have crushed them when I was not focused on where I had placed my feet. Because they appeared fragile and beautiful, I purposed not to step on them now. I registered their scent. The air was heavy and alive with their fragrance. I took in a deep breath and my lungs began to tingle from their essence.

"Jesus, did you see these beautiful small flowers all through this area? They look similar to flowers I have seen before, yet they are different. Why are they here?"

Jesus stopped and turned back to me with the smile.

With loving patience He said. "Many people walk this walk and never see them, never see their beauty, never smell their fragrance or enjoy their existence. The flowers are like some people. People who are scattered throughout our daily walk yet, they are never seen. They are stepped on emotionally. They are ignored. Because they are lowly or appear insignificant, people justify their actions and dealings with them. Although they have much to give with their beauty, uniqueness and fragrance, self-absorbed people walk right by them and disrespect them. Remember this lesson. I have put people like this all along the pathways of life. They were created to bring beauty and a smile to those on a journey. It takes a shift of focus to notice them and experience these little hidden jewels of life. Well done!"

As we walked on, the scenery didn't change and talking wasn't necessary. I continued to pay attention to all that was in the moment. My thoughts turned to wondering how far we had traveled. I also wondered why I was not getting hungry or thirsty? Hunger immediately captured my thoughts. I realized that I had not eaten or drank anything since I had walked into the cathedral. How long ago had that been? I wasn't sure. As I pondered time, I realized that the light never grew dim here. It was consistently light, always day and always a perfect temperature. These thoughts took me down many "rabbit trails" of the mind. "Don't miss the hidden jewels" drifted back into my mind at some point and brought my attention back to what was around me. *Had I crushed any flowers? What had I missed?*

Although I had not spoken the flower question out loud, Jesus commented. "No, you avoided the flowers and you ate food which you do not know that you have eaten. (39) You drank water that you did not know that you had consumed. It's always this way in the kingdom and on the River journey toward the *City*. When you are in alignment with Holy Spirit and the Father, doing their will, you are fed in such a way that the natural flesh cannot understand, yet it is satisfying. Let's continue. This part of your journey is nearly over. We are coming to a town that you need to visit."

"A town?"

The plain was flat. I could only see grass in every direction. *Where was this town?* My curiosity began to grow. *How large was it? Would I meet more travelers like myself?* It would be nice to talk to others who were on their own journey. I could find out how they had come upon the River and how long they had been traveling. Many questions started flooding my thoughts. My mind chased after them all. As we walked on, my mind was engaged in delightful thoughts of meeting up with new companions. If I could have seen Jesus's face, I assumed He was smiling.

Chapter 3

Crown Derby
Decrease

"Those who run in a race all run, to receive a
crown" 1 Co. 9:24-27

I would have walked right off the edge if Jesus had not put His arm out to stop my next step. His touch startled me out of my fanciful thoughts about the town and its people. As my heart slowed, I looked out over the edge of a cliff and saw that the land dropped steeply and abruptly to a valley below. The valley was narrow. I could see the River far below as it flowed through the valley making green spaces on both of its banks. The valley had many trees. The River looked to be back to a normal width and flow, and I was glad to see it again.

The town stretched along both sides of the River. The buildings formed a single row, side by side, on each bank facing the River. It reminded me of Old West towns I'd seen in movies but with a river rather than a dirt street dividing the two sides. A large boardwalk ran in front of the buildings and three bridges connected the two boardwalks on each end as well as the middle, making it possible to walk it as a loop. As I looked down at the town from the elevation of the plain, the town's layout resembled a racetrack, but the arched bridges gave it the appearance of a crown.

"What is the name of this place?" I asked.

"Crown Derby!"

"That's funny, that it's called 'derby' because for some reason it reminded me of a racetrack and the bridges made it look like a crown."

Jesus chuckled.

"How do we get down there, Jesus?"

"Do you see that big boulder over to your right sitting at the edge of the plain? Beside it is a narrow path that will take us down."

We turned and made our way toward the large rock. As we were walking, I had the sense that the short time we spent walking across the plain would have taken much longer had we stayed on the boat. *Boat?* I realized that we did not have a boat any longer. Apparently, I wasn't going to need it anymore.

"Another boat is waiting at the far end of the town for you at the last bridge. It is tied up and available for you when you are ready to move forward on your journey."

"Oh, I guess I thought I was done with the boat and the town was where I was going to be for a while." Although that thought had dropped into my mind, I was glad to know that a boat was waiting. I wanted to continue making my way to the *City*. Thoughts of the *City* created a yearning growing inside me more and more. I was glad because it seemed Jesus was going to continue the journey with me. I was glad to know about the waiting boat because somehow I felt that it would be the best way to get to the beautiful *City*.

Knowing my thoughts, Jesus spoke. "Your stay here will be short. There are things here for you to observe and experience. Things that will enlighten your understanding about hearts, desires and choices. This is a place of training to prepare you for more of your journey toward the *City*."

I looked up at the mention of the *City*. It was still radiating its glow throughout the plain. Its glow was blinding in its brilliance, even from this distance, you could hardly gaze upon it for long. My journey was bringing me closer, although I still had some distance to go to reach it. I could only imagine what it must be like to be up close or inside its gates.

We came to the large boulder and as I touched it, I felt the warmth of it spread from my fingertips throughout my body. It warmed me to my soul. I knew somehow that it was a piece of the rock that we had experienced with Holy Spirit. It was one of the touchstones Holy Spirit had spoken about. As I removed my hand, the stone of remembrance on my chain warmed against my neck and the warmth passed down to my heart, causing a couple of rapid beats in response. The thought that *Jesus was within me as well as He was standing beside me as my Rock* fluttered into my mind and deposited itself in my heart. It was a transforming thought and experience. As crazy as it was to think about, I knew that it was truth. Jesus smiled.

We were closer now to the town below as we stood beside the rock. "The town looks lovely! I can't wait to visit it and meet the people. But where is the path?"

"Follow me and step where I step. You will not fall or slip. It is safe."

"My feet have not slipped" 2 Samuel 22:37

I waited until Jesus went in front and stepped over the edge. Sure enough, as He stepped down, I could see a path begin to take shape out in front of Him allowing for a few more steps. It was like the earth pulled back the rocks and grass and the path was revealed. We made our way down easily and quickly without one little slip or insecure foothold. I was amazed at watching this all take place that I forgot to talk or pay attention to how quickly we made our decent.

Before I knew it, we were on flat ground again. The distance to the back of the buildings was closer than it had looked from the top. I turned and looked back to view the path we had taken. It was gone! The cliff face showed only sheer rocks. My scan went way up to the top. I could still see the large boulder where we had started our decent. As I was about to turn back around, Holy Spirit landed on the boulder. He sat down intently watching our progress. I felt I'd just experienced a supernatural manifestation of Jesus making a way where there was no way.

We walked toward the back of the buildings which lined this side of the River. The buildings were all sizes, shapes and colors. Each one unique and appealing. The buildings sat side by side lining each side of the River and boardwalk. There was just enough space between each building for walking between. As we approached, I noticed that each building was windowless and door less on three sides. *How curious.*

Catching my thoughts, Jesus explained. "No one can enter or leave except through the one door on the front. All who enter a building should stay until they have obtained the transformation that building provides. There is no provision for bypassing all that lies within. You must go in and allow the transformation process to complete you or you come back out abandoning the process. You accept or reject the transformation."

"Why does that matter?"

"People have weaknesses but they don't want others to see them. They choose to hide their weaknesses behind defenses or deflect the attention away. Transparency is rare between people. Even though each has chosen to come this far on the journey, their heart encourages them to continue hiding things. But, once you enter this town, confrontation of hidden things will take place. Some choose to ignore it becoming comfortable here. Others try to find another way around this place and attempt to make their own way to the *City* avoiding the process. Without the transformation that this town provides, deception will be strong in them and upon them."

"What's there to hide, Jesus? You know everything I am thinking as I think it. How hard could it be to keep choosing and move on in the way You intend us to go?"

Jesus smiled and this time I wasn't reassured that it was a good thing.

We made our way between two buildings and stepped up onto the boardwalk. Hundreds of people were passing by in both directions. It looked like a scene from a busy New York city street. People of every race, young, old, male, female, rich, poor, were walking. Some looked our way quickly but kept talking and walking. Some nodded to acknowledge our presence. Rarely did someone actually speak to us or welcome us. I didn't know if they were reserved or uncomfortable at seeing Jesus.

"Are all these people on the same journey as me, Jesus? Are all of these people going to the *City*?"

"Yes. Everyone comes through Crown Derby. Some come the most direct route as we did across the plain. Others stay on the River which starts meandering back and forth at the point where we got off. It can take years to reach on the River. If you choose to take the easy way and stay on the River, you will float through life without purpose or direction. Walking the plains takes only a few days to reach Crown Derby. Walking is not an easy choice. Travelers look at the plain without trees or signs of water and they fear getting out of the boat. Keeping to the River seems the logical choice. But, their logic costs them time and delay in reaching Crown Derby."

"Days!" I blustered out. My mind had stopped listening at the word "days." "We never rested or slept. How could it take days? I remembered walking with You and then we were here!" My words tumbled out.

Jesus smiled. "Time takes care of itself. Time isn't relevant here. With the Lord, a thousand years is like a day." (40)

"Lord, why did you bring me the shorter way and not let me drift through the years like others?"

"Because you always chose to take every hard challenge that came your way. You allowed Me to help overcome your fears. You faced the things that brought you intimidation. You chose to take control of your thoughts and take them captive when they tried to rise up, even when I was not there to remind you. You listened to the voice of Holy Spirit. Because of these things, I knew that you were ready for the most direct route to Crown Derby."

"Those who choose to drift on the River don't accept the invitation to challenges nor embrace the experiences that are presented as you did. Their fears keep them prisoner. Even though I am the same for everyone on the journey and deal with everyone in the same manner, not all people will respond the same or make the same choices. They move on down the River because it's the easier thing to do. I won't violate their will when I see what their heart is choosing."

"But Jesus, you mean that if they choose not to accept and embrace the challenges that come, they are doomed to years on the River?"

"No! There will always be opportunities all along the River. Places where they can choose to step out of the boat or fly with the Holy Spirit. There are always opportunities to take their thoughts captive in spite of what they see around them. If they finally choose to take an invitation, their decision will lead them to another shortcut to Crown Derby. But if they do not choose, then yes, they will become aimless until their time is depleted."

"Does that mean that some people will never even get to Crown Derby?"

"Yes. Crown Derby is designed for the next phase of each person's journey. It's another place to face hidden things and weaknesses. It's a place for divine exchanges. You decrease, and I increase. You are ready for this next part of your journey."

I didn't know if I should be excited or worried about what this town had in store. We turned and begin to walk the boardwalk. There was a slight breeze, and the walk was pleasant. I began to notice some people who were walking together decided to sit on a lovely park bench along the River and talk. Others who had been sitting got up and began walking the boardwalk again. It was a hive of activity. Across the River, I could see a group sitting under some beautiful trees having a picnic.

As we walked, I saw a younger brown skinned man excuse himself and leave the group. He headed toward a door on one of the buildings. I caught a flicker of light out of the corner of my eye as I watched this man leave the group. We stopped as I watched him enter the building.

"Why did that man choose to go into that particular building, Jesus?"

"Did you catch the flicker of light on the sign above the door?" His reply sounded weighted.

"Yes, I did catch a flicker of light."

Looking closer, I saw a neon sign. It was dark now, but in an instant, it might light up again. From this distance, I could barely make out the shape of a broken heart.

"There is always a sign for anyone desiring to see." Jesus began to explain. "The sign is the illumination of a rhema word, a 'now' God word or symbol. When a person passes by a building that can help their choice to decrease, the illumination of the rhema word activates the sign. If the person is not paying attention, they will miss it. If the person does not want illumination right now, the light will not flash at all. But, any person who desires to see, will not be disappointed. The sign on the appropriate building will momentarily illuminate."

I turned my attention back to the group the man had left. His decision to enter the building set the group off into animated conversation and body language. It reminded me of gossiping teenagers I had observed at my school many times.

The incredulous voice of one of the women came drifting on the breeze to my ears. "I would have never guessed that John needed to go in there!"

Another person puffed out his chest and said, "It's about time he chose to go in! He's needed to go in there for a long time!"

Another person said timidly, "I probably need to go in there, but not today. Let's move on down the boardwalk and make another loop."

I watched as this group picked up their pace. Then shortly, one of the ladies of the group who had not said a word earlier, excused herself, and left. Waving, she spied a friend over in another group who waved back. This group was walking in the opposite direction. As she entered the new group and passed by us, I heard her say to two of the ladies, "You will never believe what John did! He entered today into..." I lost the rest of it as they moved on behind us.

I looked at Jesus to see if He had caught the gossiping interaction. His look communicated His sadness.

We continued to walk the boardwalk and I watched people chat and sit with others. It became clear, that it was rare for someone to break out of a group and to enter a building. The majority of the people walked, talked and thoroughly enjoyed the fellowship of the stroll. I also noticed that some would occasionally break away making the illusion that they were entering a building. Later, they would double back, cross over to the other side of the River and join an entirely new group. The old group assumed the person had entered a building. The new group assumed that the person had just completed a building. It was all assumptions and deceptions. The thought came to me, *How long have some of these people been here doing this?*

"I figured you would catch onto this quickly," Jesus said. "Many people get this far in their journey and never want to leave. They find out that they can enjoy the boardwalk experience but never enter into the opportunities provided for decrease; deliverance, healing, training and correction. They live a deceptive lie. It is a deception to themselves and to others. By their choice, they never progress beyond here. All travelers must come to this town but not all will choose to yield to the process. Some will stay here until the call to the *City* comes. Others will move on, trying to make their own way to the *City* without experiencing the decrease process this place provides. Choice. It all comes down to choice. If they choose their own way, there will be great sadness if they reach the *City* because they won't hear the Father say, 'Well done.'"

Jesus's words broke my heart. People were choosing to make the motions of obedience, yet not entering in to what Jesus had for them. All of a sudden, I was gripped with thoughts like, *What about me? What would I do?* Fear and intimidation arose from possibilities of the unknown. Fear and intimidation were strong motivators. I knew their power to imprison. I had been such a prisoner many times before coming on this journey. I knew in my heart that fear and intimidation caused many people to ignore the blinking light signaling their call to enter. *Would*

I be strong enough to answer the call? Would I choose the safe route of the boardwalk with all of its comforts or decrease for Jesus? I knew my time to choose was looming ahead.

"Embrace what this place has to teach you," Jesus said with such love in His voice. "Embrace the grace that is here to answer the call when the sign is illuminated. Choose quickly to enter and decrease. Decrease is designed to transform you into the image of the One who sits on the throne of the *City* of Light and His Christ. Let hearing the Father say, 'Well done!' be your encouragement to make the hard choices. I know you can do this. Embrace and choose. Receive what this place has for you quickly or walk a time or two around the boardwalk and enjoy life for a season. But beware. Life can change what you hunger for. It is freely your choice."

I wanted to hear those words from the Father. I wanted to be transformed. But I wasn't sure I understood or wanted to really decrease. "Jesus, I understand that a building will help me confront things in my life but how do they help me decrease? Why must I decrease?"

"When you process through each building that is illuminated, you confront your weaknesses. If you choose to give them up, you and your self-will get smaller and I will actually increase because you are choosing My will. The next part of your River journey requires decrease so you can take a smaller boat–a kayak – rather than a larger rowboat. It is tied up and waiting at the last bridge. Downstream the River will make a 'Y'. One direction will be wider, deeper and have more current. The other will be narrow and have less current and volume. You must take the narrow way for reaching the *City*. The narrow way will not be an option if you only fit into a rowboat that needs more River depth. The stream with more volume and current will circle back to Crown Derby. If that happens, you will have another opportunity to get off and decrease. This is how the process goes until you have decreased enough for the narrow

63

way. Without the decrease, you stay as you are and wait for the final call to the *City* or try and make your own way through the treacherous landscape that lies between here and the *City*."

"But Jesus, I want to move on quickly to complete my journey and reach the *City*. Is there a way to process the boardwalk without coming back over and over?"

"Yes, there is a way. Walk the boardwalk with purpose. Look at every building's sign. Pause and give it your attention. Does it illuminate? If it does, go in immediately. When you complete the experiences the building leads you through, return to walk the boardwalk. Once you have walked the entire boardwalk of Crown Derby and no lights illuminate, you will have decreased to fit the small kayak and can take the River's narrow way."

"Now I must go, but I will return. I will not leave you. Remember Holy Spirit is always with you."

Even as Jesus said the words "Holy Spirit", I heard His call high above my head and I was filled with comfort. Holy Spirit was hovering. I quickly looked up and we connected. Jesus turned and walked toward the high cliff at the edge of the plain. I watched Him disappear between two buildings and for a second, I felt panic. *What if I never get this part right? What if I ended up being a person who settled for the boardwalk at Crown Derby and never decreased?* The shrill call of Holy Spirit pierced my ears and brought me back to purposeful determination. *I can do this with His help. He will strengthen me to continue. He has not brought me this far to abandon me and see me fail.*

I turned and walked in the direction of the last bridge. I wanted to see the size of the kayak, so I could get a good idea of what it might take to decrease enough to fit into it. I came to the last bridge and went over to look. Sitting in the River was one tiny kayak among many row boats. It was not long enough for my legs and I knew that my body would never fit into the tiny hole in the middle. Wow! I had my work cut out for me. With determination, I crossed the bridge heading to the closest building.

"Not as pleasing men, but God, who tests our hearts" 1 Thes. 2:4

As I approached the boardwalk, several people saw me and realized I was new to Crown Derby. They looked like any person you might meet at the mall. Jesus was not with me to intimidate them, so they stopped to talk.

A grandmotherly lady with the air of authority in her voice spoke up. "Hello there. You appear new to Crown Derby. Let us help you walk the boardwalk".

I was happy to meet these people and have conversation and fellowship since I was sorely missing Jesus.

"Thanks! Yes, I am new to Crown Derby and I want to process through it quickly."

A younger man dressed in blue jeans and a flannel shirt spoke up. "Oh, why the rush! There is always time to do a building. Come and stroll with us for a while. We are going to meet up with some others on the other side and have a picnic and some fresh lemonade. Surely you must be famished from the long walk on the plain. We saw you with Jesus, so we know that He brought you across the hard plain. Spend some time with us. Relax, and get your strength back. Trust me, you will need strength for what could be inside your next building. It is important to make yourself strong and ready to take on the challenges because you are on your own now. It all depends on you, your strength and abilities to get through Crown Derby!"

Although it sounded like good advice, his words caused a little alarm pinging inside me. I waited for my safe twin to surface and validate his advice. Now, I did feel hungry and a little weak after the trek on the plain. Lemonade would refresh me, and my flesh could use some good food right now. I couldn't remember when I had last eaten. Jenny and Germany were far removed from my thoughts. The thought of eating food and having fellowship was appealing. My stomach growled. *What could it hurt?* Besides, while enjoying the food and refreshment, I could get to know these people. Maybe they can tell me which buildings would help me to decrease quickly and fit into the kayak. I was sure there was a logical process to it all. My adventurous twin spoke up, *Don't forget decrease! Decrease!* The word of Jesus exploded through my mind.

Wait a minute! If I went along and enjoyed a big meal at the picnic, I wouldn't be decreasing in my flesh but staying the same. I might even increase. For the moment, I had lost sight of why I was here and what I needed to be focused on. Their invitation was appealing and it was logical.

Then I heard the faint call of Holy Spirit above me. I noticed that the people who were expectantly waiting for me to join them, never gave a hint of hearing Holy Spirit's call. Though I had heard it faintly, it was enough to give me purpose to remember another word of Jesus– "CHOICE". Now was a time for a choice.

My flesh sounding like my safe twin was clamoring to join the group. It was telling me I could walk with them for a time and it wouldn't matter. Besides, Jesus had said I could walk to enjoy the time if I wanted to. Time was not relevant in this place. My flesh told me that I could do a couple of extra laps and do them at a faster pace. Thus, I would work off any extra calories that I would indulge in and make up any lost time. My emotions also sounding like my safe twin were telling me I needed the companionship. My logical mind was telling me to get information that would benefit me and make it easier to do this myself. Their advice made sense. I justified going along with them. As I faintly heard one more cry of the Holy Spirit above me, my adventurous twin said, *Decrease!* Reality returned. I knew I needed to walk away.

"Hey, thanks for asking, but I think I want to do some exploring on my own. I'm not hungry right now, but I appreciate your friendly offer."

When I spoke the words every sign of hunger and fatigue left me. Hearing my words they shrugged and walked on. For a moment, I wondered what they might be saying about me. But I heard the word *choice* in my heart, and I knew I had made the right decision. I stepped out and headed down the boardwalk. I purposed to look at the sign above the first building I approached. I paused and waited. Nothing! No light came on. *Did I have it right? Why didn't it light up?*

"The light of illumination comes from the area of life where you have a weakness. Walk on." The voice of Jesus came clear and direct into my spirit.

Holy Spirit sounded above and I was secure. *Ok, I will walk on,* I told myself. On I went, slowly and with purpose. I checked out each building on my way. People would call out to me to join them and walk with their group. But I smiled, shook my head and walked on. After about the fourth building, I began to wonder what would happen when I did see the light. *What would I encounter inside?* I had been so focused on knowing how to find the right buildings that I forgot to ask what I was to do once inside.

The voice of Jesus came boldly to my mind. "Every person's experience will be different when they enter. What you will need to experience inside will be different from what someone else needs though you might enter together. Inside the building it is all about the individual and what each will need to move forward towards decrease as they make their way to the *City*."

I walked on. A group came from behind me and matched their pace to mine. No one said anything to me. Most of the group were listening to two or three prominent speakers in the center. They were talking about their dreams, hopes and promises in God. The silent ones were hanging on their every word. I noticed no one was looking at the buildings or signs. Their entire attention was focused on the storytellers. They would sigh and shake their heads as the stories were told. I wondered, *What have they missed? How many lights were illuminated for them which they missed because their focus was on a person and not on the illumination for their own journey?*

Although it saddened me as I listened, my attention remained fixed for my own illumination. The group stopped in front of a building. I looked at the sign, but it did not illuminate. I kept looking as I listened to the chattering group leaders. One was telling an engaging story about past encounters with Jesus and angels. Everyone in the group was enthralled. I positioned myself to watch the sign and still watch the group dynamics. It was fascinating to watch how many of the group were acting like hero worshippers to those calling attention to themselves with their tales of being spiritual.

Suddenly, I noticed one man's head jerk to attention and freeze. His hero worship suspended. It appeared he'd seen a light come on. His body language spoke of inner turmoil. I could tell he was pulled to leave the group and go into the building. But the pull to stay and be part of the group was strong. He had been captivated as he listened to the stories and watched the charismatic qualities of the storytellers. Certainly, he would choose the building. Certainly, he would choose to progress on his own journey. Certainly, the stories of someone else's past glory and future exploits would not be so alluring to hold him back. I continued to watch his struggle. In that moment, I realized how hard it was for him and could be for anyone who had lost focus on why they had come to Crown Derby. I wanted to push him toward the door of the building. I thought about taking him by the hand and telling him I would go with him to get him moving toward his own journey.

The shrill call of Holy Spirit was right on top of me. I could feel the hairs on my head swish from the breeze of His wings as He flew low over me. I ducked in reaction. Not a single person saw or heard Him as He flew over us. Everyone was focused on the storytellers. They never saw, felt or heard Holy Spirit. His call sent goose bumps down my neck. The person I had been concerned for, cleared his throat to get everyone's attention. *Yes!*, I thought. He was going to tell them that he was leaving to go into the building.

"Hey everyone!" He said. "Let's move on down the boardwalk. We don't want to miss anything God has for us."

Shocked and saddened, I wondered if my expression was noticed. I'm sure my mouth gaped as I gasped. I could feel the incredible loss of the divine moment. I stood there watching them all walk on. Once again, the story tellers dominated, holding the others in rapt attention. My heart sank. This man who had a "moment with God and Holy Spirit" had chosen to follow man. My thoughts were jumbled. I took a deep sigh and came to the conclusion that Crown Derby was the best and the worst of places depending on choice. In that instant I knew I needed to be doing what Jesus had told me to do. I needed to process through Crown Derby quickly, move on down the River; decreased in size as I continued to the *City*.

"As a lamp shining in a dark place"
2 Peter 1:19

I didn't want to walk the boardwalk again unless I still needed to decrease more than what one trip around provided. I didn't want to repeat steps because I chose to let my focus be captured by other things. With new purpose and resolve, I moved on. I realized I had gone the length of one side of the River and found myself at the first bridge. I crossed to the other side quickly because I wanted to move on finding my own place of illumination. My safe twin spoke up and suggested, *What if you stopped at the bench ahead? You could rest and use your peripheral vision to watch three different building's signs at once.*

Without thinking, I sat down. The weariness of years settled upon me. In that moment, I felt like I needed a nap. Yes, a nap was a good idea. I had been on the move for a long time and Jesus had never been upset when I had napped before. I decided to sit and close my eyes for a few minutes and rest. My eyes grew heavy and I was asleep. I must have begun to dream because I saw myself sitting on the bench and looking at the three buildings. As I watched myself in the dream, I noticed that my view of the three buildings was hindered. The crowds of people increased and blocked my view of all three signs. I watched myself try to be observant, but without success. I leaned right and left trying to see around or through the people as they drifted along the boardwalk.

I soon realized that it was impossible to sit there, watch three buildings, and look for illumination. The dream continued. I came to realize that the same group of people would walk back and forth in front of me. Their outfits changed. Their places in the groups changed, but it was the same people distracting me and blocking my vision. In that moment, my adventurous twin yelled, *Wake up!* I awoke startled. I thought I could get by with observing multiple buildings and rest too. It was deception. I could not sit and wait on illumination. Instantly another thought dropped into my mind. *What if these three buildings were not for you.* Logic had failed me.

I got up and resumed walking the boardwalk. As I approached the next building, my body became suddenly warm. It had the excitement of a child on Christmas morning, wondering what I would find under the tree. Expectation and butterflies filled my stomach. I turned my eyes to the next building's sign. It illuminated! I had desired this moment so badly, and here it was. Now I was afraid. *What if I'm not ready for what's inside? What if I fail the tests that await me? What if this? What if that?* My safe twin had returned. This was my first opportunity to decrease and suddenly as I faced it, I was unsure. *Was this the right test to take first? What if I had missed the first one when I had been napping? What if I had missed my flicker while watching the hero worship group? What if the decreasing opportunities had a specific order?*

I was intimidated because people were watching me. They had obviously noticed my reaction to the illumination. Now they were waiting for my choice. I felt the pressure that the groups put on a person. The group dynamics and the pressure to fit in made the choice to decrease incredibly difficult. The groups did not call people to accountability. Rather the groups gave permission for people to maintain their status quo and walk on. All the weaknesses; fear, pride, insecurities and fleshly desires could be ignored. The group gave justification to stay as they were because everyone else was doing the same. It took great courage for someone to step out and choose to decrease over the security of the group.

This was my moment and I must seize it. My spirit was telling me not to wait. Both twins were silent. Any delay would strengthen my flesh and weaken my desire to decrease. I took a quick step and turned toward the building where my light had illuminated. The sign was still blinking the words "DEATH TO SELF". *Dear God! Of all the other buildings that I could have started with, why did I get death to self, first?*

I quickly made my way to the door. Taking a deep breath, I grabbed the handle, turned the knob and went in. I closed the door with a definitive thud saying, "I'm not turning back!" Little did I know that like the old adage "All roads lead to Rome", all of the buildings in Crown Derby dealt with a form of "Death to Self". Death to self was the only way to decrease.

Chapter 4

The Mist
Completing the Circle of Life

"Things prepared the heart didn't consider"
1 Co. 2:9-11

As my eyes adjusted to the interior brightness, I could see that "doom and gloom," "dark and foreboding" were not part of this building. A part of me took flight with the hope that all painful thoughts about death, dying and decrease were not as scary as I had imagined. The building was filled with glorious light. It was sunny, warm, lush and green. Inside, the building became an expanse that looked like a mammoth arboretum. I saw birds flying. I could hear sounds of flowing water in the distance. The air was filled with the smell of life and growth. It was a picture of Eden. As my mind was taking all this in, I remembered the outside of the building. I knew this expanse could not fit inside the building I had just entered. How was it possible? People out on the boardwalk didn't have a clue what they were missing. It was beautiful. What is there to fear in choosing to decrease? Natural thoughts and perspectives didn't apply here.

I could see a small path through some ferns and stepped through them toward it. I was reminded of what the children experienced going from the wardrobe into Narnia in the book by C.S. Lewis, *The Chronicles of Narnia*. It was a portal to another world. As I began walking down the path, a wonderful sweet fragrance greeted my nose. It was attractive and caused me to wonder where it could be coming from. Just then an angel stepped out from behind a large tree. I jumped sideways from the suddenness of his large appearance. The familiar phrase "be not afraid" flashed through my mind, and before I could process that I was seeing an angel, he spoke.

"It is the sweet smell of death and flesh dying."

"Excuse me! Did you say death and flesh dying?"

"Yes, it's a pleasant aroma, isn't it?"

As my mind processed his words, my eyes were taking in his appearance. Although much larger than an average man, he was not a looming giant by any means. He was dressed in a plain and unassuming robe like you could picture being worn in the days of Jesus.

"My name is Micah. Welcome to this part of your journey. I welcome all who come to draw near the Lord. You will have your own personal ministering angel who will aid you in the rest of your journey. He will be along in a moment. Please take a seat and wait for him."

I turned to see where he was motioning when he said, "Take a seat". There was a comfortable looking bench that I would have sworn was not there a second ago. I turned to ask Micah more about this place, but he was gone.

I sat on the bench and remembered the last time I had sat down in Crown Derby. But this time I was not the least bit tired or sleepy. As I looked at all the vegetation, the thought popped into my mind that whatever was ahead had the potential to be all I needed for my total decrease. That brought me excitement. It also brought anxious thoughts about what it would take for the death and dying aspects. I took a deep sigh. *Where was Jesus right now?* I could use His all-knowing smile for reassurance of what lay ahead. I heard a flapping sound and saw Holy Spirit land on a rock across from me. Then, He directed His gaze at me. His piercing eyes brought peace but also a fluttering or a slight trembling inside of me. He didn't speak. He gazed at me. *Should I gaze back? Should I speak to Him?*

In my mind I heard His voice.

"Peace be still. Remember the times of taking your thoughts captive. Remember that what you see with your eyes is not always the truth.

Remember that you can do all things, even impossible things, like fly, when you let go of your fears and let Me enable you."

In my mind, I answered. *Yes, Lord, I remember.*

"Good, because where your journey now goes, you will always need to remember that and much more!"

With that He stretched out His wings and flew off. How had He gotten inside the building? I was amazed at how He always showed up when needed. I turned my gaze back to the foliage. As I did, I began to notice a very fine mist. I could see now that the air was full of it and it had settled upon my skin. The temperature of the mist perfectly matched my body temperature. I could feel a refreshing taking place as my skin absorbed it. My skin was plumping up just like a thirsty sponge taking in all that the mist was supplying. Amazingly, as I felt my skin and clothes, they were not damp. Another strange experience. I knew that I had not even scratched the surface of what was ahead.

The passage of time here was different. At times, it seemed to stand still. Other times, it passed quickly. How long I waited, I am not sure. But a point did come where I became a little impatient and grumbled under my breath. "What is taking this ministering angel of mine so long to show up?" Now that I was here and had already seen that all this "death to self and dying" was not what I had imagined, I was ready to move ahead.

"Any time now, Mr. Angel! Any time!"

That didn't cause him to appear. I looked around, to see if I could locate the path to move out on my own. I was impatient and ready to take off, when Holy Spirit's voice trickled down into my mind like the mist.

"Soak and wait. Soak and wait. Exchange impatience for patience."

I reasoned that I had already spent enough time "soaking" by this point, but obviously not! I took another sigh of resolve and decided to stretch out on the bench and soak in the mist. As I got comfortable, I took a deep breath and inhaled the mist. It was like tangible energy entered my nasal passages. I could feel a quickening inside my sinus cavities. I took another deep breath, feeling the mist travel on down my throat and into my lungs. With every breath, I could feel it moving. From my lungs it made its way through out every cell of my body, changing them and transforming them. It was a strange and unique feeling. *It felt like electricity charged every cell. I felt the most alive that I had ever felt. I wondered, Is this how it felt when God blew His breath into the lungs of Adam or Eve and they became living spiritual beings?* Every part of my being was full of the soaking mist and the life it brought.

I heard a sound coming from the area where Holy Spirit had sat on the rock. I turned my head and saw David.

"David????" I yelled in a loud voice. *My David from the train and Germany? He was a ministering angel? Was he going to be my ministering angel?*

"How? Why?" The words exploded out of my mouth as my mind remembered a human man on a train and now an angel. I sat up quickly. David was sitting on the rock smiling like Jesus. Now that I thought about it, he smiled the same easy smile that I remembered on the train. His outward appearance wasn't much different than Micah's. His features had not changed but now he had a glow. Not much else was different. His plain robe, cinched at the waist with a braided belt, flowed down from his shoulders to sandaled feet. They were so different from the business suit he had worn on the train.

"Are you tasting and seeing that the Lord is good? (47) And yes, it's me!" He chuckled.

I must have looked like a deer caught in headlights. Questions swirled! Yet I had come to realize that here in this place, all things could be possible. Rather than the why and the how, a peace settled over me. Having David brought a great comfort in this "dying to self-place". That connection brought me back to where I was and why I was here. Purpose of choice flowed into me like a transfusion of life. My focus became completing this mission, decreasing so I could fit the small kayak waiting for me at the River. With that new resolve, I focused on David. I found myself accepting the fact that I had a ministering angel. I realized that the role he had played on the train encounter wasn't different from the role he was now playing.

I looked at him and thought about what he said. *Was I tasting and seeing that the Lord was good?* I did feel peaceful and satisfied. I felt great! I was ready for anything, or so I thought.

"You are experiencing God with all of your being," David responded. "This is how life is supposed to be lived. Total saturation of His Presence. His Presence is His life flowing to all of creation. His Presence is what created the mist in the garden, and everything flourished in His Presence. Waiting like this and soaking in His Presence renews and refreshes. It brings new life to areas needing renewal."

"I am enjoying this, but how is this death and dying? It is bringing me life not death. Even my skin is plumped up. How does this help me to decrease? I feel more increased!" I couldn't understand it.

David addressed my questions. "Your spirit is increased. But you are impatient and the choice to wait patiently on the Lord and be renewed was death to your flesh. You are decreased by your choice yet increased by its result. It is the paradox of life in the Spirit."

David continued. "Remember to take in the mist when you need to have the Father's life power. The mist of His Presence is always available even when you can't see it in the natural or feel it on your skin as you do now. Can you feel your inner man being filled up, bringing life from the outside to your inside?"

I nodded.

"Choose to stop, soak and rest at every opportunity. Believe me when I tell you, it can take a real dying to self to rest and soak. It takes total dying to self to learn to walk in the world and in the presence of the mist at the same time. It will be one of your greatest weapons and tools if you choose to embrace what is being offered as wisdom now and master it. Remember this lesson. Waiting is providential."

I sat looking at David. I was overwhelmed by all he had said. Although I still had many questions, I felt at peace knowing that my spirit man understood, and I was changing because of it.

"Now are you ready to go forward in this place?"

All I could do was nod.

"Try soaking as we walk. It requires a deeper level of submitting and discipline than lying down and soaking."

We started down a new path, one I had not seen earlier. It was a good thing I hadn't started out on my own. I would have missed this new way. The path was only wide enough for one person at a time. David walked slowly which I appreciated because every bush, flower or tree was unique and beautiful. I wanted to take it all in. As I looked closer, I could see the mist was on everything. There was not a surface in this place that didn't have mist on it. It wasn't dripping, but it was evident. Seeing the mist caused me to become aware of my own "misting" state. Although my skin felt covered, I missed the feeling of its presence within me. I quickly took several deep breaths, refilling my lungs with the mist. Now I could again feel it flow into every cell of my being.

We walked on and on. I had to learn how to be on "auto pilot". I needed to be intentional to adequately breathe in the mist and pay attention to the path. The process became easier as we walked and at some point I discovered that both the natural and spiritual could work together. I was able to balance them both.

David didn't speak as we walked. It didn't seem strange or unnatural. Rather his presence was comfort enough. At some point, my ears recognized the sound of rushing water. The more I focused on the sound, the more I could tell that it was a large, fast flowing body of water. My mind pictured a waterfall. I continued to focus on the sound and tried to imagine the volume of water flow I was hearing. As I was pondering this, the path before us cleared revealing a rocky outcropping on the edge of a huge waterfall. The vertical drop and the width of the gorge was as large as many famous waterfalls. The sound of the rushing water was deafening. I could see mist billowing up from the thundering waters that plunged over the crest. Some water created a spray as it broke on the rocks. The rest continued downstream into the deep gorge below.

The River spray reminded me that I had lost the feeling of the mist inside of me. My skin was no longer covered with it. *How could that be when I was right here where the mist was billowing up?*

David knew what I was thinking because he answered, "As the sound attracted your focus more and more, you began to concentrate on the sounds and their source. You forgot to take in the mist for yourself. What gets you attention gets you. In this case, it was the source of that sound that captured your attention. Stop and refocus. Focus not on what is around you. Focus on the mist. Take a deep breath and purpose to soak it in."

I breathed quickly and deeply. Immediately the life flow was back. I could feel it inside and out.

"Now remember this lesson, become intentional. What gets your attention will get you. You need to discern these questions: Will what I focus on bring life or death? Will it bring the mist or not? This is what it means to live and move and have your being in the Lord."

Could I maintain all that I was hearing and learning as I moved forward into the challenges that lay ahead? I knew the principles. But I was quick to forget. David's presence helped. *But what if he left me on my own like Jesus and Holy Spirit sometimes did?*

Instantly I heard the voice of Jesus. "I will never leave you." (13) At that same time, I heard the shrill call of Holy Spirit high overhead. I was comforted and knew in whatever was ahead, I had all of them to help me walk my journey. The path ended at the waterfall. I had a feeling that a more challenging task could be awaiting me.

"For everything there is a season and a time" Ecc. 3:1

With that ominous thought, I turned my attention to the mist. I inhaled deeply and felt the mist as it moved through my nose; wetting my nose hairs. I could feel it move up into my sinuses and then down into my lungs like the tingling that comes from mentholated ointment. The mist was opening all my air ways. I could now feel things that had been restricted, relax and release. I hadn't even been aware that there were restrictions. I had a quick flashback, a memory, to my River journey. The memory of issues I had been unaware of, rising to challenge me; things I had buried deep within. *What other things were restricted, in tension or buried? Were there things out of balance, more hidden fears, I had no clue about? What else might reside still inside of me?* I had within me the feeling that if there were, my journey was going to bring them to the surface.

As I continued to breathe in deeply the mist, everything began to come alive. But this time I was aware that I was gaining strength. By taking in more deep breaths, I felt strong and invigorated. It felt like I could run a marathon and not collapse from the pain in my sides. I realized that with every breath, I was feeling younger and renewed. I felt like I did in my early 20's, full of vitality. I'd forgotten what it felt like. I thought about Caleb, in the Old Testament, as he focused on taking his portion of the Promised Land. Although he was 80 years old, he felt like 40. *Was soaking in this mist part of the provisions that the Old Testament Patriarchs had available? Could this be part of the process of being renewed like the eagle?*

I was about to turn back to David to ask him these questions, but before I could say a word, he said, "Come, it is time for the next phase of your journey."

He headed off at a quick pace, not giving me time to ask. The direction took us to another path I had not seen earlier. This time the foliage was thicker, making it more difficult to see ahead. I tried to keep up my pace and yet stay aware of breathing in the mist. Splitting my focus was hard at first. A couple of times, I lost sight of David as he continued his fast pace. If I lost sight of him, I would pick up my own pace and breathe in more deeply. My body adapted. No longer did we walk leisurely. David seemed intent to be somewhere quickly. I could tell I was expected to match my pace to his. At first the quickened pace challenged me. Rapidly my body was winded. But, as I breathed deeply, the mist improved my breathing. I had the stamina to keep up. I finally matched his pace, no longer lagging behind.

David stopped so suddenly I almost ran into him.

"Sorry, David, I was concentrating on breathing in the mist, matching your pace and paying attention to what was around me, I'm afraid I was on 'autopilot.'"

David laughed. "You will acclimate. Even now, you are being transformed and renewed in order to run and keep up with the demands put on you."

"Will I ever get to the place where I can see everything, breathe in the mist and keep pace? Will all this ever be natural for me?"

"Yes, in time. It is all about time and how you spend it, keep it and experience it. Time is relevant yet not relevant here. It is relevant to a season of the Spirit. In God's plans, time has a different relevance. Let's continue on your journey. Don't focus on doing it all. Simply keep your focus on the task at hand and that is walking this path as part of your journey. I think you will find that your body will align with the Spirit. Let's go!"

Let's go! REALLY! I wanted to shout out those words! I still had many questions. As my mind started down the path of one of them, I realized my focus had so quickly changed from the journey to my questions. I focused on David's back, now several more steps ahead. Pushing all thoughts and questions aside, I focused on keeping pace with David. Time passed or did it? I couldn't tell. The journey had taken over all my thoughts. I became one with the pace of David. I focused only on keeping the pace and breathing in the mist. I didn't know how long we kept that pace. I only know that the pace never varied, and the light never dimmed. The light continued as bright as noon on a sunny day.

"Nothing causes them to stumble" Psalm 119:165

The path that we were on varied at times. Sometimes it was straight and wide. Sometimes it was narrow and curvy. But I never lost sight of David's back and I knew that he was aware of my every move as I followed behind. I never got hungry. I never got tired. I never got thirsty. All the natural and physical things that you would think should be taking place, gave way with the energized flow of the mist throughout my body. I thought about Moses in that moment and realized that he must have experienced this same thing while on the mountain with God. Time was not relevant. Through all of this experience of miles or days or even months of walking, I realized that my breathing in the mist and keeping the pace was becoming automatic. I could let my mind be free to look around and see that the foliage had changed and that this area was different. The mist was still present.

Still feeling strong and energized, I decided to stretch out my pace to catch up with David allowing us to walk side by side. The path here was wide and taking longer strides, I advanced alongside of him. I was so pleased. Now maybe we could talk as we kept to the journey. I was about to ask David how much longer we would be walking like this, when my toe caught on a tree root. I was propelled forward, my face ready to meet with the path. David's arm shot out and broke my fall. He saved me from what would have been a hard hit, not to mention eating dirt. Regaining my balance, I stood up.

"I see that you have reached a new level in your confidence and pace." David's voice was not critical, but I could tell that he was about to mentor me in some new truths. "That's good. But when you focused on the task of catching up to me, you lost sight of the journey. When the object of your focus changes, trip-ups can occur. Every advancement has the potential to shift your focus to your own accomplishments. Take care not to fall. Always keep your eyes on the current task, words and directions you have been given. Keep your focus on His words and not on the accomplishments you have achieved while doing what was asked of you. Do you understand?"

I did. I felt corrected but not condemned. I was thankful that David stopped my fall. I knew what had taken place in the last few minutes was an important lesson to remember. Wisdom was growing in me. I continued to wonder if I would be able to retain it. I surely didn't want to lose one word of it but I feared my mind might not retain it all.

"Thanks', David, for stopping my fall. I'm sure it would have been a nasty one."

"You're welcome. As the ministering angel assigned to you, I'm here to see that you move forward with only a few scars."

His laugh at my shocked look to his "few scars" comment let me know that he had been teasing. I was delighted that he felt he could.

"Yes, you will retain the wisdom." He continued. "It goes deep into your spirit and will be brought to your mind when you need it." He chuckled again as he set off at an even faster pace.

I easily kept up now and was content to follow. Time had lost its hold on me. Contentment in completing this part of my journey came over me like a warm blanket. Completing this part of my journey was all that held my focus.

At some point the sound of a waterfall came filtering into my consciousness. *Another waterfall?* Now that thought got my attention. As we turned the corner, we came right back to the original outcropping where I had seen the waterfall the first time. *How? Why?* All kinds of questions poured into my mind. I was amazed and yet somewhat irritated. If this was the ending point, why had we gone for who knows how long through the various paths? We had to have walked in a circle! I felt agitated and angry about it all. It didn't make sense. David turned to me and the look on his face scattered all my questions and my anger. I could tell he was not pleased with my attitude. His look was stern and solemn.

"I'm sorry", came gushing out of my mouth. "It's just that I thought I was going somewhere."

"You are, and you did!"

"But we are right back where we started from aren't we?"

"Yes."

"We walked in a big circle?"

"No. We have been on many roads of life and we traveled a great distance. During every minute of the travel, you were growing, learning, and decreasing in your flesh. Nothing the Lord has you do is ever wasted. Everything, no matter how small it may seem, even walking in a circle, has a point, a reason and is valuable for your journey. Nothing is wasted. Nothing is done without a purpose. You learned how to pick up the pace and take on a new level of endurance on the journey. You kept a pace that caused you to learn how to take in the life sustaining mist. You learned the hazards of focusing on your own accomplishments. Have you quickly forgotten the lessons?"

"Oh, I'm sorry, I did quickly forget."

I took a deep breath. The mist again calmed and rejuvenated my being. The tension and the frustration from a few minutes ago fell away. With one more deep breath, all remaining frustration left my body and peace flooded in. I had peace that my efforts on the path had decreased me. Maybe now I might fit in the kayak and move on down the River.

"You have passed this small test. Now it's time for you to move to the next task on your journey."

Immediately my mind went back to death and dying. I didn't know why, but panic was starting to awaken deep inside. If that was a little test, what was coming next? I felt fear like icy fingers taking hold of my throat, threatening to squeeze my breath right out of me. Fear came rising up from deep inside me.

"Stop!" David spoke quick and firmly.

"Take your thoughts captive. Remember your lessons! Breathe deeply. Focus on Jesus! 'He is the Way, the Truth and the Life.'" (14)

"Jesus!" I cried out, but He wasn't here.

"Close your eyes and see Him. He promised to never leave you." David calmly reminded me.

As I closed my eyes and breathed extra deep, the mist began to get past the tightening of my throat. I felt a familiar warm hand on my shoulder and I opened my eyes. There was Jesus standing right in front of me, giving me that grin. Suddenly all was well. I hugged Him without thinking because I was so glad to see Him. The touchstone warmed around my neck. I realized I had not thought about it or the chain for some time. He laughed, and I could hear His laugh rumble inside His chest. It blended with the rumble and roar of the falls as the water continually plummeted down, falling upon the rocks.

"I told you I would always be here for you. You need to look to Me and for Me. Here, this is for you."

He held out His right hand, palm up. In it was another half circle of stone. It was beautiful blue with intricate carvings. In some places, I saw tiny holes going through the stone.

"This is the other half of your stone for your chain." Jesus said with joy.

I had forgotten, but now remembered He had said that one day I would get the other half. I reached out to take it. The curious look on my face told Him I didn't know what to do with it.

"Here let me help." Jesus responded.

He came behind me and undid the chain. I was seeing for the first time the chain and the gifts upon it. The chain was made of beautiful shiny gold links; smooth, flat and solid. It was a love gift from Father for starting the journey. From it hung the touchstone. It was a polished blood-red piece of the large flinty stone from the rock on the plains. That time existed so long ago. A flight with Holy Spirit! A time where I had seen things from a different perspective. As I reached out to examine it more, the touchstone immediately warmed to my touch. The next piece was the half circle from the time when I learned to take my thoughts captive and stepped out to walk on the water. This was a gift to help me always remember about walking out the impossible.

"How do I put the two pieces together?"

"Here, let Me".

He took the half piece on the chain and touched it to the other half piece in His palm. I heard a "snap" and the two fused into one flawless, complete circle. I was amazed! I examined it again as it hung from the chain. The intricate design wrapped itself seamlessly around the circle as if it had been made whole from the beginning.

"What are the little holes for?" I asked.

"They represent areas where you have decreased to the point that there is nothing left of you in that area."

"What do the intricate lines mean?"

"They represent the paths and choices you have made so far where you exercised self-restraint in your body and spirit; places you chose to bring patience to your actions and took your thoughts captive rather than they capturing you."

"Oh!"

"I had never thought about those things taking shape in my life. I was trying to continue my journey and do as You asked."

"As you continue your journey, the designs and the appearance of this stone will change reflecting what is happening in you. It is a mirroring work." He laughed a deep and satisfied laugh. "Here, let me put it back around your neck and we can go."

The chain and two stones settled down around my neck as Jesus secured it. It felt warm and natural.

"Jesus, I fear death."

There it was. No taking those words back. They blurted out without warning or thought. *Where had they come from?* The touchstone warmed. It was like the combined presence of the completed stone was working to reveal everything that still needed transformation.

The dam had been opened. "I know that I'm to embrace death and dying but I'm afraid of the bodily pain and suffering that will come with it. The unknown of what happens when I die. I don't know if I am strong enough to face it and go through to death." My words flew out of my mouth like fast balls fired in a batting cage.

"Are you dying yet?" Jesus asked.

I looked up into His smiling eyes. His question pushed back my anxiety.

"No."

"Then don't rush ahead to what might be. Stay in the moment with Me and together we will walk through this."

His words brought comfort as He took my hand.

"Let's go for a walk."

We started off following a path that was close to the edge of the high River gorge. It started at the outcropping and headed toward the waterfall. I could hear the water rushing fast and furious below. The more we walked, the louder it became. Suddenly, I remembered David. I stopped and turned around causing Jesus to let go of my hand. David was gone.

"David is doing the Father's business right now", Jesus said, "and so must we."

Chapter 5

The Great Falls
A Choice
A Step
A Leap

"My ways are higher than your ways" Isaiah 55:9

The Great Falls was up ahead. From the path we were walking I could see the majesty of it; all of its power, height and volume tumbling in abandonment to glorious perfection. Water came over the falls in one form and some became transformed, as it fell on the rocks below. I couldn't tell if there was one massive rock or many due to the rising mist. It created an iridescent fog that radiated colors of the rainbow wherever the light from the *City* intersected it.

Death waited. I knew it! I couldn't let that thought dwell. Fear lurked on its fringes, tormenting. I put it out of my mind by focusing on Jesus, His presence with me and the strength of His hand holding mine. Occasionally a "what if?" or a "maybe" would fly across my mind trying to find a spot to roost. He knew my thoughts because right in that moment, Jesus would strengthen his grip. A silent squeeze said "Trust, be at peace, I love you, you can do this, all will be well. Your thoughts are lies not truth."

The onslaught continued and a war tried to commence. Fearful thoughts appeared like specters. Thoughts returned from a distant past when I had gone through a period of great anxiety and pain. Memories flooded back into the forefront of my mind. But when they would mount an overwhelming assault, I would hear a Bible verse from deep inside. "I will hear what God the Lord will speak, for He will speak peace to His people and His saints". (15) The verse would quiet fear from barking like an attack dog trying to get my attention.

On we went, making our way around the edge of the ridge and the high gorge that fell toward the River's edge. A cacophony of voices sounded in my mind. I couldn't turn them off. The fall's loud and thunderous voice, the anxiety and past fears, along with the small peaceful voice of scripture were all playing through my mind as though each had its own microphone. The soft and quiet voice of Holy Spirit through Scripture, the peaceful voice of Jesus, an old hymn–"Trust and obey, for there is no other way" (46), all swirled like leaves in the wind gusts of an arriving storm. Words played on the screen on my mind, hinting with promise of chaos and destruction. Yet all seemed tethered by an anchor of hope. I was exhausted trying to ignore these formidable scenes, while trying to focus on Jesus my anchor of hope.

When we arrived at the crest where the River created the falls, the foliage opened up. I immediately saw a series of stepping stones leading out from the bank and into the massive River. My gaze followed the stones. I saw they headed straight to the center of the River near the edge of the falls. They led to a large flat rock, perched half in the River and half out, creating the illusion of an Olympic diving platform.

As I took it all in, a thought hit my mind. It felt like the moment I had been T-boned while driving. My mind screamed: *You are going out there and jump to your death!* My legs started to buckle. Jesus held me keeping me from collapsing into a heap. I took another deep breath. The mist flowed in heavy this time, penetrating every cell of my being. Peace came over me, bringing renewed strength that helped me stand upright and steady. With it resolve followed. I faced the end of one life and a new beginning. Death was beckoning. Its arms opened and waiting for me to embrace it and assume the same position as Jesus had on the cross. I was not afraid, which caused me to half smile. My heart knew that obedience to this was right. On the heels of that perception came the thought that I must not linger or ponder death, only focus on what lay ahead.

Jesus let go of me as strength came into my legs. He never said a word. I didn't need Him to. I took a step forward and connected with the first stepping stone. As I brought the other foot onto the stone, the waters in the River welled up and teemed around the stepping stone. The menacing swirl roared "You're crazy. Did Jesus tell you to do this? Step back onto the shore and be safe." It was deafening, threatening and intimidating. My forgotten safe twin chimed in. *Listen to logic!*

My adventurous twin spoke louder than the chaos. *Staying here on the first stone is not an option. Stepping back onto the safe shore is not an option. Move forward and do so quickly. Obey what you know is your journey.* Pushing fear away, I stepped forward onto each stone and quickly made my way to the flat boulder out into the middle of the massive raging River. I kept a quick pace, my eyes focused on only the boulder. But it was far out and far from Jesus! I couldn't give that thought a place to land in my mind.

I turned to look at Jesus. I needed His approval and reassuring smile, but He was gone! *Where? Why had He left me at such a critical point in my choice to step out and embrace death?* I scanned the shore as far as I could see looking everywhere, yet could not find Him. I was tense and stiff. My mind was swirling with disappointment and abandonment. Fear was again following me. I let my shoulders droop and started to warmly embrace self-pity.

"Why do you doubt?" The voice of Jesus was right behind me. "I told you I would never leave you or forsake you!"

His voice startled me, and I jumped. My startled movement almost cost me going over the edge. Again, Jesus grabbed me and pulled me back, steadying my stance. I was thankful. I wanted to cry and laugh at the same time. I wanted to hug Him and never let go. I took a deep breath of the mist and felt peace and resolve settle into me. I turned and stepped to the edge of the boulder where it protruded precariously over the edge of the falls.

"It is time." Jesus said calmly.

"I know." I responded, struggling for air to form my words.

I looked down to death. The distance was great. I became aware of the sounds all around me. I heard the booming sound of the millions of gallons of water rushing with abandon over the falls, and of water churning and boiling around the rocks below. The water that hit the rocks billowed up into the mist that watered all of the land; the same mist I had come to rely upon for life and renewal.

The mist obscured everything below and all I could see was a huge cloud of it rolling around looking like cotton batting used to stuff quilts and teddy bears. That thought made me smile and I held onto it. Resolved, I chose to not think about rocks and the mouth of death, but I would think fluffy batting and soft teddy bears that would cushion my long fall. A fall to certain death upon sharp, protruding rocks, hidden in the swirl of the mist. My anxious thoughts converged, *I'm facing life and death.*

"Look straight below to the thickest part of the mist? That's the place." Jesus said with a nod of his head.

I saw it! The place that had to hold the biggest number of rocks creating the biggest volume of mist from the crashing water. My mind clearly saw it all. The old safe twin with its fear of death was trying to surface and take charge of my decision. I wouldn't let it. I couldn't! I wouldn't even think about anything other than stepping off. Not giving up it said, *Turn and take His hand, maybe He will jump too.* The other twin emphatically said, *No.*

"Now!" Jesus said urgently.

With one last deep breath for courage and resolve, I stepped off to my death focusing upon soft billowing batting and teddy bears. My safe twin died in that moment and my adventurous twin embraced my inner spirit, becoming one.

"He who falls on this stone will be broken to pieces" Matthew 21:44

Time changed. I was falling feet first in slow motion. I could see the mist thickening and swirling past me as I plummeted to my death. I didn't flounder, flap my arms or resist. I dropped like a rock down and down through the mist. I took in one more deep calming breath of the mist before I hit the rocks where the water would break into millions of micro droplets. I let go of my fanciful thought of soft cotton batting. I hoped for death to be quick. I embraced the fact that I was about to take on a new form of existence. Like the water. I would become transformed.

But I continued to fall. Apparently, I had misjudged the distance. A thought that I was *falling upon The Rock* fluttered through my mind. As it left, I hit cold water. My breath rushed out from shock. As quickly as I processed "Cold!", I processed that I had not yet hit rocks. Down I went, sinking ever deeper into cold water.

I suddenly realized I needed to stop sinking and start using my arms and legs to make my way to the surface. *How had I missed the rocks?* A part of me was beyond happy. *I'm not dead!* The other part of me wondered if I had failed the mission needing to repeat it. I broke the surface with a few strong strokes. I saw that I had surfaced in water not pummeled by the raging falls. I could see rocks. It was actually a partial ring of rocks circling the area where the water came billowing over, making a large pool. I had surfaced behind the falling water.

I spied a large cave behind the falls. I swam over to where the water met the ledge of the cave floor, pulled myself out and stood up. I pushed my hair back and wiped my eyes. My vision cleared and I saw movement. It was Jesus walking toward me accompanied by a large group of people. Jesus came near and embraced me with a fierce hug. The people started clapping and cheering. Their voices echoed against the high ceiling of the large cave affirming my obedient choice.

"Come sit by the fire and dry your clothes. Now you need to eat and rest from your challenge." Jesus spoke the words with great affection.

Jesus motioned to one of the large crowd of witnesses who had observed my plunge to death. It was David and he led me over to one of the many small fires where meat and vegetables were cooking. I saw stones to sit on circling the fire's warmth. I sat down and extended my hands out to the fire but realized that I wasn't that cold. Although the water had felt like it surely had an iceberg floating in it, I was not even chilled, rather I was exhilarated. David smiled.

"Nothing like it, is there!" David said.

"No." I didn't need to ask what he was referring to. I knew he was talking about me facing the fear of death and stepping out to embrace what followed.

"What motivated your feet to take that step?"

I thought a minute and I knew. "It was pleasing Him. Not disappointing Him. I wanted Him to be pleased with my obedience. I wanted Him to know I loved and trusted Him enough to step out and obey, despite my fear."

"You had confidence that your stepping out would bring Him pleasure? Good! Pleasing Him became the joy set before you. Going after that joy motivated you to move toward death. Jesus had that same kind of joy motivating Him when He endured the beatings and the crucifixion. Enduring is not hard when you focus on the joy set before you through obedience. It becomes your sacrifice and offering that is a sweet incense for the Father." David's words settled down deep into my being.

I leaned forward and pulled a piece of meat off the spit and ate. It was the best grilled meat that I had ever tasted. I pulled off another larger piece continuing to savor the flavor. Hearing a cheer go up from those closer to the mouth of the cave, I realized that someone else must have completed their plunge. I knew that Jesus was there to greet them as He had been for me. I shoved the last piece of meat into my mouth, thinking that I couldn't remember the last time I had eaten. It seemed long ago. I wanted to get up and find the new person who had just taken their plunge. I wanted to talk and exchange all the scary details, so we could commiserate together. Before moving from the fire, I glanced at David. His look let me know that he had guessed what I had been thinking and I was not to entertain that thought.

"It is time that we moved on."

I was taken aback by the words. I had only taken two bites of food. Certainly, my clothes were not dry. David nodded toward my clothes. I felt them, and they were dry. My skin was plump and dry. I shook my head in wonder. *I'm dry, I'm refreshed and I'm not hungry*, I thought. *None of this made sense.* But a long time ago, I stopped needing everything to make sense on this journey. I chuckled.

David got up and stepped away from his seat and I followed. As he turned away from the people, I started to see if I could go congratulate the new jumper.

"No!"

But I hadn't even asked yet.

David continued. "Do not glory in what you do in Christ even if it is as significant as facing death. It will only lead to pride and you know what happens when we have pride in our actions. The fall does not end well. Now don't forget that the sustaining mist you have come to rely on is everywhere just as the light from the *City* is everywhere. Whether you see or feel them, they are always with you. Even if the atmosphere feels empty of mist or the light is obscured, they are still there. Never be deceived into thinking differently. Do you understand?" David's serious look meant business. I filed the information for later.

I was learning to take hold of every word spoken to me by Jesus or His angels and to file them away because I would need them down the road. This caused me to remember the half circle of stone on my chain and how He had completed it with the other half as He said He would. I panicked, when I thought that they could have been lost when I took the death plunge. I felt my neck for the chain and stones. My fingers touched them from one side to the other making sure nothing had been lost. They were all there warming as I touched them. But a new object had been added. What was it?

My fingers inspected it. It was horizontal like a rectangular log with a small protrusion at the top where it attached to the chain. It was larger than the other two. David noticed my curious expression as I fingered the new item on the chain.

"Every good and perfect gift" James 1:17

"He has given you another gift as a reminder of this experience. You endured and triumphed over the testing of your faith. You overcame the temptation to run from the fear of death. Because you did not love your life enough to choose it over Him, He has given this to you."

99

As I touched the gift, I wondered why the shape was rectangular. I thought it probably reflected the big boulder at the edge of the falls where I had stepped off. I began to ask David about the shape when he quickly set off toward the rear of the cave. I had to almost run to catch up. I approached him as we came to what I thought was the back of the cave only to find the path turned sharply and opened up into brilliant sunshine. Although I had moved fast to catch up, I was not winded. Like before my plunge, I had learned to breathe in the mist. As we came into the sunshine I stopped, my eyes needed to adjust.

"In time, your eyes will adjust to the light quicker. It is a process like your body acclimating to breathing the mist." David explained.

As my eyes adjusted, I noticed that everything had a new glow about it. Since the plunge, everything had a rainbow radiance. I looked down and even my skin and clothes glowed. Everything pulsated with the colors. The air reflected it, how I don't know. Intellectually, I knew this was not physically possible. But on my journey, nothing was impossible. Although, I had no clue what was ahead, I was excited to move out with David. Surely it meant another great adventure even facing new challenges.

"You have new eyes now." David laughed. "Your spiritual perception has awakened in new ways. Taking the plunge into the death experience and the unknown outcome, changes you. Now on the other side of that experience life is new and different. More life has come since you chose death to self. It is always that way!"

He walked on, and I followed, especially aware of wonderful exotic fragrances, exotic smells with elements of earthy bouquets, the aroma of musk, damp rock and dirt. In this moment I felt no hunger, no thirst, no pain, no need for rest, sleep or extra strength. These things flowed into me with every breath. I don't know how long we walked on in silence, each in our own thoughts. I was at one with everything around me. The vibrancy of it all penetrated in such a way that I could shut my eyes and still see everything clearly, as if my eyes were wide open. Eyes still closed, I saw a beautiful pear shaped tree with purple blooms and yellow-turquoise song birds singing from its branches. I kept my eyes closed and moved on toward some lush and grassy areas that looked like plush green velvet, perfect for lying down. I opened my eyes, thinking what great visions; only to realize that the tree and the grassy areas were real. I had indeed seen and walked by them with my eyes closed. *How can this be?* I wondered.

"There are no limits here" David said. "Things unseen are seen."

"I'm beginning to see that!"

My play on words was not lost on David and he smiled. On we walked in silence as if one. I was comfortable and content.

"He saw the angels ascending and descending on it" Genesis 28:12

At some point, I came to see that we had been traveling gradually upward into the mountains. The inclined path we hiked was through a nearly treeless plateau which gradually narrowed. To my right, the mountains rose to peaks that appeared to touch the sky. The view was majestic. To my left, the ground dropped to a valley far below. Short scrub trees and sparse clumps of grass dotted the descending slope as it made its steep decline down to the valley.

As I looked ahead, the pathway opened back up. I began to wonder if it was leading to a new high mountain plateau. Trees were nonexistent. Only rocks were evident. David stopped up ahead, allowing me to catch up. He had stopped at the edge of a precipice. I walked past him over to the edge for a look. We were so high! The view showed the plain with the River, now far, far in the distance. I could see the River winding its way to the *City* which was still extraordinarily massive even from this perspective. The *City* was as brilliant as ever, sending out beams of light in all directions. From this perspective, I realized that the rainbow brilliance that covered everything was actually coming from the beams radiating from the *City*. Everything in sight was tiny looking like miniatures. I turned to comment about how high we were to David, but he spoke first.

"It's time for you to go on by yourself. My assignment is complete for now. You need to continue making your way to the *City*."

"*City*! I have no idea how to get from here to way over there!" Fighting panic, I pointed to the *City*. I knew the River could take me if I could just get to it. But it was a tiny ribbon in the distance.

"How am I to get from way up here to way over there?"

I was not feigning ignorance, but short of turning around and returning the way we had come, I saw no other way.

I turned to look at David and the path we had just walked. It had disappeared behind him. A solid mountain wall now filled in the once pathway. David smiled at my incredulous stare. Looking opposite, I could see the path ended in another sheer mountain wall. Only mountain walls or the precipice with a drop to the plain far below. These were now my options. *Dear God! Was I to jump again?* Fear started to claw its way into the forefront of my mind. I felt tension pressing on my muscles and deep into my bones.

"Stop! Take control of your thoughts! Breathe!" David spoke out firmly.

How quickly all that I had learned and practiced flew away when facing a new unknown. I took a couple of deep breaths, breathing in the unseen mist. Immediately tension left my body and peace was back, bringing a clear mind. I could feel the mist's effect.

Less frantic, I calmly asked, "How do I go on from this place? I see no path to follow. I don't even see the path that brought us here! I'm trapped. There are no options!" Frustration spoke through my voice.

David turned and walked to the back of the cliff face where it blended into the mountain. Now, I could see a large bush growing out of the rock. He reached behind the bush and pulled out a massive rope ladder with round wooden rungs. My heart sank. *Surely not.* David walked to me and bent down. I saw two small rocks protruding from the otherwise flat surface where we stood. He dropped the two circular loop ends of the rope ladder over each rock and with a hefty toss threw it over the edge. I watched it unfold down and down until I couldn't see it anymore. "Surely not" was quickly becoming "surely so."

The ladder must have eventually unwound because it went taut as it pulled on the two rocks securing it firmly in place. I looked intently at the loops checking to assess the ladder's security. *Would it hold?* To my amazement, the rope and the two rocks had fused together. It reminded me of an old tree on my parent's farm's fence row. Over time the tree grew over and around a fence post and the two had become one.

"Ok, there you go!"

His words confirmed it! I'm going over and down to who knows where. My face betrayed me because David laughed.

"You didn't die before, and you won't be dying now. This is a Jacob ladder. This is what angels have used to go from one level to another throughout time. It will serve you well."

I was speechless. My mind was racing.

"How do you always know what I'm thinking? But Jesus had been there for me and He is not here now! I'm alone! This is a lot higher and more terrifying somehow than the waterfall! Besides, angels are fearless and can handle these things!" My words gushed out like water released from a dam.

David's words fired back in rapid reply, answering every question.

"He knows everything, and He tells me what I need to know. He is always present. Really? Are you an expert on angels now? It is all perspective."

His words tethered me to reality as he addressed each question.

"Facing your fears, looking death in the face and overcoming its intimidation never changes. Look to Jesus! Faith will come." David's words were now gentle and kind.

"But Jesus isn't here this time." I whined. "When He supported me on the boulder before I jumped, His touch strengthened me physically and now I don't have that!"

"But you have!" David said in earnest. "He is in you. He is always with you. Center yourself. Calm yourself and look within. Use your new spiritual eyes. Plug into the experience of your walk to this place. Remember being able to see and do what your natural eyes did not see? That is a spiritual truth you can operate in. See with your inner Spiritual eyes. You will see Him, and He will show you the way."

I closed my eyes and remembered to take a deep breath. Immediately with my first breath, I felt the mist. It brought life and peace back into me and the touchstone warmed. So, with my eyes closed and my spiritual eyes focused, I could see clearly the brilliance of the rainbow glow covering everything, including me. On my mind's screen, I could see myself turn toward the ladder and walk over to the ledge. I looked down at the ladder now swaying in the breeze.

Fear commandeered the screen of my mind. I opened my eyes and to my shock, I now stood at the edge of the cliff. The ladder was swaying and yes, there was a moderate breeze. *Now what? Was I going to quit my journey here and give up? Where was the joy set before me for this challenging part of the venture?*

Before I could let the answers formulate, I closed my eyes even tighter and inhaled the mist. Immediately, the vision was on my mind's inner screen. I locked out fear's access. I let the vision play out knowing that it would be reality when I opened my eyes. Eyes still closed, I knelt down and inched my way over the edge and onto the swaying ladder using only my spiritual eyesight. My weight slowed the sway, but I could still feel the ladder moving below me. I took my first step down onto the next rung and the next and the next. I wasn't going to open my eyes for anything because I knew that to look with my natural eyes, would likely bring fear, fainting and my death. I focused on putting one foot down and then the next securely on each rung.

I heard David's voice from high above filter down on the breeze, "You're doing great! You'll be fine."

He was an angel after all and used to this Jacob's ladder stuff. Why wasn't he leading the way? My mind whined again. I admit I did not want to think nice thoughts. That brief internal whining, brought fog to my mind's screen.

"Sorry David. I apologize. Forgive me." I yelled up.

With the words "forgive me", the screen cleared up. Faintly I heard, "I'll see you later on your journey."

I focused on the inner vision and continued down, slowly making my way to only God knew where. Thinking 'how far' brought a new thought. *What if there isn't enough ladder to go the distance? What if my arms and legs get tired and I can't hold on?*

The sound of Holy Spirit's call from high above pierced the escalating thoughts like a needle to a balloon. *Oh Jesus, help me!* My mind cried out. Instantly I felt His hand touch my ankle. It brought immediate peace and calm. I knew that what I had seen taking place on the inner vision of my mind was real. *Jesus is here with me on this unnerving ladder!* I opened my eyes to confirm His presence.

It was both good and bad. Seeing His reassuring smile gave me confidence. But looking beyond Him to the distance below challenged my peace with panic. Jesus let go of my ankle and continued down the ladder. *What do I do?* Follow, of course, but with eyes open or eyes closed? I closed my eyes. Seeing with the perception of the spirit made my world less frightening. The whole scene defied human reason. I had to put human reason aside.

I followed Jesus down, rung after rung. My spirit man did the work. My body followed. Then I felt His touch on my ankle. I stopped and opened my eyes. I looked up. I couldn't even see where I had started. Clouds now covered that part of the mountain. I looked down beyond Jesus and saw clouds also covered the view below. A welcome sight because I couldn't see how far I had yet to go.

Jesus let go of me drawing my attention. He had stepped off the ladder onto another ledge. It was the best motivation in the world. I hastened down the ladder and onto the ledge with Him. Solid footing felt great. He laughed at my quickness and hugged me. All the fatigue of descending and maintaining peace on the downward climb faded away with His warm embrace.

"It's time for you to rest and eat." Jesus' voice was sweet. "You have experienced much on this part of your journey and you have done well. Later we will do even more traveling." The overwhelming thought of getting back on that ladder brought a queasy feeling to my stomach. I knew that I still needed more transformation.

"Don't worry about what is to come! In the moment is where you must abide. It is in the moment where the provision comes as you have need. I am the God of the moment. I AM is always enough. Now come and eat."

I looked toward where he was pointing and saw a warm and inviting fire. There were pillows, blankets and the wonderful aroma of meat cooking. Suddenly, my sick stomach sensation gave way to hunger and the expectation of eating and rest.

"This is how the prophets and warriors of old operated. They moved in the nourishment and physical rest provided for them. Now, come eat. When you are rested, we will move on."

Inside I hoped for a long rest, that might be stretched into a few days, whatever that meant here. I headed over to the fire and sat down on a big pillow. He sat down and took a piece of perfectly cooked meat and offered it to me.

"Eat now. Let tomorrow take care of itself. Now we rest and enjoy each other's presence."

I took the meat from His fingers and ate. The flavor of the meat on this journey was beyond amazing. I savored each piece. As I began to let the day's activities fade, I realized that I had Jesus all to myself and I was going to enjoy this moment. No scary ladder. No jumping off boulders, no facing death. Just Jesus, like it had been on the boat. The boat and River seemed long ago; like another time. After several additional tasty pieces of meat, I took a drink from the jug sitting beside the fire. It was a little warm from the fire and felt comforting as I swallowed. I pulled a couple more pillows up around me and partially covered myself with a blanket. I looked at Jesus and He had His normal "I know" smile.

"Rest." He said softly.

"Ok, I'll rest my eyes a moment, but I want to know more about this journey and where we go from here. I want to talk with You about so many things."

I settled back and closed my eyes thinking I was more tired than I realized. It was my last thought as I drifted off to sleep.

Chapter 6

The Mountain
Facing What Resides Within

"You will show me the path of life" Psalm 16:11

I awakened to warm rays from the *City* shining on my face. I was amazed that I had slept in such light. Before my journey I could only sleep in complete darkness, even the smallest light would keep me awake. But here I had slept and never stirred. I sat up and looked all around, I didn't see Jesus but noticed a small fire going with skewered chunks of meat and vegetables suspended over the fire from two stones. I realized I was hungry again even though I had eaten before falling asleep. I found my stomach telling me it was hungry for what was cooking.

"Hungry?" Jesus said with a half laugh.

I was startled by Jesus' voice behind me although I should be accustomed to His voice and sudden appearances by now. I didn't know where He had been a moment ago as the space on the ledge was not that big.

"Come and eat. You will need strength for where your journey takes you next."

"I will?" popped out. What a crazy thing to say. This journey always required my all.

"Next you will travel to explore deep and hidden things. Remember on the River how I spoke of the deep things that can be unseen, yet they affect the course of life? On this part of the journey you will discover and learn more about the unseen in your life."

Oh joy! My thoughts were sarcastic. Immediately, my mind raced with endless possibilities and thoughts. Somehow in the back of my mind though, I knew there would be more confrontations of fears and tests of my trust and obedience. I always wondered if I would make it through the tests that were ahead.

"You worry more than is necessary." Jesus said with love, yet I could feel the need for correction in my attitude. "Take it moment by moment. There is grace for this moment and this moment is about eating and dining with me."

I determined to push negative thoughts out and not let them dance in my mind. Taking my thoughts captive was a continual lesson I had to learn, relearn and then practice. I focused on Jesus' face. His loving countenance said "I know your struggles. Together there is victory over your thoughts."

He handed me a piece of food. I was about to ask Him about the next travels when a bird flew onto the ledge. It was a dove and it waddled over next to him.

"Hello little one. And what brings you here today?" Jesus spoke to the dove with such delight and joy at seeing it.

He reached out and took the dove into His palm. The dove made cooing sounds and it appeared the Lord understood. When the dove stopped cooing, it flew off into the sky.

I must have had a curious look on my face because the Lord said, "I must go."

That was it. Nothing more. *But what about us having a leisurely meal together? What about the fact that I was going to need Him to face more intimidating internal struggles?* I was instantly anxious and agitated.

The Lord looked at me and didn't say a word. He didn't have to. His face said it all. It was saying "Yes, I know you have more fears. Yes, you do not understand. Yes, you can do this . . . for MY grace is sufficient. Trust and obey. This is the operational mode here."

I swallowed the bite of food I had taken. One bite was all I had received, but now I was full.

"Come, it's time for the next phase of the trip." Had He changed His mind and now was going to go with me?

I got up and started to walk toward the edge of the cliff. The ladder was still swaying slightly in the breeze. In that moment, I determined to not show Him my fears or apprehensions of taking the ladder on down to where ever it went.

"Breathe in deeply of Me. Breathe in deeply of the mist. Relax in this moment and trust that you are headed on another great adventure. Every place I lead you has an upgrade for your transformation."

I turned around and looked at Him. How utterly beautiful He looked in the rays of light coming from the *City*. There was an iridescent glow all around Him. In that moment, looking upon Him, it was easy to relax and breathe in deeply. I could sense and feel His strength, authority and power all wrapped up in the radiance of His presence.

"Come, we go." He said as He walked to the back of the ledge where a huge boulder rested against the back wall.

"But Jesus, the ladder is here." I pointed behind me to the ledge.

He stopped and said, "We are finished with the ladder. It served its purpose."

"But how do we get down from here?" I turned and walked closer to the edge and looked down at the ladder. Only four more rungs dangled beneath the ledge. *How had I not noticed that before?* My mind raced with endless thoughts, as I turned back and walked to Jesus. Jesus responded to my queried look.

"You see what you need to see when you need to see it. In mercy, things are veiled. In mercy, they are shown to the extent that is necessary. In the case of the ledge, that is what you needed. You made the trip and passed your test. You overcame your fears and now we go. We leave by a new way."

My eyes were scanning. *What new way?* There was nothing to get me down from here. Then I thought, *Oh dear God, not bungy jumping, parasailing or free gliding? What's awaiting me now?*

"He came to the tomb ... a cave" John 11:38

Jesus didn't say a word. But I could have sworn that His shoulders were shaking in silent laughter. He turned and walked toward the large boulder. I followed quickly and purposed to stay close. He slipped around the edge of the boulder and was gone. I stopped in my tracks. A path around the massive rock was nonexistent. The boulder was tight against the mountain face. It was perched on the edge of another ledge. I inched closer with trepidation. I could not see around it to even determine if there was any ledge on the backside. Where had Jesus gone? How had He maneuvered around this obstacle?

"Jesus?" There was so much question in speaking His name.

"Yes, I am here. Come on. Come around." He said like it was nothing.

"But I can't. There is no way."

"I always make a way. Come on." He spoke with firmness in His voice.

"But how? How do I get around this huge obstacle when I can't see where to put my feet or what to hold on to?" My voice quivered.

"You hug the rock." He said it like that was not a hard thing to do.

"What?" *Why was He stating the obvious?*

"Hug the rock."

I looked at the boulder. It was wider than my arm span with nothing to grab on to. My palms began to sweat. I rubbed them and wiped them on my pants.

"Of course, you can do this. I would never ask you to do something that you can't do. Do you trust me? Do you trust what I am saying?" I heard the tender firmness in His voice.

Well, of course, I did. Well, of course, I wasn't sure. I was a mixed bag of a mess.

"Remember to take a breath of the mist and do it."

Well, I reasoned, He hadn't taken me anywhere that had harmed me so far. Even the places where I believed death was imminent, I had only to die to my fears. I took a deep breath, then another, and one more for good measure. I moved without allowing my analytical side to engage. I was starting to understand that logic didn't usually work on the journey. I hugged the rock and put my right foot around as far as I could. It was firm and hugging the rock give me balance and security. I inched my way hugging and hugging, taking small inching movements with my feet. Slowly but surely, I inched around the boulder. I still couldn't see around it. Unexpectedly, Jesus took hold of my right hand and pulled me. I was embraced in His arms and on the other side.

114

"See, you did it. One step at a time. It's always one step at a time." He said as He let go and took me by the hand.

He led me forward on a narrow ledge winding its way around a couple of bends on the new mountain's side. I was thankful for His hand in mine. I had no fear of falling although there was nothing but empty space for what looked like miles below. Then we stepped onto another ledge. At the back of this ledge was a cave.

"Here we are!" Jesus said with joy in His voice.

Here? Where was here? A cave? A very dark cave with a small opening awaited. *Now what? What lurked in the darkness? What was I to confront in this cave?* My mind sought answers.

As Jesus spoke, He handed me a smooth piece of wood that was about the length of my arm. "Here is a torch. It will serve you well as you traverse the darkness."

I noticed as I took the torch from His hand that it wasn't heavy. Jesus reached and touched the upper end of the torch and it immediately ignited. The burning fire was different than I had ever seen. It possessed an almost white glow brilliant like a bright LED, yet it danced like a flame. There was no heat and no smell, only light.

"What do you mean, traverse the darkness? You make it sound like I'm going into that cave alone."

"You are."

He said it so matter-of-fact, I was taken aback.

"But how will I find my way? What if there are twists and turns and even other multiple pathways on the way. How will I know which way to choose? Jesus, what is the purpose of this? How will I find my way out?"

"So many questions My child. Have you not come to know that you are only given what you need for each step? Have you forgotten that I am always with you? I'm always with you in the moment. Where is your faith? Has it not grown so you find me faithful, considering all that you and I have walked through already?"

"Yes Lord." I acknowledged the truth as my mind quickly but methodically flashed from each frightful event to the next. As I focused my attention back on His words, I suddenly felt faith and strength rise. I was beginning to feel courageous enough to actually stop whining and take on this next adventure. *Adventure?* Had I reconciled the unknown and probable death on this next part of my journey, as an adventure? Maybe I was changing after all.

Jesus smiled, and I knew that He was aware of my very anxious thoughts.

Jesus replied accordingly. "I never let a test come that you cannot pass. I supply and equip you with the provisions for great victory. The problem is not the training but your confidence in Me, and your confidence in what I see in you. Fear always challenges and taunts. Remember, I give you all authority."

"Ok!" Even as I acknowledged that I understood what He had spoken, inside I doubted. I wanted to just get the whole thing started so I couldn't back out. I took a deep breath, straightened my back and quickly asked, "Any last-minute instructions, directions, words of guidance before I do this?"

Jesus spoke. "It is well with your soul. (42) Even though you walk through the valley of the shadow of death, fear no evil. (43) I have gone before you. (44) I surveyed the land. Every step you take, I have already taken. Nothing will in any way hurt you." (36)

Bible themes and truths. Many hidden there in the recesses of my mind, even as He had been speaking them. But would they be there when He was gone?

"I will meet you again at the River".

It was assuring to hear that He would see me again at the River. It meant somehow, I was going to make it out of this cave and find my way there. While pondering these things, I took one more peek into the cave. I wanted to see if I needed to ask Him anything else. I couldn't see much because it was pitch black. Stalling, I turned to speak to Jesus but He was already gone.

Before moving on, I stood a moment letting my mind flit back to Jenny, Germany and a simple vacation; a vacation that was in another place and time. I was now far removed from that reality. But in this new reality on my journey, I never felt more alive. None of it made sense. Surreal as it all seemed, with its formidable, supernatural and fantastic events, I knew I was in the right place at the right time. *I just didn't know where or how.*

I let out a breath I didn't even know I had been holding, then took a firm grip on the torch and walked a short distance into the mouth of the cave. Darkness surrounded me like a funeral shroud. There was a tangible presence wanting to envelope me in its darkness. Only the light from the torch kept it at bay. I was moving forward with God, to only He knew where, yet I wanted to turn back and run out. I turned to look at the opening. I wanted to see the light and radiance from outside, but the opening was gone! I panicked. I ran to the place where the opening should have been. It was gone, gone! I ran my free hand along the wall of stone. Seconds ago, what had been an opening was now cool solid stone. I lifted my torch higher, and scanned for an opening, thinking maybe I lost my sense of orientation. But there was nothing but utter darkness and the light from the torch. Only one way now and that was forward. Nothing like having your path set before you! The thought of being swallowed alive by a mountain was real in that moment. Very real!

I began to move forward, thinking in my head, *Let's move on quickly and get this over with.* With every step I took I felt the darkness. It was so tangible, I believed I could reach out and touch it, had I the courage. But I didn't try. I feared that it could be worse than my mind was telling me. I didn't want reality to confirm my fears. I thought about closing my eyes and walking forward using my spiritual sight as I had done with David or on the ladder with Jesus. Nevertheless, there was also part of me that felt that there are seasons when darkness surrounds us, that require having both eyes open and aware.

Then I noticed that the more I thought about the darkness the less light was produced from the torch. Startled with this new revelation, I quickly took control of my thoughts and began to focus on His last words. I knew that He would have told me what I needed for this test and to focus on that. I began to meditate over and over on His words. They came back as clearly as if He was speaking them to me in the moment.

Reminding myself of His words made the torch burn bright. I knew I needed to walk in the light of His word. I lifted the light higher and began to repeat His words out loud. As I did, the light got even brighter than when He first gave it to me. The thick blackness retreated and became less intimidating. I purposed to continue speaking out His words.

I walked for some distance through a long winding tunnel, around rocks, over rocks and past other tall formations. Time again stopped as it had many times before on the journey. I had no idea of how long or how far I had hiked. I focused on His words and meditated on understanding as much as I could. The torch continued to stay bright and strong, projecting light to my path.

Unexpectedly, the tunnel became wider, branching off in three directions. *Which direction? How will I know? What if I pick wrong? Could I get lost in here forever?*

"Jesus, you didn't tell me what to do here," I whined out loud. "Why have you brought me here? Don't you care?"

With each word, my torch grew dimmer. As darkness grew and got stronger, I saw movement in my peripheral vision. Fear tightened my chest and brought a chill deep in my soul. I heard scuttling behind me. I spun around lifting the dim torch, broadcasting hardly any light on the path I had been on seconds before. A large dark hissing creature now crouched, lurking, following, waiting. I couldn't make out what it was, but I could see piercing yellow eyes and smell its rotten odor. Instantly I knew that it came to harm me.

"Jesus! Help me!" It was out of my mouth without a thought.

Instantly, the light blinked brighter. The sudden brightness caused the creature to back up. It retreated and hissed louder.

"Jesus, help me, please help me to get away from this thing and out of this place!"

Strange! When I called on His name, the light got brighter. But when I asked to flee from the threat, the light diminished. My mind and emotions raced. I didn't understand why the light only grew momentarily bright and then diminished.

"Do what you have been taught. Remember again my words to you." Holy Spirit's voice came to my spirit. His words flooded my mind and I knew I had again let fear take control.

Yes, Lord. My inner being spoke the words in agreement. I closed my eyes. I took a deep breath and felt the mist even here in the tunnel in spite of the beast's foul odor. In my mind's eye, I was with Jesus on the River in the boat, safe and slowly floating toward the *City*. Peace came over me and I felt strengthened. My mind was clear. I needed to recall and trust His words.

With increased confidence I spoke, "My soul is very well right now. This is a test. He knows that I can pass it. He knows me. He has walked this way before me and knows all about this place and its tests. He knows that this creature is here at the point of my decision as to which way to go. All things are created by Him and for Him. This thing, whatever it is, has a purpose for me. I'm done allowing it to intimidate me and I will use His authority and make it go away."

I was angry and livid at the creature for intimidating me and irritated at myself for allowing it. I was mad that it was challenging me and His authority in me. I looked at the creature with new eyes. I stared right into its piercing, yellow eyes. I took another deep breath of the mist and closed my eyes for a second. In that second, I saw the creature for what it was, a tiny thing. An enlarged shadow of itself, cast by the torch light, had tricked my perception. Nothing scary, only pathetic. Before I closed my eyes and saw its true stature, I had been determined to run toward it, like David had toward Goliath. But now it wasn't worth the effort.

"Be gone from here and away from me. Do not come back and trouble me again". I spoke the words out with total loathing.

Right before my eyes, the creature diminished even more. It turned and melted into the darkness. I was amazed and confident that what was ahead, I could conquer with the help of Holy Spirit and the words of Jesus. The touchstone warmed.

I must move on. I had spent enough time on the creature. As I turned to continue walking, I viewed the three tunnels. Jesus had not set me up to fail. He knew I had learned enough on the journey to pass this test and find my way out of this mountain.

"I will meet you again at the River." His words filled me with strength and determination.

"Ok, Lord, which way do I go?"

I shut my eyes and took a deep breath like David and Jesus had taught me during fearful and uncertain times. A memory came back of David telling me the mist was always present and brought life. It was a clue. Opening my eyes, I walked to the first tunnel. I scanned it for signs of life such as moss and took a deep breath. It was dank and musty smelling without the freshening mist and no life. I walked over to the middle tunnel and did the same. It was the same, smelling like an old attic or basement. Again, no mist. I went to the third tunnel wondering if it would be the same. I didn't know what to expect.

"Now faith is assurance of things hoped for, proof of things not seen." (35) The scripture popped into my mind. As I held up the torch, I saw moss here and there on the walls. I took another deep breath. The air was soft and fresh. It was moist with the mist. No dank or musty smell. I knew I had found the right tunnel. I had confronted things that lived in this dark place, in the bowels of the mountain. As a result, I was becoming more aware of how to traverse the deep things of my own inner darkness. I knew I needed to file this away, as I built up my understanding of life on my journey.

I walked straight forward for a long time. The way was smooth and unchanging; no rocks to climb, no real obstacles. The torch gave out a steady light that lit the pathway and warmed the walls of the tunnel. They took on a dark chocolate hue. I became lost in the monotony of my rhythmic strides. My mind was on auto pilot. Chocolate! How delicious that sounded right now. My stomach growled as I wondered how long I had gone without food or water and how special that one bite of food had been to strengthen me this far. I took another step. From above me a wet drop hit me squarely between the eyes. It brought me to a quick halt and out of thoughts of chocolate. Another drop hit my face. I wiped it and saw it was clear. *Water?* Now I was hungry, thirsty and exhausted. I looked around for some place to sit. I saw a small boulder up ahead. It was perfect to sit on. I could lean against the soft moss on the wall and rest.

I shuffled over to the rock, my legs and entire being suddenly exhausted. I could barely pick up my feet and collapsed onto the rock. I leaned back against the moss with a weary sigh. It felt warm like a soft, fleecy, green blanket. Exhaustion hit, and my eyes felt heavy with fatigue. *I'll take a second, close my eyes and rest.*

I fell instantly asleep but was abruptly awakened as the torch hit the rock I was sitting on. My eyes flew open as adrenalin rushed through me. *What might have happened to the light if I dropped the torch?* I fought to keep my eyes open and hold the torch. I did not want my light source to go out. Looking around I saw a small ledge about shoulder height where I could lay the torch. With scant strength, I pushed my body up and laid the torch on the ledge. The flame continued to flare making a nice glow to the area. Great! I'll sit here and take a quick nap and regain my strength. Another breath of the mist and I was far away in dreamland.

Dreams came and went across my mind. When I did awaken, it felt like I'd slept for days. I awoke groggy, disoriented and not sure where I was. Eyes still closed, I stretched remembering I was in the tunnel reclining on a rock. I had been making my way out of the tunnel finding my way to the River to meet up with Jesus. I opened my eyes and realized with a quick start that I was in pitch blackness. So black that I could not see my hand in front of my eyes. Panic was back. *Where was my torch? Why was there no light? What was I going to do? Where was Jesus? Was something lurking in the darkness waiting for me? How would I go on without the light?*

I was overwhelmed by all the thoughts. Tears began streaming down my face. I was quickly overcome with panic and fear. Everything went tight inside my chest. Even the air I was breathing was harder to take in. Suffocation felt as close as my next breath. *When will I get the victory over this?*

"JESUS!" was all I could get out.

Nothing.

"DEAR JESUS, COME AND HELP ME!"

My eyes saw only darkness, except for a flicker out of the corner of my eye. I was uneasy about looking in that direction for fear I'd see the glowing eyes of a new monster waiting to devour me.

"JESUS! COME AND HELP ME!" I screamed, more for my own comfort and maybe frighten the possible monster away. But, as I continued with, "Jesus, Jesus, Jesus" even faintly, my eyes caught the flicker of light again. I felt compelled to look this time. It wasn't beastly eyes. It was coming from the ledge where I had placed the torch. I repeated it. "Jesus, Jesus, Jesus" and the slight glow of light remained. It was not my imagination.

As I said "Jesus", I saw that darkness surrender to His name. With three more emphatic, "Jesus, Jesus, Jesus", the glow of light steadily brightened and increased! When I stopped speaking His name, the faint glow of light diminished. I spoke "JESUS!" out with more force. The glow of the light intensified. "JESUS! JESUS! JESUS!" Three times with fervor. More light!

Ok, I understood.

A scripture popped into my mind. "Then Jesus spoke to them again, saying, 'I am the light of the world. He who follows Me will not walk in darkness but will have the light of life.'" (4) Apparently, the torch was manifesting this truth literally. It was His light given to me for this part of the journey. He was The Light and He was my light. The torch represented His essence. A new set of Scriptures flooded my mind. "A little while the light is with you. Walk while you have the light, that darkness doesn't overtake you. He who walks in the darkness doesn't know where he is going. While you have the light, believe in the light, that you may become children of light." (16) The touchstone warmed as well as the rock pieces in my pocket.

I didn't understand how it was all working. Memorizing scriptures wasn't a part of my life. But I quickly connected several things. First, whenever scriptures were in action or Jesus spoke a spiritual truth to me, the touchstone warmed. Now the rock pieces had added their emphasis. Second, that speaking the name of Jesus made the torch glow and manifest light. I needed the torch to glow brightly. I needed my pathway lit to move on and meet up with Jesus.

"Thank You Jesus, that I'm seeing your words and promises come to light. Thank You Jesus, that You are the light of the world and my light. Thank You Jesus, that somehow those rock pieces are transferring their power to me. You have not failed me, and You are always with me. Sometimes I get Your presence, sometimes I get Your words that transform me and the atmosphere around me. Sometimes You send Holy Spirit. I am never alone."

With every word of praise and declaration, the torch on the ledge became brighter and brighter. I understood that speaking of His faithfulness and of my thankfulness made the torch burn the brightest. Soon the torch was glowing and disseminating its light.

I stood up, grabbed the torch and lifted it high. I looked around in every direction to expose any other beastly thing, big or small. I saw nothing but the walls of the tunnel. As I completed the circle, I saw the tunnel dead ended ahead. Thoughts of never finding my way out came rushing and with every thought the light diminished.

"Ok, no dwelling on the thoughts of fear and doom!" I spoke out to encourage myself. Dwelling on fearful thoughts stole my light and my help in the darkness. I took captive my fear of being lost forever inside the bowels of the mountain as quickly as it came. Immediately the torch glowed bright.

Jesus said He had taken this very route Himself. *Ok, what did He do?* Different thoughts vied for my attention such as, *He might have transported Himself out of here right to the River's edge.* As a science fiction reader, that had great appeal to me. But every thought that came to me took a measure of faith I didn't think I possessed.

The voice of Jesus again ran through my mind and the rock pieces and touchstone warmed. "The problem is not the training but your confidence in Me and the confidence in what I see in you."

Ok, the problem is my confidence. Yes, that much was obvious. He is big enough to get me through this. "I have all I need to pass this test." I vocalized His words.

Either the torch would be enough, or I would be given more than I now had. Sighing deeply, I raised my torch and took a step toward the dead end ahead. With the first step, I had the thought *He is going to help my weak and conflicted brain find the way out.* After a few more steps, I saw that "things are not always as they appear." The dead end was really just a large bolder blocking the way. As I approached it, the torch light revealed that there indeed was a "narrow way of escape" to the right side of the boulder. I quickly inhaled a deep breath, pulled my stomach in and held it, making myself as thin as possible. I started to squeeze around with the torch leading the way, but two thirds into it, my chest got stuck. I couldn't move forward or backward. I was stuck literally between the rock and a hard place.

The torch lit up a chamber on my right. Tangible darkness was pressing against me on the left. Going up on my toes didn't help. Wiggling didn't help. My mind wanted to panic. *Was I doomed to be sandwiched here in the bowels of this mountain?* But if I had learned one thing repeatedly, it was "not to concede to the impossible".

One more time. I took my thoughts captive and prayed out loud. "Jesus, you said I would make it through this tunnel and meet you at the River. Therefore, I believe that somehow you will help me to figure this out. I yield to Holy Spirit for wisdom and creative thoughts."

126

I wanted to take a deep breath of the mist, but my chest was pressing tightly against the rock. I relaxed, exhaled and let peace come over me. My legs felt weak and for a moment I wondered if my restricted air intake was making me light headed. The story of Balaam's ass dropped into my mind. "Yahweh's angel went further, and stood in a narrow place, where there was no way to turn either to the right hand or to the left. The donkey saw the angel, and she lay down". (17) That was a strange scripture to think about. *Maybe there was a connection Holy Spirit was trying to help me see.*

"Lay down" seemed to resonate. *Ok, what could it hurt?* I began to let my legs go limp. The first effort didn't yield a result. I relaxed more and let peace take over. As I did, I moved down a little lower in the crevice and the gap between my chest and my back grew. I continued going lower. When I reached my leg's limit to squat, I became free enough to move and lean into the next chamber. I clumsily slid out onto the floor. I rolled onto my back, torch high in hand and laughed. It was a humbling experience. I was thinking how Holy Spirit had to help me with the example of the dumb ass in Scripture. Now that was going to be a funny but great testimony if I ever got out of the bowels of this mountain. I lay there on the floor a few more minutes, all the while thinking of the humor of the Lord. He has so many ways of helping us stay humble.

Get up and move on. Make some more progress. I told myself. Doing so, I used the torch to scan the chamber. I saw baskets of bread, jugs of water, fresh fruit, and many unlit torches attached to the chamber walls. I cried out, "Thank You Lord for this provision" then went around and lit the other torches. The small chamber was now bright and welcoming. I noticed a holder for a torch right in the center of a small rock table beside a wooden chair. I put my torch in it and gathered food and drink.

Everything was fresh! The cool water quenched my thirst. The bread smelled like a fresh French baguette, hard and crusty on the outside and soft inside. As I stood over the fruit basket, I could smell the fragrance of ripened fruit. I took out a peach, a few grapes and a crisp apple and sat down. I ripped apart the piece of bread thinking that I would never taste anything as good again. It didn't disappoint. It tasted fresh, warm out of the oven, with melted butter. Of course, it wasn't but in my mouth, it felt like it was. The peach and grapes were perfect; juicy and sweet. I decided to take the apple for later. Finishing the bread, I got up to get another drink and wash the peach juice from my hands and arms. When finished, I felt full, like I'd finished a full course meal.

"Jesus, you are the best!" My outspoken words caused all the flames to flare for a second. Time to move on. I picked up my flaring torch and looked for the way out. Beside the boulder where I slid in, I could now see that the tunnel continued. Refreshed, I moved out to see what was in store for me next. I left the other torches burning. Perhaps, they would light the way for another traveler.

I continued on and wondered how long I had been making my way through the bowels of the mountain. I had a humorous thought of how human bowels started up high and made their way down and out. I laughed at the symbolic comparison. I certainly hoped I was making my way down through the mountain, even though I couldn't tell. At times it felt that I was going up because of the pull on my calf muscles. I chuckled to myself thinking "How would I tell anyway?" This tunnel path had taken many twists and turns. Occasionally I had to climb over several large rocks, but at least the tunnel had not branched anymore.

Suddenly my feet started to slide apart. The tunnel floor had become damp and slippery. I stopped and pulled myself together, going forward with cautious steps. As I proceeded, I encountered more wet patches. I became wary, not wanting to fall. The more attention I paid, the more I noticed that the tunnel floor was starting to run downhill.

At first it was gradual and scarcely noticeable. I said a quick "Thank You, Jesus" that my focus on my pace didn't diminish the torch. In time, the grade of the tunnel floor increased markedly downward. It became necessary to slide my hand along the tunnel wall for support. It was then I realized that the moss no longer grew on the tunnel walls. They were damp like the floor. If the tunnel floor continued this grade downward, I wondered if I could stay upright and walk on what was now a continual slippery slope. I was pondering all of this when I suddenly heard sounds ahead. I hoped for people or an opening from the tunnel. I made my way onward as quickly as I dared wondering, *What's up there?*

The sound grew into a thunderous roar. Now I could hear the distinct sound of rushing water. My wondering thoughts wanted to bring some anxious feelings with them. *Is it another waterfall that I had to jump into? Is it a veil of water covering the cave opening to the outside?* I hoped for the latter! Without warning, the floor of the tunnel made a steep drop. I quickly sit down on the floor to proceed without falling. This concern took my attention away from the anxious thoughts and a torch that was starting to dim.

The water was now more than a trickle covering the floor. Inch by inch I made my way down the steep tunnel. It was a challenge to hold the torch and keep my balance. I used my legs to pull myself gradually along the tunnel floor. The tunnel took a sharp left turn, then a sharp right. The walls and ceiling had narrowed considerably as I had made my way in what was becoming a chute. It reminded me of tubes that you go in at the water parks but without as much water to move you along. I held the torch close to my body since there was not much head room, thankful for less flame. I continued making my way down the chute as it twisted and turned like a huge cork screw, spiraling downward.

Suddenly the tunnel chute ended onto a large flat floor that formed another chamber. The water trickled out onto the floor, spreading in all directions. I stood up as water ran down my legs inside my soaked pants. As I held the torch high, the source of the rushing water came into view.

I could see a rushing stream in a channel of stone emerging from a hole in the chamber wall. It was a giant trough of fast-moving water that exited out a large hole across the chamber. Similarities from the start of my journey came to mind, reminding me of the channel in the cathedral basement. I held the torch high to survey my options. There were none. No other way out and no other way down. Only a rushing stream of water in a trough that went, God only knew, where. *No way.* I wasn't going to consider that as an option.

I noticed that my torch sputtered a little and was even less bright. As I quizzically looked at it, the flame became half as bright. "Praise You Jesus", I glorified the name of Jesus, expecting the flame to once again glow bright as before. The intensity of the flame didn't change. I spoke louder. "Jesus, Jesus, Jesus". Nothing changed. *Why isn't this working?*

"Ok, what is going on here, Jesus?"

"I'll see you at the River" Jesus's confident statement flooded my mind. *Ok, why those words? What was He expecting from me in this impossible situation?* Instantly I knew, and a knot formed in my stomach. He expected me to be obedient and follow His words regardless of what I saw or feared. Provision for success was in obedience. I needed to jump into the rushing water and see where it took me in order to get out of this mountain and meet Him at the River. I needed to plunge into that black hole and trust that I would come through it unscathed and in my right mind. The more I thought about taking that plunge the more anxious I became. I began to pace and rub my sweating palms. The knot got bigger in the pit of my stomach.

"Your fears want to make you think the worst." His voice trumpeted like thunder vibrating through my being. "You have all that you need to make it. Every step you take, I have taken. Nothing by any means can harm you."

I was hearing it and understood what He was saying, but I didn't want to listen. To hear meant obedience, and I was afraid to take that step. I began offering more pleas to convince Him He was wrong in this case. I paced back and forth looking at the gaping hole of the tunnel's mouth. My mind raced for a different way out.

"I don't have all that I need." I emphatically spoke out. "I need to see where I am going. I need to know that the chute is large enough for me all the way down, otherwise I could drown. I need to know that the chute will not be too fast or deep. I need to know! Will I go under water and drown? Will I suddenly drop to my death? What if the water surrounds me and extinguishes the torch for good, leaving me in total darkness? I need to know Jesus!"

I heard His chuckle first before I felt His tangible Presence behind me. I turned around and there He was, standing tall and confident. Even though the torch light was half as strong as it had been, He glowed. I rushed toward Him and squeezed Him tightly, not caring that I was soaked.

"Oh, you need to know do you?" There was a hint of laughter in His words. "I told you that nothing by any means can or shall harm you. What part do you not understand?"

I understood in my head. It was my heart and my emotions that the fear was intimidating, like an ugly Gollum from J.R.R. Tolkien's *The Hobbit*. I didn't answer.

"Oh, I see, it is the fear of death or bodily harm that brings you fear and intimidation again, right?" His words of truth hit me. Suddenly the reality of His words overcame me and my chest tightened.

I couldn't breathe. He had put into words what my mind had been entertaining. I was still afraid of pain, suffering and death. Simple and clear, yet powerful. Didn't I get victory over that when I jumped in the waterfall? I let go of Him and took a step back. I looked up into His face and lost it. My tears let loose like a floodgate. The tunnel adventure with all its stress swirled inside of me right along with the truth and power of His words. Although hearing the truth was freeing, at the same time it was formidable and confronting.

"Let's walk over to the water channel."

He took hold of my right hand. His touch flooded my soul with peace. My tears were gone in the few steps it took to get to where the water gushed down the hole. I looked at it and with a fleeting thought, pictured it as an open black mouth of a demon, ready to swallow me whole. A chill went through me that attached itself to every bone, muscle and fiber of my being. It felt like icicle hands had seized my heart.

"This is where you look into the face of everything dark and daunting. Face every Hellish thought. This is where you take another step toward dying to everything you still can't see inside your heart and mind." The voice of Jesus was quiet and loving. Yet, the power of His words restrained and muted the rushing waters passing by us down into the dark hole. But the icy hands kept their grip.

Step? I remembered His past words of "Every step you take, I have taken."

I let go of His hand and faced Him looking Him squarely in His eyes.

"Jesus, You said, You have taken every step that I will take. So, have You gone down this chute before?" I thought that if He had taken the wet plunge and made it, I would feel more confident in taking it too. I shook as the cold chill went through me again.

"No, I have not taken this particular plunge".

Great! I thought. *I have Him! He will need to go down first to honor His word to me. Then I will follow.* My mind was already racing with the thought and the assurance it would bring. Perhaps it would bring warmth for my chilled heart.

"But I have taken this step."

"What do You mean Jesus? If You have not gone down this watery chute, how have You taken this step?" As I spoke out the words, my teeth chattered from the cold breath of death that wanted to turn me into a frozen corpse.

"I mean that I have already looked into the mouth of pain, suffering and death. I have already taken the route of a dark gaping hole to an unknown confrontation with things I could not see or discern. I already took steps that led to pain and suffering and found out death could not swallow Me."

"You see, this is the step I took that night in Gethsemane. This is the step that took Me through the beating of My body, the carrying of the cross, the piercing and the agony on My body. This is the step that brought Me face to face with the greatest fear of all; separation from God Himself. God could not look upon any sin and I carried the sins of all mankind, for all time. I feared. I felt forsaken. Would death be able to hold Me? That was My dark tunnel that took Me down the black gaping mouth to Hell. It was there I was confronted with lasting death and eternal separation from God. But Hell could not take hold of Me. The prince of this world could not claim any legal right to hold Me in death's prison. Instead, I defeated death and took the keys of Hell making sure no one else has to ever be afraid of pain, suffering and death."

The distant voice of a past Sunday School teacher reading scripture about this exact thing, flew into my mind. I didn't even remember her name, yet her voice came resounding into my mind as if she were present reading from her Bible once again.

"Because, we God's children are human beings, made of flesh and blood, Jesus who was immortal, loved us so much, He became flesh and blood too. Because only as a human could He die and experience all that we would experience in our flesh. He had to become like us. Only by dying and shedding His blood, could He break the power of the devil, who had the power of death. Only in this way could He set us all free. We who lived our lives as slaves to the fear of dying needed rescued from the fear of death. Jesus died to help free all who call Him their Savior from the fear of death forever." (18)

That's me! I thought!

Jesus didn't speak. His loving look warmed my soul and took away the icy hands from my heart. The rock pieces and touchstone warmed, removing the last chill that had entered me.

The teacher's voice from the past continued. "It was necessary for Him to be made in every respect like us, His brothers and sisters, so that He could have mercy on us and offer up His blood as our Priest before God. His perfect blood could become the sacrifice that would take away the sins of the people. Since He knows all we have gone through with the suffering and the testing that the fear of death can bring, He is able to help us when we are being tested by that fear." (18)

What could I say? Truth was standing right in front of me. Truth began resonating inside of me. Truth was filling the atmosphere in the small chamber with hope, warmth, strength and life. As it did my torch grew bright. I could do this. I could face the dark mouth of death because He had, and He overcame. I would take the step into the watery chute and come out on the other side wherever that was, in victory. I turned away from Him and looked into the dark mouth of the chute. It wasn't scary now. Now I saw it as it was. No longer was it a gapping mouth to swallow me but the possible portal that could lead to freedom.

"I can do this, Jesus, I can."

As the words left my mouth the torch flared and went to its brightest strength yet. It became a confirmation that I chose life and truth. With the flaring of the torch, I felt a warmth begin to arise, melting every last doubt. I was excited to possess this victory. I quickly turned to smile at Him and get His nod of approval. He was no longer there. For a fleeting moment, I wanted to return to despair.

But I remembered. "I will meet you at the River." I wasn't going to let doubt and unbelief diminish my faith. Besides, Jesus had moved on to meet me and I didn't want to disappoint Him. I took a deep breath and held my torch tightly. I took the step of faith and jumped right down into the black mouth of the mountain.

Chapter 7

Valley of the Shadow Land
Overcoming the Fear of Death

"Though I walk through ..." Psalm 23:4

The current was swift, propelling me rapidly through the chute. The chute was about four-foot-wide like at a water park I'd visited. But that chute had been translucent yellow allowing sunlight to pass through. Here it was pitch black except for the light the torch was shedding. The rushing water soaked me from head to toe. It also caused the torch to hiss and sputter, but the light's intensity never diminished. I could only see a foot or two past my feet as the chute twisted and turned me at will in its downward spiral. Another thought about the waterpark came to mind. One of the rides was called the "toilet". I chuckled at the comparison and water splashed into my mouth. Reality instantly returned. This wasn't a leisurely waterpark ride. *Where would I end up?*

Unexpectedly, the chute leveled out and the water jetted me out of the mouth of the mountain onto a flat sandy beach. I landed hard in sand, pushed forward by the spewing water hitting me squarely in the back. It almost extinguished the torch. I rolled to my side to escape the discharging water and managed to stand. I looked around and saw that I was out of the mountain. It was dusky here, wherever here was. *Where were the shiny rays from the City?* No sun and no moon, only ambient light. The torch helped me to see, but only minimally. I held the torch high and walked along the water stream flowing like a creek from the mouth of the mountain. It ran toward what appeared to be a lake.

The lake was dark, flat and smooth like a polished black stone. I was finally out of the mountain but now facing a lake that hindered moving forward to the River, with no sign of a boat anywhere.

I was confident that Jesus meant the River that flowed to the *City*. This was definitely not that River. In fact, as I took a deep breath, I caught a definite putrid smell. It was the odor of decay and rot. Death! I held the torch high to the left and could see in the distance the lake touched the side of a mountain range. My mountain was part of that chain. The wall of mountains rose up like the sides of a giant cauldron. It was not possible to travel in that direction. Looking right, I saw that the beach continued around the side of the lake. There had to be a way of escape from here or provision had to come. Jesus promised that, so I started walking to the right, wet and chilled. The chill I felt was from being wet and cold. *Or was it?* The sand was firm but slightly damp, compacting as I walked. It was easy to travel at a good pace and a brisk walk would warm me up and dry my clothes.

"Lead me to the Rock ...I will take refuge in the shelter" Psalm 61:2-3

I had walked a great distance before I could see that the beach did not touch the base of the mountains on the right. I had been deposited at the intersection of two mountain ranges. The remaining dim light revealed both too steep and impossible to climb. I was glad for the option to walk on flat land.

I wondered how much time I had before total darkness set in and hoped I could find a secure comfortable place to sleep until the morning light. The thought of morning light caused me to contemplate that up to now on the journey, I had never experienced night or darkness. But here, the light from the *City* did not seem to break through. I was uncertain why the rays of the *City* couldn't penetrate in this place as it had in other regions on my journey. As I looked up, the light seemed obscured by a solid cloud bank. I didn't want to contemplate what all that could mean, so I kept walking.

Moving on, I looked for a secure and comfortable spot to sit and rest. On and on I walked, encountering nothing but boulders and a narrow stretch of flat land between the lake and the wall of mountains. The land morphed at some point from sand to hard flat rock. Boulders littered the pathway, making walking a straight path impossible. Most of the boulders were taller than me and four to six feet wide. No tree or other living thing were visible. It was a dreary path. A black, bottomless lake, laid silently on my left and a wall of sheer rock stood on my right. The twenty foot pathway snaked its way between the boulders.

The boulders here did not feel the same as those I had encountered before. They were not the touchstones I had come to know and appreciate. No, so far they looked like obstacles with one purpose and that was to hinder my journey. About then, I realized that the "dusky" light had not changed. I laid the torch down on a small rock and walked away from its light to look at the unending dark black cloud impeding the sun's light. It stretched in every direction as far as the eye could see, seamless and massive. It looked exactly like the cloud created by a massive volcanic eruption I had viewed on a National Geographic special. With that memory, a little bit of my hope leaked away. This was a cloud created by fire and smoke.

How long would I have to walk under this dark, brooding cloud? I quickly hurried back to my torch fearing it would have begun to diminish. But surprisingly, it was as bright as ever and glowing with a steady light.

"Thank You Jesus", I whispered half hoping that I would hear His voice like times past.

Only silence surrounded me, eerie silence. Now sensing that I was not going to find a comfortable and secure shelter, I looked for a boulder that might be concaved at the base so I could curl up under its protection. I walked onward for a long time and almost missed what I was looking for.

It was exactly what I needed but was situated on the back side of a boulder. I found it quite by accident when I kicked a small stone that went sideways and observed it disappear under the boulder ahead of me. I approached to discover exactly the alcove I was searching for. *Could I fit?* The scooped-out base was small, but it would be perfect. I stopped and crawled back into the little alcove. Here, I would be secure on three sides. The surface of the boulder was smooth and the ground was sand. I nestled snugly into the soft sand, happy I didn't have to be lying on the bedrock I had been walking on. I scooped out an area to secure my torch and shored it up with more sand. Perfect! Rock on three sides and my torch in front of me.

My clothes were now dry and walking had warmed me. I laid down and curled up comfortably in the sand which molded to my body. As I snuggled in, I looked up at the rock above me and noticed that it had a different hue from the other rocks. I knew instantly that this rock was indeed another touchstone rock. Jesus had provided once again. In this place of shadow and darkness, Jesus let me find Him as my resting place. I reached up and touched the stone. It was warm to the touch. The rock pieces and the touchstone on my chain warmed in confirmation. I had forgotten the chain during my watery escape out of the mountain. I touched the chain ensuring that all the pieces were still attached. They were.

"Thank You Jesus. You are always so good to me!" I sighed and took a deep breath in spite of the overpowering odor. Yes, even here, I found the mist was present. I filled my lungs and promptly fell asleep.

I was awakened by a horrible stench. I actually felt startled awake, but didn't think that the awful odor carried on the breeze, could cause me to feel so apprehensive. My eyes turned quickly to the torch. Thankfully it had not dimmed. It burned bright. The air around me was foul, damp and stunk terribly. I pulled the torch from the sand and with one more deep breath of the mist, I crawled out of the little space where I had slept. I stood, my legs cramping as I stretched after the long sleep in a fetal position. I walked a few steps from my rock shelter and felt a damp breeze, pungent with the stench. As my eyes acclimated to the dim light,

I held up the torch and noticed smudge and drag marks on the stone path ahead. The offensive smell was coming from the direction where the drag marks and smudges appeared. My imagination conjured up what rotting meat and fermenting garbage might smell like. It was horrific. *What was it? Was it coming from the lake or something else?*

Somehow, I knew that the lake, as well as these spots and smudges were contributing to the offensive odor. I was also sure that the main source had yet to be discovered. That thought stirred anxiety. Realizing that was not a good emotion to allow, I focused on eating. I reached into my pocket for the stored apple, it was gone! I checked the other pocket. Nothing! *Did I lose it in the water chute coming out of the mountain?* Resigned that I would have to do without, I began to walk onward for my "second" day–if you could count endless dusk as a day in this dark valley. Breathing in the mist again, all anxious thoughts faded.

Nothing had changed since I went to sleep. Awaiting me was the endless lake to my left, the sheer hopelessness of the mountain wall to my right, unyielding boulders in my path and now a sickening odor that gagged me if I inhaled too deeply. I felt on edge. I captured the thought and smiled. *Now why would I be on edge? I'm out taking a walk to meet up with Jesus, right? What could be so bad?* Little did I know what was waiting for me ahead. Had I known, I would have begged Jesus to transport me out of this place or crawl back under the touchstone and hide. But, in order to meet Jesus at the River, I must follow this pathway and go where it leads.

"Clouds, foaming waves, roots and blackness of darkness" Jude 1:12-13

I soon found the source of the foul stench. As I walked to avoid the black smudges on my pathway, I came to a large boulder that almost barred the entire path. To move forward, I needed to walk around this obstacle.

Halfway around, the odor hit me, like a gut punch taking my breath away. I gagged and would have lost my cookies had I eaten some. Thank God I had not found my apple, nor had I eaten anything. I continued around the boulder finding the pathway littered with dead things. By "things", I mean the decaying flesh and various bodies that appeared human, animal, insects and plants. Huge tree roots and branches were lying on top of bodies. Other places bodies were draped over trunks of trees and mounds of what looked like rotting grass. Some piles were seven to ten feet tall. These piles of dead things went from the edge of the lake on my left to the wall of mountain on my right. The unending scene was absolutely grotesque and overwhelming.

At the lake's edge, the piles tumbled into the water. I noticed a strange undulating in the water. The water churned and foamed around the immersed piles. The foam was dark brown and had churned itself high onto the piles at the lake's edge. It was ghastly to behold. As my gaze followed the foaming piles away from the lake's edge back toward the mountain wall, I saw that the piles caused a dark black stain to appear on the stone face of the mountain. They looked like the dark smudges on the path but different. Seeing them brought a foreboding deep in my inner core.

Compelled to look more closely, I walked on toward the mountain's stained surface. The light from the torch reflected off the mountain's surface except where the dead things touched it, causing the black stains. I crept closer to take it all in. I was grossly fascinated and wanted to see it up close. When I was a few feet away and gagging from the smell, I saw that the torch light was literally sucked into the black smudges on the wall. The smudges resembled slowly growing black holes. These black holes were like stars that imploded upon themselves and absorbed all things. The black smudges absorbed the torch light at this close proximity. I could even feel it pulling at me, wanting me to touch it or worse yet, touch it with the torch. It wanted to pull me into its pooling abyss. It wanted to extinguish the light.

I felt that if I yielded to this curious desire to touch the black hole, I could be sucked into something where I might never emerge. Then I had more gruesome thoughts! *Was the lake another form of a black hole? Was the lake made of blood and sap? Had liquids from many dead things oozed out forming this lake of death as well as these black holes? Was the lake a larger manifestation of death in this place?* I recoiled in disgust and fear. As I did, the torch flickered.

"Jesus, You are the light of the world and not even death could hold you captive!" (19) From deep inside me that popped out.

I snapped to attention and focused on how to walk through this valley that had the shadow of death everywhere. I held my torch up. As far forward into the distance, as far as the dim light would let me see, piles of bodies stretched on and on. I needed to edge my way close to the piles as I walked the pathway set before me. Sometimes the passage between piles was so narrow, I could hardly pass without contaminating my clothes and body with the foam or oozing liquids. This close to the piles I saw they were covered with large fat, black flies and maggots. Swarms of the flies ate the decaying rot. They looked like a black blanket moving over the rotting piles. When disturbed, they flew up choking me and reducing what little ambient light I had. They tried to land on me as I frantically swung the torch and my free hand at them. Many of the piles looked to be moving as the maggots crawled and ate. It was ghastly! In that moment, I wanted to vomit again, but only dry heaves racked my body.

I quickly turned and went back around the large boulder. The air was a little better. I took in a deep breath hoping for the mist and was not disappointed. It filled me with resolve and strength to go on. As the dry heaves eased, I leaned against the boulder while many questions flew across my mind.

Why wasn't Jesus here? Why was He not concerned for my safety? Was this punishment? With every thought, the torch would sputter. But its sputters quickly brought my wayward thinking back on track. *NO! I will not allow this place to stop me from meeting with Jesus at the River.* My focus had to be on His words to me. "I will meet you at the River."

How was I to get past all of this?

More of His words came to mind. "Yea though I lead you through the valley of the shadow of death, fear no evil. (43) Nothing by any means can harm you." (36)

The words fluttered like a butterfly on a summer day even in this place. In that second, the stench diminished or was it my imagination? I thought about all I had experienced to this point. Time and time again, He had proven His words to me when I faced the impossible. He had shown me that in Him I could do all things. It was about His faithfulness. He had always been with me in word or tangible presence.

"Ok, Lord. Your words have come to me, and I have learned that Your words are truth and life. Jesus You are the living word, so when I have Your word, I have You. 'God is my refuge and strength, A very present help in trouble. Therefore, I will not be afraid.'" (28). As I spoke out the words, I felt the touchstone and rock pieces warm. My inner spirit became encouraged and strengthened.

"Through the water, fire and flame" Isaiah 43:2

I closed my eyes and breathed in deeply. It was the opposite of what you would think to do. But nothing operated the same in this place. Truths in operation on my journey were far different from the world I had left behind. Either His word was true, or it wasn't. I was going to put it to the test once again. I took in a deep breath of the stench that had caused my dry heaves. Logic told me this was a crazy thing to do. But obedience, without allowing logic to rule had served me well on my journey so far.

Surprisingly, the smell didn't cause me to gag. Instead I had an ever so slight hint of a high meadow filled with wild flowers. It was moist with the hint of the mist. I closed my eyes. I was no longer in the valley of shadow and death, but on a high mountain plateau full of wild flowers. I twirled and breathed even more deeply. I chuckled at myself for thinking of breaking out into song like in "The Sound of Music". I stayed in this mental experience for some time. I sat down on the grass, I rolled in the flowers, I stuck them in my hair, I let the clear mountain breeze blow away the scent of death. Watching this on the inner screen of my mind, this opposite spiritual act, brought joy. Again, the spiritual truths at work in this place were beyond amazing and comprehension. I was in no hurry to return to the shadow place of death.

At some point, I realized the need to return and walk through the shadowy valley of death on this pathway that had been set before me. This wonderful place in my mind's eye was not leading me to the River; I needed to find the River. I must return to confront death. I needed to find Jesus big enough to lead me through this place of shadows and death just as He had led me through the places of life and joy.

The mental experience had refreshed me. Somehow, I knew inside that I would not be overcome by the things that would soon encompass my walk through this place of death. I could do this now, so I opened my eyes to proceed. In my heart of hearts, I hoped that I had been transported out of the foul place or that its awfulness had been neutralized. One can always hope. But I was not, and it had not.

Rather, I had a new sense of peace and purpose for the steps that lay ahead, so I started my trek through the shadowed valley on the narrow gross path. Nothing had changed here, but me. I was different in my attitude. I strode out with purpose and power. With each stride I determined to get through this shadowy place of death and meet with Jesus at the River. On and on I walked, not focusing on the smell or the never-ending piles of undulating bodies. Time was lost to me. I kept my mind on pleasing Jesus, and the joy He would have when I finished this trek without once "losing it". I was changing, and I knew it. The easily intimidated woman who had begun a journey was no longer around. With every step of my journey, I was being transformed into a new creation.

Then my path took a sharp turn to the left and I was brought face to face with my worst nightmare yet. I had come to a large area filled with bodies towering higher than any ones before. Some were on fire and others smoldering. In other piles, the contents oozed out and fueled the fires like wild fires, flaring up and out of control. *How was I to make it through?* The only visible path led between two towering, burning walls of fire as far as I could see. The flames from each were joined across the path. There was no other pathway and no way around or out of this God forsaken hell filled valley of death. Suddenly, pictures of my flesh catching fire and my skin being turned to black ash appeared on the inner screen of my mind. The images rose like terrifying giants wanting to intimidate and stop my passage through this land of death.

"Jesus, show me what to do". The words came out of my mouth and took me by surprise.

Before my journey, asking Jesus for help wouldn't have entered my mind. Yet, I had sensed that I was changing. Yes! I was changing even in this place of death. Before, I would have screamed, "Jesus, do something!" As I mulled over those two different expressions I suddenly saw movement.

Something was coming through the flames. I was stunned to see Holy Spirit and hear His piercing call. His call quieted the crackling sound of the fire. He passed through the consuming tongues of flames and flew right at me and landed at my feet! Not a feather was singed! His beautiful feathers showed no evidence of fire. Untouched! I looked at Him in wonder, processing what I had viewed. *Holy Spirit could do it, but could I?*

I heard His voice inside me. "Shaddrack and his buddies survived in greater flames than these! You can do this! Let's go!"

Holy Spirit flapped his wings, stirring up the flames of the piles beside me. He flew right back through the flames that filled my path and disappeared. I faced the flames wondering how far I must run within the raging inferno before me. I could see no end. I paused and breathed in the mist, then another deep breath, then a third. I asked myself, *Will it be enough?* When I heard a gentle voice say, "Just go." I took heed and began running. *It's no time to waver, just obey,* I told myself. As I ran toward the huge flames, I felt the intensity of the heat. Part of my mind from the deep recesses, told me I was going to die a horrible and painful death from the flames burning off my skin. I pushed that thought out of my mind and I visualized I had a fire proof blanket around me. I retained this mental image of the blanket and headed where Holy Spirit had flown through. I kept running on the path leading into my personal glimpse of Hell.

The next instant, I was through the flames and on the other side. *How?* The flames were only smoldering on this side. *How had I passed through such an endless fiery tunnel in the blink of an eye? It was a miracle.* Holy Spirit was gone. But I was thankful for His Presence to get me through. The threat of death that had appeared so real was once again defeated. I held up the torch, looked at what lay ahead, and moved on to meet with Jesus.

My next sight caused me to stagger to a halt. The bodies before me no longer burned instead, they were tumbling into the lake where the path ended, right at the water's edge. Foam from the bodies piled up on the shore covering all that tumbled into the lake. *Who were the people forming this decaying wretchedness? Where did they come from? Were they people on the journey who somehow failed the quest? Would I ever know? Did I even want to know?* Inside I knew that my questions would hinder my own journey, so I refused to let my mind entertain them.

I approached slowly to see if there was a hidden path that might become apparent as in the past. When I reached the foam where the path met the dark foreboding lake, I looked slowly all around. I saw nothing that offered a way of escape. I held the torch higher and the light showed that the lake narrowed here.

Across the lake from this narrow place, no piles of bodies, no foam could be seen. Crossing the lake was the task at hand. There was no getting around this. My only way forward was through the dark and foul lake; the very lake that was made by foul blood, body fluids and who knows what else. *How deep was it? What kind of creatures might live in its depth that would be attracted to live, warm flesh? What if the chemicals in the water were so acidic from the dead flesh and other things that fell prey to its grasp, my own flesh would be dissolved away? I could die a thousand ways.*

A flutter of the torch reminded me to put an end to that train of thought. I took a deep sigh. Death! I had faced it in many ways already. This would be just another test, however daunting. Jesus had promised me that He would see me at the River, this was not the River! That meant I had to make it through to continue and find my way out of this dark, shadowy valley. Only then would I come back into the brightness of the radiant *City*. I had to make it to the River. I needed feet and legs to do that. So somehow, someway, I would make it across.

I walked toward the foam. When I reached it I stopped, putting one foot over the foam and down into the water. It came up to my ankles. I picked up the other foot and placed it into the water. Both shoes were now soaking up the foul stench. I could feel it penetrate and touch my skin, but nothing burned me. Nothing came to eat me. I took another step and found it was the same depth. The black water was thicker than I expected; soupy. I couldn't think of that. I took another step forward, then the next. All shallow! *Could it be?*

The density of the water in the diminished light had hidden the fact that the water was only ankle deep. I quickly walked on, trying not to splash my clothes with the foul stinking stench. My feet and shoes would be hard enough to get cleansed. Soon I was across. I stopped and turned to look at the dimly illuminated smoldering piles of flesh on the other side of the lake. Smoke continued to rise, keeping the solid cloud of darkness overhead. The light of the *City* was still obscured. But I knew, without doubt, that I would find my way to the River, a waiting Jesus, and see the light of the *City* once again. May it all come quickly!

"The people who walked in darkness have seen a great light" Isaiah 9:2

Holding up the torch, I scanned for a direction to go. I looked for the path. Nothing! I studied the walls of the mountain and noticed that ahead, to the right, might be an actual opening in the solid wall. If it were, it would be the first that I had found. I walked toward the opening. With every step, my feet would slip inside my soaked shoes then slide forward. The left shoe made a squeak and the right made a swoosh. So much for stealth if I needed it. As I walked on the smooth stone pathway toward the hoped-for opening, my wet feet became cold.

Continuing on, I held the torch up again for a better look. There was definitely an opening or crevice of some kind. *Would this finally be my pathway out of here? Would I need to continue on in this shadowy place of death, skirting the lake on this side?*

I finally reached the opening and was able to squeeze through the small crevice in the mountain wall. It continued and was just wide enough for me to barely pass so long as I stayed sideways. It was not a direct path by any means. Turning first this way, then the other. I inched my way sideways, holding up the torch. But after about ten minutes or so, my thighs were burning. I stopped for a moment to let my legs rest and leaned against the smooth, cold, pathway wall. I closed my eyes for a moment. The next thing I knew, my hand holding the torch dropped and hit the side of the other wall. With a start, I quickly stood. Apparently, I had fallen asleep and my body had gone limp. I took a deep breath to awaken myself, remembering that the mist was always around even in the most unlikely of places. My strength came back a little with each breath. Feeling strong enough to continue, I moved on.

As I took my first side step, the torch flickered. Not with "it's going out" but from a sudden gust. The breeze blew intermittently, but it was coming from the direction I was going. My heart leapt with joy. A breeze meant that there must be air coming in from an opening on the other end of this narrow pathway. Heartened and encouraged, I moved forward. The pathway continued to zigzag, and I inched on. I could tell from the torch flame that the breeze had increased.

Suddenly, as the pathway took another of its many turns, it opened into a large circular shape area. Two steps into it I found a soft sand floor rather than the hard stone. I could see another opening on the other side of the room and moved toward it. But as I took a couple more steps in the soft sand, I was suddenly overcome with exhaustion. I stopped to take a few deep breaths to gain strength. It came. But such a peace came over me, I reconsidered continuing on. I decided a nap was needed instead.

My feet were like blocks of ice, so I took off my wet shoes and stood barefoot in the sand. Surprisingly it gave a measure of warmth. I found a part of the wall hollowed into a cozy little niche, so I sat down and snuggled into the soft, pliable sand. I positioned the torch handle securely in the sand beside my feet. I felt a gentle breeze coming, keeping the flame burning bright. The torch had not produced heat before, but now it was giving off warmth in my time of need. I laid on my side in a fetal position and moved my cold feet close to the radiating warmth. As my feet began to warm my last thoughts were pondering the sights, smells and the events of two days walking through death. "Days" of course was a relative term on my journey. Tomorrow, the third "day", I hoped to be out of this prison of death and back to the light. I drifted off to sleep. Sleep came easily without the foul smells and presence of the abhorrent valley sights.

As I was still in the twilight place near dreams but waking into consciousness, I realized I had been dreaming about the River, the shining sun and the brilliance of the *City*. Unfortunately, it was simply that, a dream. I was still in the niche, resting in the warmth of my makeshift bed. The flame was still burning bright and full. Its light further clarified where I was and what I needed to be doing. However comfortable, I needed to make my way to the light.

My feet were warm and dry but stained by the foul contents of the black lake. *Would they ever come clean?* I didn't want to think of the odor on my skin. I found my shoes. They were still wet. *Should I put them back on? Should I leave them? Should I carry them? Lord, only you know what lies ahead for my journey. Will I need these shoes, or do I trust that I will somehow get another pair?* I questioned in my mind. Hearing no answers, I decided to carry them and walk barefoot, hoping they might dry.

I picked up the torch and shoes and made my way to the other opening. It led to a wider path, but it still meandered. I had only gone a short distance, when the path turned ninety degrees to the right and I was confronted with a pile of rocks blocking my progress.

"You've got to be kidding me" I said out loud.

"No!"

I jumped backwards at the sound of the voice. It was the voice of Jesus loud and clear. Clear in sound as well as in meaning.

"Jesus?"

"Yes, I am here on the other side."

"Oh, I'm so glad you are here. I have so much to tell you!"

"Yes, I know everything that you have faced on this part or your journey. You have done well. You kept your strength in Me, and you found your way out of the valley of the shadow of death. You persevered on every pathway set before you." But His words of encouragement didn't settle into my heart. Instead frustration arose, blocking the life from His words.

"Out of the valley! Obviously, you must not be looking at what I see. I see a large pile of rocks blocking my way. I need some dynamite or a jack hammer to get these things moved!"

"Remember the story of the fig tree and what I said in that situation?"

It took me a minute to refocus from the obvious pathway blockage to a mental concept of what Jesus had said in a Bible verse.

"You mean where You said to speak to the mountain, and it will be moved?"

"Yes."

"Ok, is that what you want me to do? Tell this pile of rocks to move? Ok rocks, move!" I was a little rude and impatient speaking with overemphasis.

Nothing moved. The pile didn't shake, there was no earthquake, there was no landslide. The rocks remained; piled high and tight.

"Jesus, I did what you said, and nothing happened!"

"But did I say, 'Melissa order the rocks to move'?"

"No, but isn't that the point of the story you had me remember?"

"No, the point was for you to recall that faith and the resulting actions are all connected to what the Father is showing you to do in the moment. Remember, I said and did only the things the Father was showing Me to do in that moment and in that particular way."

"SOOO, do I need to ask what you want me to do in this situation?"

"Yes, the faith and believing will come into play with what I show you or tell you to do."

"Ok, Jesus, what do I need to do to get out of this place? Do I need to move these rocks? Do I need to close my eyes and let the Holy Spirit transport me to the other side? Do I need to ask you to move them out of my way? Tell me Jesus what to do."

"Move the rocks".

This time I did not assume to speak to them. I knew I needed to ask more details.

"Jesus, how do I move the rocks?

"Begin with the biggest and heaviest one you can see and move it."

Now His instruction was opposite my logic. I looked over the pile. The torch illuminated them clearly. I could see that all of them were big and heavy. Where to start? How to start? Would I be able to even budge the biggest one? As I looked for the biggest rock, my eyes quickly found it. It was the key rock at the bottom of the pile and appeared to hold the entire pile in place. My school physics classes came to mind. I knew that the weight of the other rocks pushing down on the biggest key rock would make it that much harder to move. Upper body strength was not one of my attributes.

I took a deep breath. The thought flitting through my mind, *even a champion weight lifter couldn't pull it out!* Even as that thought filtered its way out one side of my mind, in came a still small voice that sounded like mine saying *I can do all things through Christ who strengthens me.* (20) Taking one deep sigh, and breathing in the mist, I chose to listen to that small voice. I moved to the biggest rock to get into a position to pull it with all my body. I put the torch in a small crevice beside the pile of rocks and got into position, both hands on the monstrous rock. I squatted to get the best leverage with what little strength I possessed.

"Jesus?"

"Yes?"

"I want you to know that although I probably can't move this big rock, I believe that somehow you will give me the strength to do it. Ok Jesus?

Jesus? Jesus?!" No answer. "Jesus are you still there?! You said you would never leave me. Jesus did you leave me?"

From the other side of the pile of rocks I could hear Jesus laugh. "No, I will never leave you, but I am moving on ahead to meet you at the River. You've got this!"

"Wait! You mean you are leaving me stuck behind these rocks? How am I supposed to ....? Jesus!"

His fading laughter rang clearly on the breeze.

"He is always with you in the instant you need Him. He knows you've got this. So, He will meet you later at the River."

I literally jumped and would have fallen had David not caught my arm and steadied me from behind.

"Oh David! Thank God! He sent you to move the rock."

"I'm to let you move the rock. I'm instructed to minister to you as needed."

"Well, the ministry I need right now is for you to use your super angelic powers and move that rock!"

"Sorry, Jesus said you've got this."

I could tell from the tone of his voice and the serious look on his face that he was not going to lend a hand. My mind seethed. *What good are you!* I shouted in my mind. I turned back to the rock, and took a squatting position, ready to try and budge the rock. Behind me, I heard David chuckle.

"Jesus shared your thoughts with me, and I have to say, I'm a little surprised by your attitude! Did you think that since I had served and ministered to you as directed by Him before, I would do this task for you now when He has directed you to do it? When I gave you an answer that you didn't want to hear, you devalued my presence. Do you honestly think my presence here is worthless? Apparently so! I guess I'll take my leave and ...."

Without any need to think, I shouted "NO!" I stood up and turned around facing David. "I'm sorry David, I am so tired of the continual struggles here in these miserable mountains. I want to get back on the River and be with Jesus. Please forgive me."

"In the world you will have trouble: but cheer up, He has overcome the world." (21)

I guess his response meant David had forgiven me.

"Does He abide within you?"

Without hesitation I responded. "Yes!"

"Then He is here. He is in you, and He will help you overcome whatever hinders your walk with Him, if you let Him!"

Now that was the ministry I needed. I constantly needed to be reminded of the truth. I felt strengthened, not in body but in the hope that somehow, someway, my pile of rocks hindering my progress, would be moved.

"Ok, let me get on with this. The sooner I move this obstacle, the sooner I can make my way to meet Jesus at the River."

"Now, that is the person I was hoping to re-engage with." David replied with joy.

Squatting to tackle the rock challenge, I placed my hands on each side of it. I had a brief thought that the width of the rock was wider than I could grasp. Moving this monster of a rock was not possible in the natural. I quickly stomped down that logical observation and strengthened my grip on the rock. As I did so, I noticed that the surface of the row of rocks above it did not appear like all the other rocks. *These rocks must be a type I've not encountered before. Everything here is so different*, I thought to myself. With two energizing deep breaths of the mist, I pulled with all my might and more. I felt like I had willed even my toes to pull. The rock still didn't budge.

My mind said, *Not surprised*. My spirit said, "Giving up?" I took a couple of deep energizing breaths and pulled again. I drew on every ounce of my being. The rock still didn't move but my hands did. They slipped off with such force they hit the rocks above it, and I fell back in the soft sand. The rocks that my hands hit loosened and moved. Strange, but now I was on a mission. I had found what might be a weak link in the pile of rocks.

I got up quickly and took hold of the two loose rocks that I had struck. I gripped each one and pulled. The rocks not only budged but pulled right out. I stood holding them in my hands, looking down at them in wonder. They felt like Styrofoam but looked like porous volcanic rock. How strange! My attention turned back to the pile of rocks drawn by the peculiar cracking and popping sound they were making. I was trying to process what the sounds meant and watched with wonder as the pile of rocks began tumbling down like dominos. I would have been buried, if it hadn't been for David. He pulled me out of the way even as I continued to stare in amazement. Praise God for David! Once I was back on my feet, I remembered my shoes and the torch. I scanned the sand and found them moved. Obviously, David had taken care of them.

158

"Amazing!" I was astounded and delighted. *How?* Certainly nothing I did should have made that kind of difference. The biggest and heaviest rock still sat in its place, unmoved. But all of the others had crashed down around it. I moved my gaze to the opening. Through the now open narrow passage I saw the reflection of sunlight. Hope flooded my soul. I was encouraged, full of joy. Light! I was going to get out of the shadow land where I had been for who knows how long. I turned to look at David, thankful he saved me from being crushed. He was smiling. It reminded me of how I felt when Jesus smiled. I longed to see Jesus again and get one of those big hugs.

"I'll see you at the end of the passage." David's words brought me back from my thoughts of Jesus.

David climbed over the large rock taking my torch in one hand but leaving me my shoes. Without another word he vanished.

"Not my feet only, but also my hands and my head"
John 13:9-10

This time I wasn't troubled by his disappearance. Things like this were becoming my new normal. I turned around and proceeded toward the scattered rocks. I picked up my shoes. They felt dry. They were still stinky, but I put them on anyway so I could climb over rocks and not cut my feet. I quickly made my way over the rocks and down the narrow passage. The further I traveled, the light became brighter and the air fresher. I was overjoyed even giddy like a kid going to the fair. I was excited about meeting with Jesus.

Continuing through the passage, the light got brighter and brighter. I knew in my heart that I had finally come out of the bowels of the dark mountain. I was on my way toward the light from the great *City*. I quickened my pace. An aroma of grilled meat came on the fresh breeze. The instant I smelled it, my stomach growled. I felt I hadn't eaten in weeks! Well, it could have been weeks, I didn't know. I quickened my pace. Whatever was cooking smelled like fine steak. I turned a corner and unbelievably, I was out of the passage and the shadows. I walked into the brilliant light from the *City*. Its rays shinning out across the land were so bright, I had to cover my eyes. The light was blinding because my eyes had grown accustomed to the darkness.

"When your eyes adjust, come over and sit down. I have food." David's voice carried on the clean breeze.

I gradually opened my eyes. The light no longer blinded. I walked over where David was grilling a large piece of meat over a fire. I saw a water pitcher sitting beside a loaf of bread and some fruit. Vegetables were cooking on top of some rocks in the fire ring. Then I noticed a large cushion perfect for sitting beside the fire where David was cooking. I went over and joyously sank down into the comfort of something this soft for the first time, in a long time.

"So much better than rock and sand". I didn't even realize I had said the words out loud.

"Yes, I'm sure! Now, hold out your hands." David's words brought my focus back.

"What?"

"Hold out your hands. They need washed to rid them of the foul remnants from your time in the valley of shadows. Decay and death contaminate. They need washed with pure water. By the words of Jesus, I am directed to sanctify and cleanse you with the washing of this water."

"No arguments here!"

As David poured water over my hands from the pitcher, I saw that the clean, clear water lifted the dark stains and foul stench from my hands. Every remnant from the shadow valley was being washed away! I was amazed as I watched my skin become clean and my normal skin tone return, no soap or bleach needed.

"Do you have more water other than in this pitcher?" I asked.

"No, why?"

"I was hoping for a bath because I have that foul stuff all over me. I picked up so much contamination by walking though the valley and the black lake."

"There is enough to wash your feet." David emphasized.

"Well, that is better than nothing!" I was grateful.

"Oh, you will be amazed at what the water can do. There are also some new clothes and shoes. Jesus directed that you have new clothes that have no spots or wrinkles."

"I hate to put on clean clothes when I'm so dirty. But I could use the shoes once I wash my feet."

David smiled and turned to dish up the food.

"Here you go. It's already blessed." He handed me a plate with a big, thick, juicy steak on it. Alongside were some roasted root vegetables, a huge chunk of bread with butter and a fork and knife. I was giddy with expectation. As I took the plate and utensils from David's hands, he began to pour me a glass of water. As I watched him pour the tall glass of water, I secretly hoped there would be enough left over for more than my feet. I needed washed from head to toe!

"There is always enough with Him."

Yes, that truth brought hope.

The food was the best. I marveled how every meal tasted better than the last. Who would ever believe the story of my journey? I found it hard to believe myself at times. *Was I really experiencing it?* I had already encountered too many supernatural things to think that I was dreaming. I ate slowly, enjoying every bite and was grateful. I could feel it strengthening my body and my soul. I finished the last bite and was full. I took the last sip of water from the glass and handed it back to David.

He took the glass and sat it to the side. Next, he pulled out sandals, some clothes and a small towel from beside the cushion where he sat. Handing them to me, he stood and picked up a wash basin and the remaining pitcher of water.

"Follow me. There is a secluded place where you can wash your feet and change your clothes."

As I followed behind him, my mind was inundated with questions of how I might somehow stretch the water enough to wash my whole body. But there wasn't a wash cloth. Only a small towel to dry my feet. David went around a large boulder. Behind it was a small alcove perfect to change clothes and wash my feet. There was even a small flat stone to sit on. David laid the basin and pitcher on the ground beside the stone. Following his cue, I laid my clean clothes on the stone, leaving enough room for me to sit. He bent over and poured the remaining water from the pitcher into the basin. It was only enough water to cover the top of my feet. Thoughts of a whole bath vanished.

"Leave your old clothes, the basin and towel on the stone when you are finished. Then come back to the fire." David casually spoke as he carried the pitcher back around the large boulder and went from sight.

"Thank you, David." I spoke out so he could hear.

I meant it with all that was in me. I was thankful to be out of the valley of shadows and here in the light. I was thankful to have a little water for my hands and feet and the clean clothes. How I longed for a shower and some good smelling shower soap. Yet I was thankful for what I had.

I sat down on the rock and pulled off the shoes. *Do I get out of my current clothes or wait? Would I find fresh under garments in the pile too?* I hadn't thought of that until now. *Maybe I could splash some of the water on my legs, while my feet were in the basin, making my ankles a little cleaner?* That thought led to another thought–*take off everything now*. I did.

I spread the towel to sit on and placed my feet carefully into the basin. I didn't want to splash or spill any of the precious, clean water. In seconds of my feet being immersed, I could feel the cleaning process beginning to take place almost like dipping into a warm effervescent pool; first on the soles of my feet, then spreading up through my toes and onto the tops of my feet. It felt like a relaxing pedicure. I closed my eyes and savored the feeling of my feet getting clean. When I closed my eyes, to my surprise, I could feel the sensation of my body being cleansed beginning with my ankles. Not wanting the feeling to end, I kept my eyes closed. I could feel the sensation of warm water flowing up over my lower legs, then my knees. I opened my eyes to check. No, I wasn't in a pool of water. But my lower legs were getting cleaner even though the water was barely covering the top of my feet. I couldn't comprehend how that could be, but I didn't want the sensation to end. So, I closed my eyes and leaned back, letting the feeling make its way up my body and to my face. I finally felt submerged in the warm sensation, hair and all. I simply relaxed and enjoyed the process. It was incredible, and I didn't want it to stop.

I sat for a long time. I didn't want to open my eyes and stop the warm, clean feelings that I was experiencing. My logical mind said *There is only enough water to wash my feet* but my spirit and my entire body was reveling in the supernatural cleansing process I was feeling, regardless of logic. I felt clean from head to toe. Inside and out. A slight breeze chilled my body and brought me out of the warm, clean dreamy state. I needed to get dressed. Having experienced the incredible supernatural bath experience, I longed for the real thing.

I opened my eyes. *What? How?* I couldn't believe what I saw. My legs were clean. My arms were clean. I was thoroughly clean from top to bottom. Even my hair was wet and squeaky clean. Miraculously, the water had somehow migrated from my feet up and had removed all the foul stench of death from me. I was now clean. Putting my arm to my nose, I took a sniff. I even smelled clean and fresh. How, I couldn't imagine. I felt as clean inside as well. I laughed at the pleasure the bath had brought me. I marveled that it had all been by the power of washing in this special water. I was thoroughly clean.

I stood up. I didn't need the towel to dry. I was not wet except for my hair and my feet that were still in the pan of water which still looked as pure as before. I took the towel from the rock and rubbed my head. A few quick rubs with the towel and my hair felt dry. I laid the towel down to step out on and dried my feet. I looked at my dry soles once so horribly stained from the foul lake water. Incredibly and wonderfully my feet were fresh and clean as if I had had the best pedicure money could buy. I smiled and rejoiced, *Only Jesus can make these things happen.* I picked up the pile of clean clothes and out fell undergarments too! I smiled as I realized, *They will all fit perfectly.* Only excellence in every detail. I was learning more about how the Kingdom operated.

As I finished slipping into my sandals, David spoke from the other side of the large boulder.

"Leave it all there. I will take care of it later. It's time now for rest. Later you head out for the River."

I had not felt sleepy until now. But when he said the word rest, a tiredness fell on me like I had worked a long but profitable day. I didn't need convincing.

"Thanks, David. I didn't feel tired, but when you said rest, I was instantly overcome by fatigue."

I walked out from behind the boulder with my perfect fitting new clothes and plopped down into the large and comfy cushion. I made some nesting adjustments, took a deep sigh and rubbed my eyes. David brought over a fleecy blanket and covered me up. I was asleep in seconds, dreaming of seeing Jesus and heading home to the *City*.

"Where then does Wisdom come from?"
Job 28:12-28

Well rested, I awoke to the aroma of fresh coffee and freshly baked sweet rolls. I opened my eyes and looked up into the bright light radiating all around from the *City* and smiled. No more death from the shadowy valley of stench. I was on the other side of those tests and moving on. Finally, I will make my way to the River, see Jesus and travel on to the *City*. As I gazed at the brilliant light radiating from the *City*, a deep peace settled over me. I was looking at my new home. It was an exceptionally strange thought for one who had never gone too far from her apartment. But on this journey, I was transforming. I was becoming a different person from the one who first stepped into the row boat at the ornate, ancient cathedral. This new me felt more alive and connected here in this strange land than I ever knew in my comfortable life back home. The *City* was pulling me to my real home and that is where I was headed. Yes, Jesus and the *City* was all I needed. Putting those thoughts to the back of my mind, I stretched, sat up from my restful position and turned toward the fire.

David sat there smiling, an "If only you knew what was coming" smile. It filled me with mixed feelings. A part of me was honestly looking forward to another adventure. At the same time, a part of me was a little apprehensive not knowing what the adventure would bring. Curiously, I used "adventure" for past experiences. History so far on my journey, spoke of the opposite; danger, intimidation, confrontation with fears and supernatural provisions and experiences. *What was next?*

"Finally, you are awake! I have coffee and fresh sweet rolls." As my stomach growled loudly, David and I both laughed. Had I slept that long? Obviously, my stomach thought so.

"You need to eat and get ready to move out. Today you will be crossing through the wilderness on your way to the River. You will want an early start because it is not a place to linger long. Wild beasts inhabit that area and you won't want to encounter any of them." David's voice carried a note of seriousness.

My mind jerked into neutral. Seeing wild beasts would be scary enough. Beasts that might eat me, brought a different kind of fear. I was quickly falling down a rabbit hole of no return when I heard Jesus speak in His authoritative but loving voice from behind me.

"Peace"

Hearing His voice, pulled me back from fear immediately. I began taking control of my thoughts. My heart leaped with joy at the sound of His voice. I was coming to know the reality of "I will never leave you or forsake you. My Presence is always with you." He knew what I needed. But I still wondered, *Would I ever learn? Will I ever come to trust?*

My mind jumped from Him never leaving me, to touchstones, to the forgotten rock pieces I had carried in my old pants pocket all this time. I needed them back because of the strength of their presence when my journey led to places without Jesus, David or a large touchstone for security.

In panic, I turned to David. "David, I forgot to take the small pieces of the rock out of my old pants. Do you have them? I need them! What will I do without them?"

"Peace!" Jesus spoke to me with more emphasis and authority. "I will transfer the essence of those rock pieces and that of many other scriptures into your heart. They will arise in your spirit as you need them. They will be with you forever, a ready source in battle any time you need truth as a weapon, a two-edged sword.

I turned back to Jesus, His eyes locked with mine and a feeling I could not describe came into my heart. Whatever it was, I knew the transference had taken place in that moment. With peace renewed in me and the strength of the transference, I let out a sigh and squared my shoulders.

"Good! Now come and see what I have for you before you start your trip through the wilderness."

I got up and walked quickly over to where Jesus was standing.

"Give me the chain with the three gifts."

As I touched the chain, the touchstone warmed as always. I found the clasp, took the chain off and handed it to Jesus.

"I want you to know you are my beloved daughter. You have walked boldly through the valley and in death's shadows victoriously. You have gained a portion of wisdom on this part of the journey. It will be a great tool for you ahead. Wisdom has great value and its beauty is multifaceted beyond measure. Just like light can be refracted from the *City* and sends its brilliance throughout the land, so too does wisdom. It has many diverse divisions. Wisdom takes the LIGHT and breaks it down into a myriad of many facets. Light refracted creates the colors of the rainbow. Wisdom refracts spiritual light. It breaks down the Truth of Father's Words. It colors and affects everything that it comes to rest upon."

From a hidden pocket on His robe, He pulled out a beautiful, perfect round crystal. He laid it on His open palm and it immediately caught the rays from the *City*; its appearance like a multifaceted diamond. It had a gold loop for placement on the chain. Some of the facets caught the rays from the *City* and shot out from His palm in rainbow colored streams. Other rays were magnified and concentrated like lasers.

"This is your gift for gaining wisdom. Because you overcame the intimidation of death and have been washed in the pure water, you are now like this crystal. It will remind you when you need to call to remembrance that death can be stripped of its power to intimidate and impose fear. Remember, longing to see Me again, is what got you through every hideous and fearful place. All of this insight will be wisdom later on your journey."

He continued to hold it in His palm while speaking of the crystal's comparison to wisdom. With each point He made, a laser beam flashed out. "This symbolizes your refinement. As you went through the fires and as you went through defeating the fear experienced in the valley of death, you were forever changed. You have been made into the likeness of this crystal. You faced all of those deep inner things that had never seen the light of day as you walked through the bowels of the mountain and the valley of death. The pressures you faced successfully created its beauty."

He took the chain and placed the crystal on it. Then he handed the chain back for me to put on.

The ball was hard to look at because the light from the *City* refracted in its clarity. Laser lights flashed in all directions. I looked into the eyes of Jesus to avoid the brightness, so I could secure the chain around my neck and place it beneath my shirt.

"Now, let's eat together so that you have strength for this next leg of your journey. It is time for you to move on."

Time! When I was with Jesus or Holy Spirit or even David, I was so at peace that time wasn't important. I also remembered many times in the bowels of the mountain and in the valley of the shadows, how I longed for time to pass quickly so that I could escape. Time here on the journey expanded and contracted. I couldn't figure out the why or the how of it all. But with those thoughts passing on through my mind, I enjoyed the presence of Jesus and David in the moment.

Chapter 8

Equipping of the Saints
A Rod, A Staff & More

"Your rod and Your staff" Psalm 23

I was about to drift off in a delightful nap, when the pleasing, assuring voice of Jesus pulled me back to the moment.

"You're going to need a couple of things on your journey to the River where we'll meet up again."

"Oh! You're not here to go with me?"

"No, this wilderness crossing you must walk on your own. Everyone must walk through the wilderness just like the Valley of Shadows and you must be alone. Don't forget, you are my beloved daughter. I am well pleased with you. I know you'll come through this wilderness crossing victoriously and with new levels of power. But here are the two things to take with you."

David handed Jesus two items lying at the foot of one of the large rocks. I had not even noticed them. As Jesus touched them, they instantly changed from about 16 inches in length to about five feet.

"These are My rod and My staff. You will find them useful on this leg of the trip through the wilderness. You will experience comfort by having them. My Father gave them to Me and they comforted Me during My wilderness times especially with the wild beasts. They will come in handy for you too. They have delegated power and authority attached to them, so do not lose them or give them to anyone else unless I tell you. Father told Me that you are ready to manage them."

In one of my hands, Jesus placed a long walking staff that was straight and sturdy and smooth to the touch from much use. It was the right height for helping me walk on uneven or rocky surfaces. Fitted on the top was a piece of deer antler that made a "Y". Both antler ends were pointed and sharp. The sides of the stick were indented allowing my hand to hold it securely. It was a perfect length for my height, yet my stature and that of Jesus were not even close. That was a curious thought to ponder. Every provision provided for me was sized and proportioned perfectly to fit my needs. From His other hand, He gave me a heavier piece of wood which resembled a thick, oversized baseball bat. It was weighty and long enough to use defensively. You could strike a good blow with it if necessary.

"I'll see you at the River." And with that, He quickly hugged me and turned toward the crevice leading back to the bowel of the mountain and the shadow of death. A little sadness came over me because He walked off so quickly. I already longed so much for His Presence to be with me.

"Come." David said. "I will show you where to start your wilderness trek."

I followed David over to the edge of the ledge where we had been resting. A few feet below the ledge, a large grassy plain began, spreading out toward the horizon. In the distance I could see the *City*. It's radiating beams colored the grassy plain with rainbow colors. I could see the River making its way like a tiny blue ribbon running toward the *City* from the left and then threading its way away from the *City* to the right. From here the River appeared to run right through the *City*! I filed this picture away and focused on what lay before me. The grassy plain, or the wilderness, as both David and Jesus had referred to it, flowed from the edge of the mountains to the distant River.

"Look back to your left and scan the horizon. You will see a large dark mass along the River. Do you see it?"

I turned back to the left and began a thorough scan from the edge of the mountains where I could first see the River. My eyes followed the River till I saw the dark mass that blocked the ribbon of blue.

"Yes, I see it. What is it?"

"That is Crown Derby. The dark mass you see are the trees of the town which grow along the River. You need to make your way there. That's where you will see Jesus again. Remember the small kayak you were not able to fit into?"

"Yes"

"Well, it's still waiting to take you down the River. Keep your eyes fixed on those trees and they will guide you across the wilderness. Now don't delay. Go in the strength of your meal."

I knew not to ask David if he would go with me, so I just smiled. He smiled and walked to the crevice and back into the bowels of the mountain.

I was going alone as Jesus instructed. Yet, not alone. I knew that Jesus was always with me and never left me. It was truth that I had grown to understand and believe by the experiences on my journey in spite of occasional feelings of insecurity. I took several deep breaths, instantly filled with additional strength and invigorating energy from the mist. I used the staff to make my way from the stone ledge down onto the floor of the grassy plain. It brought comfort to my mind and heart to think of it as a grassy plain and not a wilderness. One image brought cute critters like prairie dogs, deer and maybe buffalo. The other held man-eating beasts like lions, tigers, bears, wolves and…. I abruptly stopped that line of thinking and focused directing my eyes to the trees that lay in the distance. I had a job to do and I was determined to do it. Off I went.

I lost track of how much time passed, but the mountains were now far behind me and the distant trees were much closer. I had put my mind on other thoughts like seeing Jesus again, getting on the River, and making my way to the *City,* my new home with Jesus and the Father. *What would the City look like up close? What were the wonders waiting inside?*

"Don't give place to the devil and stand against his wiles" Ephesians 4:27 & 6:11

My imagination of the *City's* splendors was in full motion when a horrible sulfur smell grabbed my attention. I stopped short. *What was that smell? Where was it coming from?* It was not the smell of death but actually smelled worse. I had not forgotten the smell of death and wondered if I ever would. No, this was different. It was a smell that set all my senses on alert. It was a smell that made the hairs on the back of my neck stand up. I walked cautiously. The ground dropped off suddenly making a bowl like depression in the grassy plain. You couldn't see it until you were right up on it. Inside the bowl, the grass had been scorched away. In the center, I saw the most hideous, yet intriguing creature ever, sitting on a rock. No movie, no creatures from Hollywood could compare to what this creature looked like. It was hideous to look at, yet it intrigued your mind to study it. I could feel a hypnotic pull upon my mind. I quickly looked away. Yet I was curious and looked back. It was a man, yet not. It was a beast, yet not. It was hideous, yet compelling. I felt drawn to come closer. I took a step forward without thinking. The sulfur smell became stronger and began to burn my nose.

"Yes, come closer. I will not harm you. I only want to talk with you. Few people come this way. Most people on their journey take the River route. I am so happy to see a person here in my area. I have been so lonely."

Its voice was smooth and pleasing to the ear. The enticing and hypnotic fascination grew stronger. Part of me said *Run.* A part of me said *What could it hurt to stay and talk a few minutes. Poor lonely thing. It's all by itself.* I certainly understood what being alone felt like in this place.

"Yes, come closer and let me talk with you a little while. So, you have been on a journey, have you? You have been through many things, I'll bet. Rest a minute and tell me about some of them. Why did you come this way and not take the River like most?"

I wanted to start telling it or him about all my horrible and fantastic experiences. I wanted to tell it of my love for Jesus, my desire to be close to Jesus and how that love for Jesus led me on this pathway. But as I looked at its grotesque sympathetic face, I began to feel uncertain about everything. Doubt about decisions and directions started to creep in. I felt pulled to want to tell it all the near-death experiences. I wanted to tell it about the horrible valley of shadows. I felt pulled to sit and talk about how traumatic my journey had been up to this point. Its eyes and its smile seemed to say "Yes, focus on the hard and frightful things. Yes, tell me how your flesh has suffered. I will give you pity. I will give you sympathy."

"So, you have faced some deathly experiences, I sense. I'm so sorry that you had to encounter them. Too bad you had to do all those things alone or because you were blindly following Jesus. I bet Jesus told you that you would never be alone. Yet it seems that during every fearful thing you went through, Jesus wasn't there for you, was He? You faced them alone. Now here you are in the wilderness all alone again. It is truly sad. I'd say it was only your sheer determination and strong nature that got you through those things. I'm so sorry. You must be amazing, given all the things you have done for yourself. I would never have let that happen to you if you were walking through all that on a journey with me. I would have never left your side."

With each statement, I walked closer to it. Drawn, I was pulled in by the look of sympathy in its red, pitiful eyes. The sulfur burned my nose even more, but I was so focused on its words, I didn't care. My mind shifted into full debate, like two opposing lawyers in court giving conflicting statements to sway the jury. I felt confused and afraid. I began to feel abandoned by Jesus and to think that this unsightly beast was right. A part of my mind wanted to agree with its words. *They were true after all, right?* My flesh began to feel sorry for what I had been through. Feeling mistreated and abandoned like an orphan, I began to feel sorry for myself and everything that I had encountered, because of blind trust in Jesus.

Holy Spirit's piercing call high above brought a halt to my wayward thoughts. David's quiet voice caught my ears. I turned away from the beast, David was standing on the bowl's ridge, steps away.

"What are you doing?" David said with concern in his voice. "Why are you listening to the lies of this liar? Where is your discernment?"

With David's voice, deception lifted. I looked sheepishly at David. The beast made a low and faint hissing behind me, but I caught the sound. Clarity returned instantly, and I turned toward the beast.

"I know you," I said. "You are the father of lies. You are the one who tempted Adam and Eve to doubt God with half-truths. I'm not listening to you anymore."

I turned to leave the scorched bowl, but as I turned, my way was blocked by another hideous beast. It was not so much a person but more of a large, appalling animal. Fangs, tusks and claws stood before me. It had a head like a giant warthog, but the body build like a hyena. It snarled and tried to nip at my legs. Without thinking, I instinctively took the rod and swung at the thing. It yelped and ran away. I moved to depart, and the retreating beast was replaced by three more equally as hideous. One came at my legs and one at my hand that held the rod but the third hesitated. I took my staff and thrust the sharp antler into the closest beast, then swung the rod at another. I struck both beasts and my arms reverberated with the solid impact. The antler pierced the chest of one and it yelped, running away leaving a bloody trail through the scorched grass. I hit the second beast squarely alongside its large furry head, causing some of its teeth to break off. It too left, yelping and bleeding. The third snarled, crouched to lunge, its intimidating eyes focused on my throat. Again, without thinking about it, I took an aggressive step toward the beast. As I did so, it retreated with a yelp, its tail between its legs.

"So, you think you can ignore me and win, do you? You think you have power to drive away my demons?"

The sulfur man-beast hissed causing me to turn back to where it had been sitting. Now it was standing right behind me. It loomed like a tower over me. It stood erect like a grizzly bear, snarling and hissing out its words. I could smell the stench coming from its pores. Foam was forming in the corners of its mouth, reminding me of the foam at the lake in the valley of the shadow of death. I almost vomited my meal from that morning at the thought. Fear tried to settle over me. I backed up. The man beast stepped forward. I retreated, it advanced, toe to toe at this point. From high above I heard the distinct shrill of Holy Spirit. A righteous anger from deep inside me rose up at Holy Spirit's sound. It continued to bubble up. I could feel the pressure of it building inside me like a geyser. Holy Spirit called again, and the righteous anger escalated. A third time, Holy Spirit's call pierced the atmosphere around me. I looked squarely into the man-beast's eyes not flinching, blinking or thinking. I felt a hatred for it welling up within me. I saw a hint of fear come over its beastly face for a second. It masked it instantly. But I saw it. The hideous thing knew that I saw it. It tried to posture up more intimidation by its stance toward me, appearing almost pitiful in its attempt. Laughter started to bubble up within me now. The mixed emotions of righteous anger and the laughter felt curious. Together, the two emotions strengthened me. I let out a loud chuckle and the man-beast jerked like I had jabbed it with a red-hot poker.

"Do you see these?" I held up my rod and walking staff, both covered with the blood of the demon beasts. "These were given to me by Jesus. They were His from His Father. I am the beloved daughter of that Father. He is proud of me because I have overcome the fear of death and the fear of you. He has never left me or abandoned me as you want me to think. I know who you are Satan and I do not fear you."

As I said his name, more shock shone in its beastly eyes.

"You are defeated. Jesus saw you fall as lightning and I'm getting a picture of you falling now as well."

I felt more joyful laughter well up. It brought me strength, confidence and assurance knowing that this thing before me was long ago defeated. It knew it. Now so did I. Not only did I know it, but he knew that I had the revelation of the truth. Intimidation and fear were now reversed, his to own.

"Do you see these!" I pulled out the chain with the gifts. The diamond ball caught the light of the *City* and sent out blinding beams of pure white light. Bands of rainbow colors also danced in all directions. One of the pure brilliant light beams magnified by the crystal hit the beast squarely in its red eyes like a laser beam. Blinded and screaming, it fell back, but caught itself on the rock where it had been sitting.

"A table in the presence of my enemies" Psalm 23:5

"Put it away! Put it away! I can't look at that light! Put it away, put it away! I beg you. It's blinding me! It's blinding me! I can't look at it!"

Part of me honestly wanted to make it suffer more. But as I was contemplating that idea, David walked up.

"He is already a defeated foe. God the Father and Jesus will deal with him soon. You need to regain your focus and move on toward the destination that was set before you."

"Ok."

I tucked the chain under my shirt and prepared to move out. I gave a last look at the man-beast, defeated and pitifully holding its eyes. With David leading the way, I turned and left the scorched area.

I had only walked a few feet when aromas of wonderful food smells came wafting in the air. I no longer smelled the horrible smells from the beast. Instead my attention was on the wonderful food aromas. *From where, I wondered*? David walked and I followed. There in the midst of the grassy plain under a giant tree was a round, beautifully decorated, dining table with two chairs. Jesus sat there waiting. On the table were every one of my favorite foods displayed in beautiful dishes. In the center sat lit candles and a vase of my favorite flowers.

"Jesus? How? Why?" I looked at David for answers but didn't give him time to reply. I hastened over to the table where Jesus sat. He looked up at me smiling that incredible smile I felt was only for me.

David pulled out the other chair, beckoning me to take a seat. As I sat, David took the bloody rod and walking stick from me and handed them off to another angel that I only now noticed. A pitcher of water was brought to pour over my hands, washing away the drops of blood splatter from the beasts. I was given a towel to dry them. Jesus smiled and poured some kind of red liquid into my glass. He poured it away from the table until my glass overflowed, and the liquid fell on the grassy ground. I heard a moan coming from where I had left the man-beast, Satan. I turned toward the sound. From where I sat, I could see into the scorched depression and noticed the man beast was being forced by some big angels to look our way.

"He has to watch us enjoy this meal together, because you overcame him with your words and your testimony. Wisdom has shed her light. You discerned the deception of the enemy and thus defeated him and his demons."

Jesus turned His attention back to the table. So, did I.

"Let's give thanks for this food Father provided and enjoy this time together."

Jesus prayed, blessing the Father and the food. As I said, "Amen" Jesus began to serve up the food. He took my plate and put the right amount of each of my favorite foods on it. Then He filled His plate and we began to eat. As we ate, Jesus spoke of the Father and how He loved me. He told me the Father was taking a special interest in my journey. He shared how the Father was so pleased with my progress toward Him and the *City*. His words filled me with joy, peace and comfort. I was overwhelmed with the expression of Their love. I could feel it deep in my innermost being. I was satisfied in body and spirit.

After our leisurely time of fellowship, an angel came up to Jesus and whispered. I could not hear what was spoken. Jesus shook His head in acknowledgement and the angel left. Right then David returned with the clean rod and staff. He took a hold of my chair, indicating I needed to stand up. As I did so, he handed the rod and staff back to me. The rod and staff were half their size and tied together with a rope making it possible to hang them from my shoulder, freeing my hands. My amazed look caused David to laugh.

"They will adjust their size and length as needed for the current situation. Right now, having them small lets you walk a faster pace."

"Your travel time to the River is shorter than it appears. It won't be much longer till I see you there." Jesus finished with a smile.

David took my arm and led me to another pathway through the tall grass, I could actually see it this time. He motioned for me to follow it. I took one last longing gaze at Jesus. His smile warmed me from head to toe as He waved good-bye.

"They will follow you the rest of the way to the River."

David's voice pulled my gaze away from Jesus. Now I noticed two beings approaching from the side.

"We are Goodness and Mercy. We will follow you the rest of the way to the River and see that you return to the kayak."

Goodness and Mercy had human-like forms although I knew that they were supernatural beings. However, they were different from David and the other angels that I had encountered on my journey. They weren't frightening or intimidating. They were just different enough that you wanted to stare and ponder. Each was uniquely beautiful. I must have been staring, because Goodness laughed, and Mercy said very sweetly, "Shall we go?"

"I must decrease" John 3:30

The trees were within a short walking distance and I could see Crown Derby and its boardwalk. I was approaching from the River where the last bridge crossed over. The small kayak was still tied there.

I was excited to get here and yet apprehensive. Was I going to fit? I had recently eaten several wonderful meals, with bread and sweets. I worried I may have put on a few pounds, increasing rather than decreasing. I quickened my pace to reach the bridge and to hopefully burn off some calories.

"You fear you won't fit?" One of the beings asked from behind. I stopped and turned around, having forgotten that they were following. Their question reiterated my anxious thoughts that had troubled me for several miles now.

"Yes, what if after all of this, I'm still too big, and the boat won't float? What if I can't even get in it?"

"Don't think about the food and forget about the past," said Mercy.

"Yes, if that is the case, then you choose to decrease and take another trip on the boardwalk."

The words from Goodness were like an unexpected bucket of cold water in the face. I gasped at the thought of another trek on the boardwalk and processing through more buildings. *Could I? Would I choose to take yet another journey already knowing all that had transpired since the last odyssey through a building?*

"Don't worry for what may not be. Remember not to be anxious for anything." Mercy commented.

With an apprehensive sigh, I turned toward the River and the bridge. "Might as well get this over with."

We found the kayak tied up at the last bridge. I looked at the small hole. I looked down at myself and thought that I looked the same. I wasn't going to fit.

"I knew it!" I said in frustration.

"You won't know until you try." Goodness spoke a little too chipper for me.

"Yes, there is no time like the present to move out for God." Mercy said. "Here, let me hold your rod and staff."

I handed them over and walked down the steps to the landing where the kayak was tied up. I didn't believe that I was going to fit but I needed to confirm it. I might get a clue to how many more doors I might need to pursue. I held onto the dock and stepped down carefully as I put one leg in the hole, then the next and tried to sit down sliding both legs forward. My legs were too long to slide up into the bow of the kayak. I then tried bending my knees, folding them behind me under the seat. I sat down and to my amazement, I did fit into the small hole. I was thrilled because I had decreased enough to fit this much.

"But you are sitting too tall." The truth of their words echoed into my inner being. They were right. Not being able to put my legs forward meant that I couldn't sit properly balanced on the seat. I needed shorter legs, not just the decrease in weight, which had been my focus. I pushed myself back to a standing position and stepped out. Short of cutting off my legs, I didn't have a clue how to make myself decrease in height.

"Walk the boardwalk again." Goodness's voice grated on my ears.

"Yes, that is the answer to finish the decrease." Mercy chimed right in. "We will carry your rod and staff as you walk."

I didn't want that advice or that method. I wanted another choice. The three of us stared at each other. Goodness and Mercy only smiled and nodded toward the boardwalk.

"Trust us. Would Jesus send just anyone with you to back you up? No, He sent us, Goodness and Mercy to follow you because we are the resources you need to help you at this time. We are named after attributes of the Father. Which means that His goodness and His mercy will follow you as you need, until you can get into that kayak and leave for the next part of your journey."

Even though I didn't want to hear it, everything they said resonated as truth. The solution to my situation was walking the boardwalk in obedience. So up the steps I went, onto the boardwalk with Goodness and Mercy right behind me. As I walked and looked at the buildings waiting for a light to go on, I encountered several of the same people I had walked with before. Some of them acknowledged me with a nod of their head. Some walked past me as if they had never met me. I knew they recognized me, by the way they hung their heads. I began to wonder if the presence of Goodness and Mercy on my heels caused this reaction.

"No, it is not us", Goodness said. "They can't even see us. Only you can. They are reacting because you are now almost decreased enough, and they can see it by your stature."

Only then as I passed a bench, did I compare my height with the bench height. I was definitely shorter in comparison from my last walk around the boardwalk. *Thank God!* I said in my mind. *But how?*

"All things are possible." Mercy reminded me.

Encouraged, I passed another building, watching to see if the sign came on. Nothing. I continued walking around the boardwalk continually looking for the sign in each building to illuminate. Nothing, nothing, nothing! *Had I missed it?* By now I had completed the loop and was approaching the last bridge where the kayak was tied. *Now what was I to do?* I turned to ask Goodness and Mercy that question when Mercy spoke up.

"You are finished."

"Finished? But I never ..."

"Yes!" Mercy proclaimed. "Even as you chose to walk and watch, watch and walk, you decreased in stature. Each time you chose to keep going you decreased a little more. Every decision to endure what your mind said was not working, brought decrease. Decrease came even while you embraced more potential prospects of death. Now you are ready."

"Did I hear that she is ready?" Jesus spoke as He walked over the bridge and approached us.

I turned with such joy and found that He appeared so much bigger and stronger than before.

"Oh Jesus, You came like you said. I'm so happy to see you. Do you have your own kayak to join me on this next part of my journey?"

"No, now you will be navigating the River without me. I have to take care of some of Father's Kingdom business. But Holy Spirit is always watching over you and David will show up from time to time, as well as Goodness and Mercy. We will meet again as needed. I always know where you are and what is taking place."

I couldn't help myself, I ran and hugged Him tightly. "Oh Jesus, do You really think that I can do this with my own decisions and navigations? I don't feel as confident in myself as You make me out to be. Do I stay on the River? Do I ever get off and follow a path? How will I ever know?"

"Remember that My Father and I will never move you toward your destiny and future without the promises, the provisions, and the permissions you need. (48) They are already provided for you. We know that you have the ability within you with Holy Spirit's help, to do what is set before you. We have confidence in you. Have faith. Now let's get you settled into the kayak and send you on your way."

He took my hand as we walked down the steps. I turned to say "Thanks" to Goodness and Mercy for their help, but they were gone. I turned back to a smiling Jesus who was now holding the rod and staff from Goodness and Mercy. I knew I needed to move forward. I needed to step out in faith. I had to trust that I could do this, just as I had embraced and survived every past challenge.

"Now let's see how you have decreased."

I stepped down into the hole of the kayak and bent one leg to go toward the front. I then positioned the other. They fit perfectly. I settled down comfortably on the little seat. I was in completely and balanced. I had decreased to the right size.

"Now remember from our discussion, when you come to a "Y" in the River, you need to take the more shallow, narrow way. Going the other direction would bring you eventually right back here. I know you don't want to lose time doing that. You have decreased enough to be able to take this small kayak, so you will do fine navigating the shallow, narrow section of the River. It's time. Off you go." With that He handed me the looped rod and staff.

I placed them securely by my leg in the hole, glad for their smaller size. Jesus untied the kayak and I began to drift out into center of the River.

"But Jesus!" I screamed, "What about a paddle to steer with?" I started to float under the bridge and into a faster current. The kayak was not going straight but had begun to drift sideways.

"Here!" I heard Mercy's loud voice from the bridge above. As I passed under the bridge, a paddle was dangled down to me. As I reached up to take the paddle from Mercy, there was a "thunk" from a small cloth bag dropped on the bow of the kayak in front of me.

Goodness called out as I was being carried away by the fast-moving current. "That's to eat and drink along the way." I secured the bag under my seat with my rod and staff, safe and dry. In that moment, the fast current took me around a bend. I found myself suddenly in new territory.

"Still waters and green pastures"
Psalm 23:2

The River moved fast. I was thankful for the paddle that helped me keep the kayak steady and centered. Without it, I would be at the mercy of the current. The River was wide and deep, and the current fast and strong. Since leaving Jesus and Crown Derby behind, I had decided to stay in the center of the River. I wanted to be able to move out in either direction quickly if needed. I wasn't sure which side of the River the narrower and shallower portion would branch from. I was comfortable on my own at this point and actually enjoyed the beauty of the River's scenic banks, noticing the trees along the River had thinned out. There was a bend to the left coming up, and the River's current picked up even more speed as I approached it. I rounded the bend and came unexpectedly to the "Y" going off to the right. I saw it and quickly realized, I needed to do some hard paddling to navigate across the strong current over to the narrow passage. The stronger current swept to the left. Anyone not paying attention or putting in the effort would be swept in the wrong direction. I remembered what Jesus had said. The direction of the main current would take me back to Crown Derby. I didn't want that. So, I paddled with great effort aiming the kayak toward the straight and narrow way on the right.

It took greater strength than I had anticipated. My muscles were cramping from the effort, yet I maneuvered across the strong current, avoiding its persistent pull to the left. Finally, I entered the narrow branch on the right but not without expending most of my strength. The narrow branch's flow was the opposite. It was tranquil, smooth, with no current.

The momentum of the River current along with my laborious paddling to break free had me moving full throttle. I was going way too fast when I entered the narrow stream. The kayak began to spin. I tried to correct it, but it was out of control and headed toward the bank and a large fallen tree. With a rather hard "crack" I hit the tree. I let out a yelp as I quickly ducked, trying to keep my head and arm from hitting the tree's trunk. My arm was lucky, but my head was not. The hit propelled me backward causing me to almost pop off the seat and out of the kayak. The paddle flew out of my hands and landed a good distance away floating in the water. There I was sitting dead stopped in the middle of the narrow stream with my head reeling. The paddle didn't move. Everything was at rest. I checked my head for a lump or blood; I was surprised finding nothing. The spot on my head wasn't even sore! Thank God I didn't need medical attention. Refocusing, I realized I needed to retrieve the paddle but how?

"Jesus, this is why I wanted you or David or Goodness and Mercy to be with me. I can't make the journey alone. I don't have the ability! I'm always messing up and failing."

Holy Spirit's piercing call from high above corrected me about my little pity party. As Holy Spirit called out again, the rod and staff bumped my leg. I looked down at them inside the kayak and wondered what made them bump my leg. As I stared at them, I thought that they might help with the paddle problem. I was about to throw out that idea when a new thought came to mind. "Look down into the stream." I did, not thinking about where the thought came from. To my amazement the water level was shallow. The kayak barely cleared bottom. Reason said I could get out and walk, pulling the kayak while retrieving the paddle. Holy Spirit sounded from high above and the rod and staff bumped my leg again. *YES!* At full extension the staff would work like a pole. I could pole my way toward the floating paddle and retrieve it.

I liked the idea of not getting wet. I quickly pulled the looped rod and staff out. The staff grew to its original size, but the rod stayed small. I used the staff as a pole and maneuvered the kayak to the paddle, retrieving it. The staff, no longer needed, shrunk when it touched the rod. I placed them securely by my leg. With my paddle, I now headed to shore, thinking this would be a good time to take a break and sample the provisions that Goodness and Mercy gave me.

I saw a place along the bank where I could easily navigate the kayak to shore and get out. There was a little alcove where the water had eroded the bank, creating a sandy beach. The kayak crunched as it rubbed against the sand and small stones. I stood up, stepped out and tied the kayak to a tree branch with the rope at the bow. I grabbed the bag of goodies, leaving the rod and staff in the boat.

Suddenly tired and hungry, I made my way up the bank into a beautiful grassy valley, enjoying everything sight. I could see the *City* sparkling on the horizon, looking closer than ever before. I couldn't wait to get there and see what made it so beautiful and special. I knew it was the home of Jesus and the Father and wanted to make it my home too. The sun was warm and the breeze coming through the valley felt perfect. I sat under an oak tree, leaned against the trunk, and opened the small cloth bag to peer inside. I discovered a stoppered flask of rose-colored liquid, a round loaf of multi-grained bread, an apple and a piece of meat that was dried like jerky. I gazed at the provisions and thought that this apple looked exactly like the one I had lost. My stomach growled. I realized that I had not eaten since I last ate with Jesus. *How long ago was that?* I wondered. In this place, time was not measured in any way I could discern. It was eternal day with the brilliance of the *City*.

I started to tear off a huge piece from the loaf of bread and then thought better of it. With no clue how long it was going to take me to get to the *City*, or to wherever I'd meet up with Jesus, I knew it would be wise to limit what I ate for now. So, I tore off a small piece. The apple was going to be a problem since I didn't have a knife. I bit off about a fourth and saved the rest. I did the same with the jerky. I chewed slowly although it was so tasty, I wanted to devour it all. In between I took a few sips of the juice. I was amazed at how full I felt as I took my last sip and corked the flask. I carefully placed the items back into the bag and decided to rest my eyes. I felt like I had eaten a full meal of pasta or mashed potatoes and pot roast, and needed a little nap.

As slumber overtook me, off into dreams I went. I found myself following Jesus through crowded streets in a city full of people. The city in my dream was beautiful, almost like the *City*, yet somehow missing the mark. People were busy, but I saw sadness and emptiness in their eyes. I watched from behind Jesus, as He encountered small groups of people and spoke with them. I noticed He had the full-sized staff and rod with Him. I observed how He used it to almost herd people this way or that way and isolate a few by His side who would allow Him. I couldn't tell what He was saying but His body language showed He was passionate. Sadly, most of them appeared apathetic about what He was saying. Occasionally I would be able to read their lips and they seemed

191

to say, "Yes, I'll get around to it," or "Yes in a little bit, I'll do that." Some would say, "Thanks, but I'm good."

I watched and followed Him through many streets, then on to other areas like suburbs, one after another. He walked and walked, in every place He visited, not a single person was missed. Sometimes in some of the small groups that He spoke to, people would start to cry and then hug Jesus. For these people His words had touched their hearts; their response was visible. He would hug them back and move on to another group or place in the city. I noticed that those who would cry and hug Him would be met immediately by David, Goodness and Mercy. Together they walked out of one of the city's gates onto a large bridge and headed to another location. I couldn't get a handle on why people reacted so differently. I continued to watch the interactions between Jesus and the people in my dream. I was about to move closer to Jesus to hear clearly what He was saying to the next group, when I was startled awake.

There was a "swoosh" with air fanning across my face and hair. It woke me. Holy Spirit was standing right beside me holding the rod and staff from the kayak in His beak. He dropped them beside me on the grass and flew off over the narrow stream. I watched the gracefulness of His flight and wondered why He had brought me the rod and staff. When I lost Him from view in the trees, I pulled my gaze back and as I did so, I noticed the kayak was gone. The rope was still tied to the tree branch, but the kayak was gone. *What happened? How?* The stream's movement was as flat and calm as before. I jumped up and ran down to the water's edge. Certainly, the kayak was resting on the sand. Frantic, my eyes scanned up and down the shore line. Nothing. The kayak was gone, and I was without a way to continue on my River journey. *Now what would I do?* In bewilderment I walked back to where I had been napping.

When I picked up the rod and staff, they immediately regained their full size. I put the loop over my shoulder and picked up the cloth bag of food, scanning the valley that lay out before me. I could see the *City* on the horizon and figured that walking across the valley toward the *City* was the best decision. There wasn't a path, but the brilliance of the *City* was not hard to keep in view. So onward I headed. As I walked, my mind floated back to a time, when I would have panicked over this situation and would have been crying or pleading for Jesus to come and rescue me. Yet now, here I was with a "situation". Although it was not what I was thinking would take place, I was calm and at peace. I knew that I was going to be ok. So far, Jesus always made a way and provided the help or provision that I needed for every step of my journey. He had never let me down. As I walked, I let my mind create possible visuals of what the *City* might be like or how Jesus's face would light up when I saw Him next.

Time as usual held no importance. I was encouraged because I could tell the *City* was getting closer. The light continued to grow brighter like the noon sun. I decided to stop and take another break as I was making good progress toward the *City*. From here, I could see that the *City* was larger than anything I could image. Sometimes I caught glimpses of what appeared to be structures behind the radiant beams. These structures rose into the clouds. *Was that even possible?*

I sat down beside a large rock and pulled out the food from the bag. The rod and staff collapsed on their own as I laid them down beside me. The rock made me remember the large flint rock so long ago and the small touchstone on my chain warmed. I ran my hand across this new rock's surface. It also warmed to the touch. I recognized this was another one of the touchstones that I had encountered throughout the journey. That meant His Presence was here. I looked back at the food and to my amazement all of it had replenished itself. The bread was whole. The apple was whole. The jerky was whole, and the flask was full of delicious red liquid. My heart was thrilled. I ate my fill this time and was amazed once again, at how little I needed to feel full. When finished, I watched the food replenish its self miraculously. Witnessing the food restored to wholeness, I thought about when Jesus broke the loaves and fishes and they continued to multiply. "Thank You Jesus!" I spoke out loud.

"Blessed are those invited to the wedding supper"
Revelation 19:9

"I always delight to show My goodness to you." Jesus's voice startled me as it came from the other side of the rock.

"Jesus! I so missed You. Have you come to walk me to the *City*? What happened to the kayak? Am I on the right path, going in the right direction?" All my questions gushed out.

"I love you." His words immediately brought peace. His words brought an end to all worry in my mind.

Everything became ok with His spoken words. Peace settled over me and with a deep sigh, I took His hand that was reaching out to me. Now on my feet, I hugged Him tightly.

"You are doing well. Do not worry about the kayak. It served its purpose. Yes, you are heading in the right direction. The *City* is your destination. Here, I have some things for you."

From behind the Rock, He pulled out a small basket. Inside it, I could see a rolled-up piece of paper with a ribbon tied around it and a square object. It looked like a stone tablet with beautiful lettering inscribed on the surface.

"Sit with Me for a while and we will talk about things that are ahead."

We sat down. He reached into the basket and took out the rolled-up paper.

"This is from Father for you. It is an invitation to a big celebration feast that He is going to put on for Me in the *City*. This is your special invitation. We both want you to be there."

Then He handed it to me. It was the purest white I had ever seen. Perhaps it appeared so white because it was tied with a single crimson red ribbon. I untied it and rolled it open. I began to read.

"As the Bride of Christ, your presence has been requested by the Father to attend the special feast being given in honor of My Son, Jesus, to celebrate His upcoming marriage. Do not miss this celebration. Please make your way to the *City* where you will be directed to the great banquet hall and your special seat of honor for this event."

Then Jesus began to speak. "To seal you as the Bride of Christ, I have given you a betrothal ring. It was on your finger from the first time you said yes to Me as your Lord. But you wanted Me in your life on your terms. You couldn't deal with the level of intimacy I desired, so the ring was never visible to your eyes. It was veiled by many things. Now look at your finger."

I looked down, to my amazement a perfect gold band encircled my ring finger. As I moved my hand and finger it glistened and reflected the light rays from the *City*.

"Do not take it off, ever!"

With that, He took the invitation, rolled it up to secure it with the red ribbon and placed it in the basket. "You will need to show this invitation for entrance into the *City* and the celebration. Will you 'rise up, My love, My fair one, and come away with me?'" (22)

"Jesus! My heart feels like it will explode with joy. Yes, I will come with You to Your home in the *City*. I never want You to leave my side. I know You have proven to me that You never leave me nor forsake me, but I want to look upon Your face always. I never want to be away from Your Presence."

Jesus pulled me close and kissed me on the forehead.

"Soon you will be in the eternal *City* in Our Presence. I desire it as much as you."

"The days that were ordained for me … in Your book" Psalm 139:16

"Now I have a destiny gift for you."

From the basket, He pulled out the square stone tablet with writing on it. Jesus took it and laid it upon His lap. I had a sense that what was written on it had to do with me personally and my journey. Jesus rubbed His hands across the writing. Then He rubbed it again with the fingertips of His right hand. As He did this, I saw Him close His eyes, tip His head back and take in a deep breath. He exhaled slowly as His fingertips moved from top to bottom across the writing on the stone. It reminded me of seeing a blind person read the Bible in braille for the first time as the words become alive.

"Come see the words! They are important and full of life and power. I can feel their life and power as strongly as I did when they were written before the foundation of the earth. They have been waiting words. Words whose timing and season are now, Kairos words. Words ready to be spoken into time, so they can take flight and perform what was spoken by Us over you in ages past. Come, run your hand across them and feel the life from them yourself! Unite your being with the confirmation of their truth."

I put out my hand and slowly put it on the stone tablet. It was cold to my touch yet where my fingers encountered the engraved script, the words were warm. The more I moved my hand across the words, the more I could feel power building up. It was strange and uncomfortable. So, I started to remove my hand before it got stronger. Jesus immediately put His hand over mine and pressed down, preventing me from retracting my hand. But with His hand on mine, the sensation passed harmlessly through me and into His warm hand. He didn't react to the pulsating power from the words. As my fingertips completed tracing the inscription on the tablet, I stopped on the last character and sensed that it was a period. I couldn't remove my hand because Jesus's hand was still on top of mine holding it securely in place. I waited and didn't try to remove my hand. I felt that I could have, but I sensed that Jesus wanted us to continue resting our hands together on the tablet. So, I relaxed my hand.

"Did you feel the life?" Jesus asked.

"Was that what I was feeling? It felt like electricity!"

"Why were you afraid?"

"I didn't want to get shocked."

"Do you remember the machine at the Center of Science and Industry that you visited with your class?"

"Yes."

The memory promptly returned to mind. A memory of how the students tried to withstand the increasing pulse that came through the handle. The goal had been to see how long you could endure and not let go.

"The tighter the grip, the longer you could endure the pulse upon your hand. But did you or any student ever get shocked? Did anyone receive so much pulsing that it harmed the hand, the body or heart?" Jesus questioned.

My mind was processing His words. I knew from being on my journey that His words relayed parables of spiritual truths. He was talking about choice and endurance. He was talking about keeping a strong grip on the power. Here in this moment, the power was in the tablet and the Words of Life it contained for me. Jesus smiled knowing that I had understood His words.

"You must take hold of the Words of Life written for you and hold them tightly. They contain the life force of creation for you. The life force of creation is everywhere. It is in the atom, in the sun, in life all around you. It directs and energizes everything that it is moving toward its purpose and destiny. Now is the time for you to begin to receive the life force of your words written for you before time began. Going forward, you will have their power propelling you toward the fulfillment of your destiny."

"But Jesus, I can't read the words and I can't hold onto the life force without Your hand helping mine."

"Yes, your hand always needs to be in Mine. You keep your hand where it needs to be, and I will keep My hand upon yours. The words written are full of life and power. They are your personal rhema life words from the Father over your life. Remember, they were written in these books by the Father's good pleasure for you, long before you were created and born into time. It's time now for you to hear and receive these destiny words."

"Let's begin again and read the words out loud. Speaking them out allows them to take shape and design. Cooperating with the Father's creative force will bring them to pass. When Father spoke out 'Let there be light', those words began to create light in all of its intended fulness. They formed the sun, moon and stars. But there is always multiplication in the words of the Father. So those words went on in time to create candles, torches, oil lamps, electricity and light bulbs. On and on it went. It will not cease until everything that the Father had determined would be created to provide light is complete. Now you have lasers and LED's. Even more light technology is coming."

"That is how life words are for every child of the Father. He speaks before their existence could ever be comprehended. He sees them and knows them and plans that His goodness shall be for them and upon them. Those words are recorded in His scrolls, books, and tablets awaiting the timing for them to be decreed, spoken out and then brought to pass. Through them, the Father has been in every moment of your life – past, present and future. Now speak your words out loud and begin their activation."

My mind had landed on "tablets". I smiled thinking the Ten Commandments had been written on stone, yet symbolic of today's electronic tablets.

"Jesus, I can't read the words. They are in a script or language that I don't understand."

"Close your eyes and allow your inner spirit man to read. This is the language of the Spirit and your spirit knows it well."

As I was closing my eyes, I glanced down and saw that as we moved our hands into position on the engraved words, they appeared on fire with a red-orange glow. I shut my eyes tight and pushed my hand firmly into the palm of Jesus. I wanted to make sure that Jesus's hand helped me absorb the power that lie within the words on the tablet. He began to move my fingers slowly over the words. Without looking or knowing the words, I had an immediate knowing what they said. My mind knew!

"Speak out what it says!" Jesus encouraged me. So, beginning with the first word, my eyes still closed, I began to speak forth what was written on the tablet.

"In the beginning was the Word and that Word was the creation of all life. The breath of the Father gave life to all that He spoke forth and it breathed life and destiny into man. All creation was designed to bring forth the Father's good pleasure. One of His good pleasures was to create me in the fullness of time."

The words went to a new paragraph, but a warmth began to spread inside of me with the words "of His good pleasure to create me". I wanted to hear more and eagerly moved my fingers down to take in the next set of words. Jesus didn't have to move my hand.

"For I am wonderfully made." I paused for a second letting my fingers rest on the tablet. Had I read that correctly? The tone had changed from a general word to a specific word for me. Jesus laughed that wonderful, all-knowing laugh.

"Yes, you are reading it correctly. This is personal for you. The Father is speaking about you personally."

So, I sighed because I struggled with absorbing these words of being wonderfully made. It was hard for me to relate to the words I had read. I could have given a list of all that needed changed. There were many things I didn't like about myself. In my opinion, I would not call myself wonderfully made. Yet the Father was saying that very thing.

"Truth is always seen correctly by the Creator of the creation. There are no mistakes in what He chooses to bring forth on the wheel of creation. The Creator says that you are wonderfully made and that is the real truth. Man would say that "Beauty is in the eye of the beholder", but the Father Creator does not see as man sees. Man looks at the outward appearance and judges based on a fallen perspective. Man's eye is flawed from the fall and influenced by the enemy of his soul. God looks with true eyes upon the inward and secret parts. Only the Creator has to be pleased with the beauty and form of His creation. If it pleases Him, then it stands to the end. Nothing leaves the wheel of the Creator that He isn't at perfect peace with."

Jesus's explanation settled down deep inside of me. With that, my list went "poof". All my arguments were gone. I continued reading with more purpose to hear and see what the Father saw in me.

"I'm designed to resemble and reflect the true image of the Father to all flesh. He created me and is transforming me into that image. He sets me upon the high places to rule and reign in strength and power. It is His strength and power. It is my designed nature to triumph over evil. It is my created design to put to flight, the enemy. I am created to be a weapon of warfare to drive the enemy away. I was designed to root out the evil encamped forces and then bless the land to multiply. Fruit is in abundance in my DNA. It is the <u>D</u>ivine <u>N</u>ature <u>A</u>ssigned to me. I am royally decreed to be victorious. I am The King's daughter and He denies me nothing that will advance His Kingdom and bless His people. I will always have an audience with Him. Always! Nothing is ever too important on His agenda that I cannot interrupt Him and have His attention. Nothing is too little, too hard or too stupid to bring to Him. If it is a concern to me, then it is a concern to Him as well. He loves me like no other. I am His favorite. I have favor with Him and with man. Angels are at my discretion to utilize for help with the battles. His word is a two-edged sword in my hands. The angels enforce His word that I speak forth as Holy Spirit directs. 'Praise Yahweh, you angels of His, who are mighty in strength, who fulfill His word, obeying the voice of His word.'" (29)

"He always knows where I am. His GPS in me was installed when He created me. He always knows what I am about and where I am. Others may get their needs meet from other sources or another's hand. But my source is the Father. It is personal with Him. The source of all I will ever need comes from Him and Him alone."

I was again at the period at the bottom of the tablet. Jesus removed His hand from mine. When He lifted His hand, I felt a fluttering deep inside like thousands of butterflies all taking flight at once.

"What you sensed and felt was the life of these words taking flight. They go to bring about the fulfillment of what you read. Nothing will ever be the same again because you have chosen to take into yourself the seed of Father's words like Mary did when the angel spoke to her the words of new life. Those words were seeds of life in her inner being. Your words have taken life and rooted, though unseen right now, they will be birthed in time. There are more words and more tablets for you. But now, it is time for you to go forward toward the fulfillment of these words."

He stood up and placed the tablet back into the basket, creating a moment in the atmosphere. It was like a "hallelujah chorus" had finished and there was a divine "Yes and Amen" spoken out, reverberating throughout the land. The Father had spoken and that settled it! I knew my encounter with Jesus had crafted a commissioning, my commissioning. It set forth His purpose for me. I had no clue as to its full end. I stood up, knowing it was time to move out.

"I can't wait to get to the *City*! I know I am close. Are you coming with me the rest of the way?"

I was optimistic, full of hopeful anticipation that He would, because if there were more tablets to read, I needed Him to help me read them. Even though I wanted Him to go with me, I had also come to realize that my journey was simply that. It was "my" journey. Even though He was with me, He needed to let me proceed through each phase as if on my own.

"No, I have other Kingdom business to do just now, but you already have all that you need to move forward. Even as you mused in your inner spirit, this journey is for you. Remember I never leave you, I am with you always. Goodness and Mercy are around as needed, so is David and Holy Spirit. You will do fine."

"Jesus, I assume I am to walk toward the *City* since the kayak is gone?"

"You are to walk forward. Holy Spirit will direct as needed. You will know what to do because My voice will whisper behind you, "'This is the way, walk in it'. (30) Remember?"

"Yes, I remember."

"Good." Handing me the rolled up invitation, He continued. "Now make sure you hold onto the invitation you have for the wedding feast. You will need it to get inside the *City* gates. Hold onto the life from the words on the tablet and you will be strengthened toward your destiny. Remember you are a chosen vessel, perfect for the tasks that Holy Spirit leads you to do."

With that He gave me a big hug and a kiss on the forehead. I heard the shrill call of Holy Spirit over my head and looked up to see where He was. He had landed in a nearby tree. I turned to tell Jesus good bye and take one last hug but, He was already gone. Holy Spirit swooped down from the tree and landed right in front of me. I never grew tired of looking at His magnificent eyes, stature and plumage. It always amazed me that He had His way of appearing right when I needed to be reminded of a spiritual truth or refocused. It was such a comfort to me to know that He was always helping me to get it right.

"The path that lies before you will pull upon all that you have learned and all that you have been given up to this moment. Remember it is always about the moment."

Holy Spirit's words entered softly into my mind. They took up residence with warmth and a weightiness.

"Watch where I fly and follow after me."

With that He took off and mounted up, catching an air current that, thankfully, was low enough for me to easily keep sight of His flight. He headed off in the direction of the *City* and then disappeared where the River went through some dense trees out of my sight. I walked over to the bag of food and the rod looped to the staff. I stowed the invitation in the bag, placed the rod and staff over my shoulder with the loop, and walked in the direction Holy Spirt led.

Chapter 9

Decision Ville
Seven Cities of Deception

"We were foolish, deceived, serving various lusts
and pleasures" Titus 3:3

I walked at a good pace to the River's edge. Surveying the River, I noticed a cove that could be reached by boat. It was only accessible from one side because the other bank was too high to scale. Many empty boats and kayaks were pulled up and stacked. Obviously, others had come before me by the River, as well as by land, because I was on a well-worn path. Ahead, I could see rocks jutting out of the River spaced so that they blocked even a tiny boat from passing. They reminded me of the posts that prevent shoppers from taking their grocery carts beyond a certain point. Apparently, no one could continue advancing on the River. I continued walking toward where the path disappeared into a dense stand of trees lining both sides of the River. They literally canopied the River, obscuring the light from the *City* and cast such a shadow I had not seen since the Shadow Valley. Was there a connection? Nothing felt right or good where the light was not shining brightly. I wondered how Holy Spirit had navigated through here but realized that He was excellent in flight regardless of obstacles. I hoped to pass through this place as fast as possible.

At the edge of the trees, I noticed the path meandered into the stand of trees.

"Thanks, Jesus, for setting the path before me." I spoke out as if He were physically present.

My own words began to bring to mind one of the few set of scriptures that I had ever put to memory–the 23rd Psalm. On this journey, I had definitely lain down in the green pastures and been led by still waters. I smiled at the thought of how a kayak had disappeared on still waters. He had and was restoring my soul moment by moment. I had walked through the Valley of Shadow that was full of death. I figured I was probably 50/50 on not fearing the evil that was all around. But, I was getting better at being reassured that Jesus was always with me. The rod and staff brought me comfort and security, especially in dealing with Satan in the wilderness. I could testify that the table Jesus set was the best ever. There in His Presence was where I always longed to be. He had indeed made my cup run over at the meal and had also given me two supernatural beings that followed me periodically as necessary. I laughed because I had not seen or heard from them in a while. But Jesus had promised that if I needed them, they would show up. He had never lied to me. His words always proved true. So, I didn't doubt that they would be around at the right time. I had my invitation to the *City* where the Father made His home and I was looking forward to being in the Presence of the Father, Jesus and Holy Spirit! These truths came and settled down in the recesses of my mind, causing the warming of the touchstone on the chain. Its warmth jolted me back to the task at hand. I realized I literally had stopped walking when I had begun to meditate on the Psalm. It was a good thing, because walking in the obscured light needed my full attention.

I could really use the torch I used in the belly of the mountain to help me see right now, I thought. The *City's* light barely shone through the tree canopy. As I stepped into the dusky pathway, I found my thoughts returning to all I had experienced with Jesus on this journey. The meditation on truths had released new thoughts. *It's amazing how I have changed and how I have made all these correct decisions along the way.* Suddenly, I stumbled over a root that stuck out of the ground. My staff instantly became full size and snapped into my hand. Grabbing it firmly, I felt more secure in maneuvering the dim path. Holy Spirit's call high above the canopy spoke to me and broke through my thoughts of my personal successes. In that moment, I suddenly remembered another time I had stumbled shortly before my waterfall experience. David had connected the stumble to focusing my thoughts and attention upon my personal achievements. Pride always goes before a fall. The truth of David's words stirred my heart. "Every advancement has the potential to shift your focus to your own accomplishments and that's when a trip up can occur." His words once again proved true.

"Forgive me, Lord! I have only been successful because Your grace and mercy have brought me this far. Help me to never forget this lesson again."

Peace settled over me and I continued with my confidence in Him and not my skills. The path suddenly took a sharp turn to the right, going away from the River. Sitting there was Holy Spirit. He held the torch in His large beak, lit and shining brightly.

"Oh, Holy Spirit, thank You for this".

I reached out as I said the words and took the torch, raising it high so that I could better see the path before me. It was going to be a great help to light my path. He took off flying swift and fast. In a blink of an eye He was gone. I never tired of the astonishment from all the supernatural things I experienced on my journey. I laughed with joy.

With the torch held high making the path clear, the staff immediately went small. I walked onward and finally came out of the tree canopy and into the light of the *City*. It was even more brilliant and blinding. So much so, I needed to stop and close my eyes for a moment to let them adjust. As I did, my earlier dream immediately began to replay on the screen of my mind. Jesus was in a city with many suburbs. It was so much more real now. I quickly opened my eyes to see if I had somehow been transported there. Sadly no, I was still standing at the edge of the trees where I had come into the light. I looked back to the trees with their shadowy canopy and wondered why this stand of trees was a part of the path to the *City*?

With the torch, I had been able to make my way through the dark canopy without tripping over the many roots and stones in the path. But someone traveling without the light, could trip or fall repeatedly. *Curious!* I made a mental note to ask Holy Spirit or Jesus about all of this.

My eyes now acclimated to the presence of the light, I noticed the light of the torch had gone out. It was like someone had flipped a switch. No smoke, no sputter, just out. *How did it make that pure white light?* My mind queried. I touched the end of my torch where the light had been. It was cold to the touch. I found that fascinating because I knew from experience that it could radiate warmth. I put it into the sack with the food and invitation and pulled the string closed. As I did the staff and rod went to full size. I had become aware that when the rod and staff transitioned in size, a spiritual action was about to take place. This transition spoke to the atmosphere I was coming into. It was the Father's way of giving me advanced discernment. Apparently, I was going to need them as I went forward on this next part of my journey. Grasping the staff firmly in my right hand, I scanned the land in front of me and saw a path heading back toward the River.

"Jesus, You said, You would tell me which way I was to go. I have learned to not assume that what appears obvious is always correct. So how do I proceed?"

Holy Spirit swooped down from out of nowhere, headed out flying low over the path and flew out of sight.

"Thanks, Holy Spirit!" With that, I headed off.

The path came to the River then skirted its banks. I noticed there wasn't access off the River on either side, even if someone had made their way around the sentry rocks on the River. The path was flat and easy to walk, yet the rod and staff maintained their size. I filed this information away in a back corner of my mind along with the reason for the shadowy canopied trees. I could see that the path along the River was heading between two large mountain ranges. As I walked toward the mountains, the River was now far, far below, running faster than I had ever seen. I could hear the roar of rapids coming from ahead. Even though I could not see them, their sound was undeniable. I was glad that I wasn't on the River. On I walked keeping a steady pace.

Soon the source of the roar came into view. As far as my eyes could see, the River was full of rapids and the flow was extreme. It reminded me of pictures of the New River Gorge or the Grand Canyon in the rainy season. The path and terrain began to climb upward, dropping the River even farther below. The terrain was changing. It took the shape of a high mountain valley that had parts of the mountain range running like fingers through it on both sides of the River. The mountains climbed high into the clouds and snow lay on top of some of the peaks. They all appeared rugged and impassable.

I began to wonder how I was to make my way to the other side where the *City* was located. Rays from the *City* created a halo effect around the mountains peaks. I scanned the horizon. The mountains went as far as I could see in both directions on each side of the River. I hoped that I didn't have to scale the mountains or find a passage through them because they appeared daunting and formidable. I had never seen the range of mountains where Mt. Everest is located, but these looked like they could be as high. I hiked on, thankful for the support of the staff to steady me. I came up over a ridge and there it was! Not "The" *City* but nevertheless a grand and magnificent city. It was large. It appeared as brilliant as the *City*. Every square inch of land that wasn't too rocky had dwellings. These buildings extended far into the heights. The dwellings were painted and looked bright, similar at first glance, to the *City*. But as I walked on, I could tell something wasn't the same. I stood and gazed from one mountain range through the valley across the River's gorge to the valley area on the other side of the River. This city spanned between the mountain ranges on both sides.

I wondered how the people had gotten over the deep gorge to the other side. As I gazed at this sprawling city, the layout resembled a giant candelabra or menorah. The River divided the mountain ranges therefore, the city was split in two and had grown like the candelabra arms with the River making the stand. I could imagine what it would look like at night in the darkness. But since nightfall was not an event here, I could only imagine. It had the potential to be a magnificent light on a hill.

A thought dropped into my mind. A city meant people. With this city so close to the *City*, they would certainly have knowledge to share about the *City*. I couldn't wait to talk with them about the home I was headed to. Questions came. *"Why would these people stop here and build a city when the City was right on the other side of the mountains? What could this place offer that The City did not?"*

I continued walking the pathway as it inclined. The River looked like a tiny ribbon far below. As I crested a small hill, I saw a magnificent bridge that spanned across the River gorge. The bridge was sturdy and wide so many people and goods could flow from one side to the other. People were making their way on the bridge, walking into what I considered the suburbs or the arms of the candelabra where they developed on the flat spaces between the mountain's stony fingers.

The bridge was massive. In the middle, over the center of the River, the bridge expanded creating a large circular plaza. It reminded me of the chief market areas, the agoras, mentioned in texts about ancient Rome or Greece. There were so many people, yet no one had spotted me. I was still excited to meet all of these people who lived so close to the *City*.

At this distance, the *City* appeared to be located on the backside of these mountains and you could begin to see how massive it was. The *City* skyline stretched above the highest of the mountain peaks into the clouds. *Could it really reach up into the heavens?* Well, all things were possible here. I quickened my pace toward the bridge and the people. I wanted to hear about the great *City* that was now so close. Certainly, these people could share many things about it.

As I walked on, the path became a small paved street, painted with the same material as the dwellings and other buildings. It too reflected the light from the *City*. The street led to a large wide road that became the bridge. I was captivated by this city's beauty and radiance. Everything reminded me of the traffic reflectors marking the road lines and signage; the type that caught and reflected back headlamp lights.

"This must be some special place." I spoke out loud. The immediate shrill call of Holy Spirit from high above answered my statement. It was a different sound than I was used to hearing. It was not the normal agreement or acknowledgement sound. I felt a check inside my inner being and stopped walking.

Lord are you telling me that what I said is wrong? The soft emphasis on "wrong" settled over me.

But why Lord? By all appearances, this place appears fabulous and blessed. Again, the soft flutter of "Not all things are as they appear," settled down into my spirit.

Ok, Lord, then I need you to guide me in this since what I am seeing, you are saying is not reality. I need wisdom and I need discernment.

The touchstone on the chain warmed and I reached up to finger it. Doing so, I touched the crystal ball that Jesus had given me, representing wisdom. I pulled it out and it caught the brilliance of the *City* with its rays of white light. Rainbow colors shot out almost like a light saber in a sci-fi movie. It was then that I caught the first concept of understanding. The city of suburbs, as I was now thinking of it, created its glow with external paint on the dwellings. It didn't generate its own brilliance and it didn't magnify or intensity the brilliance from the *City*. Rainbows and laser light were not being reflected by the suburb city. The crystal around my neck magnified the *City's* brilliance. Somehow the suburb city created a substitute brilliance that I had not discerned. There were no rainbows. There were no laser shafts of light. Had I not questioned the Lord and Holy Spirit about the check in my spirit, I never would have caught the difference. I would have been deceived. The word "deceived" resonated inside of me like a megaphone blaring.

"Not all things are as they appear. Beware of the wolves." The Lord's voice was strong and clear. Even though Jesus was not present, His words came clearly to my inner spirit.

Wolves? My hand went to the rod instinctively. What did all of this mean? Although I had set my hopes on going into the city and having fellowship with other fellow travelers on the way to the *City*, I instinctively knew I needed to pull aside and get more understanding.

Lord, does any of this have to do with the darkness of those trees back there and the fact that the rod and staff are remaining full size? Holy Spirit swooped down close and circled. His voice came clear to my inner spirit like those of Jesus moments before.

"The canopy of trees was a loving gesture from the Lord. It was created to get the attention of those traveling who never chose to decrease. It is a last warning that they needed the presence of the light. Because they never experienced the presence of real darkness and its seductive deception, they thought they could skip what God required. Deception led them to find a way around Crown Derby. When they entered the canopy of trees, each trip up was an opportunity or a wake-up call that light was necessary for their journey. I longed for them to cry out for light. Few did. For the ones who made their way through the trees without light on their journey, they continued in their deception. Deception led them to this city. Now they have fallen prey to its ultimate deceptions."

With that, Holy Spirit flew away from the city of suburbs and headed in the opposite direction. My eyes followed. I scanned the area He had headed toward, looking for a place where I could be alone and not discovered. I wasn't ready to encounter anyone from the city just now. Thank God, no one had noticed my approach.

My eyes caught a small hill in the distance. With better focus, I realized it was the crest of a rock or boulder. It was away from the broad paved path I had been walking and I felt drawn to go there and check it out. The touchstone on my chain warmed with the thought, so I quickly set out. As I approached the rock, I saw that it was mammoth, located in a large sunken area that formed a natural arena. Its depth masked the rocks size. Only the top crested above the plain's elevation. I walked down the steep decline and headed over to it. Reaching it, I put my hand on the surface and ran my palm along the side of it, it felt warm. Like many times before, I knew this was another touchstone for the travelers on the journey. A place to take refuge.

This was a secure place. It was a place to mediate, engage with the Lord and receive His words. I walked around to the other side and found a large alcove making a perfect shelter. *Only you Jesus,* I spoke internally, as I sat down on the soft grass. The rod and staff transformed into their small state and slid off my shoulder onto the grass beside me. I laid my bag on top of them.

"Not just Me, but Holy Spirit, David, Goodness and Mercy are all here too!" They all appeared from the other side of the rock.

I jumped back up and closed the short distance, hugging Him fiercely. Jesus laughed His deep engaging laugh. I embraced David, Goodness and Mercy as well. Holy Spirit eyed me, keeping His distance, but He did make a sweet eagle-like "EEK" sound and flew up on top of the rock like a sentinel to watch what might come our way.

"Love you too, Holy Spirit!" I laughingly spoke.

A strong single eagle call came forth. I loved His greeting.

"So, if you are all here, I must need a lot of help. Is that place such a bad place?"

"Multitudes in the Valley of Decision" Joel 3:14

"Come let's sit and talk. There are still many things for you to understand." The voice of Jesus was filled with love, but I caught a seriousness in His tone. We made our way back to the alcove and sat down.

"What lies before you is Decision Ville. It is called that because everyone who arrives there will have to make a decision. Their eternal future is in their own hands. If they haven't been transformed into my image by decrease they will be confronted with every area of temptation: the lusts of the eyes, the lust of the flesh and the pride of life. (45) They will have no power to stand against the strong temptations. Sadly, Decision Ville will seduce them because they look to themselves, their own strengths and their own wisdom. They are deceived to think they can overcome their fleshly desires. I have not been asked to be Lord of their hearts so I can't empower them to see through the deceptions they are confronted with."

"There is also an enemy of mine who comes in like a thief to steal away My people. He does not care for the people. He only wants to hurt Me by taking people from Me, from Us, because of his pride and jealousy. Here in Decision Ville, he has set up his last big efforts to steal away as many people as he can and keep them from coming to the *City*. When they come here without decrease, they are all under deceptions. Those deceptions allow them to be enticed to trade what they have been given as love gifts from Me, in exchange for temporary pleasures or power. Those trades enslave them to this place and the enemy of their soul. They are not able to leave for the *City* where they were destined to live."

"Why would they do that? Don't they understand what they are missing by not experiencing Your love and Your Presence?" My pondering look caused Jesus to explain it a little more.

"They choose because the pull to just enjoy life and stay as you are is very strong. People do not want to confront what lies deep inside in their secret places. They would rather try to work out their own way to reach the *City* and avoid the confrontation to decrease."

In that moment, I could understand how hard and how scary it could be to face the dark and intimidating things that are buried deep within. I had struggled with it many times myself in my life on my journey.

"Jesus?"

"Yes, my child?"

"Isn't it confusing for people to encounter each other and not really know who they are deep inside? It's like those people in Crown Derby acting all spiritual and strong when they really were weak and afraid. They are actors, pretending to be something they really are not"

"Yes! You are seeing now with a deeper understanding. Without the love and intimacy that comes through decrease, My image is not seen. You can call yourself a "Christian" but without decrease, you will not look like Me, speak like Me, act like Me. This confuses the world. To bypass the transformation of decrease allows the religious and hypocrite spirit to manifest a contradiction to the world. I want all of mankind to know Me, the real Me. You cannot share or reveal what you do not know or have no knowledge of."

His words were beginning to open my eyes of understanding in new measure. So, I said, "Jesus tell me more!"

"Avoiding and escape brings separation in their hearts from Us. Separation allows deception and deception leads to their love growing cold. Therefore, 'seeing they don't see, and hearing, they don't hear, neither do they understand. For this people's heart has grown callous, their ears are dull of hearing, and they have closed their eyes.'" (23)

"'But blessed are your eyes for they see; and your ears for they hear.' (24) Your eyes have chosen to look upon the deep and dark things that lie within. For you that process started on the River. You have had ears to hear. You have heard what the Father, Holy Spirt, the ministering spirits and I have said to you. As a result, you are transformed and are being transformed into the Father and My image. You are being made free from the lusts of your eyes, the lusts of your flesh and the pride in your life. You have overcome them as I did in the wilderness on My journey."

"Is that why I eventually understood that not all things are as they appear when I was gazing at Decision Ville? Is that why I was able to pull away from its alluring seduction at the call of Holy Spirit?"

"Yes, you saw how Decision Ville was deceptive in its appearance. Even through your transformed eyes you saw it grand and bright. Had your ears not picked up on Holy Spirit's warnings, you might have fallen into the deception of this place yourself. Only by your transformation where you chose to decrease, did you have open ears to hear what Holy Spirit was warning."

"Here I am! Send me!" Isaiah 6:8

I understood, yet I was sure I didn't get the total depth of it because Jesus was at the point of tears as He spoke. Seeing His passion for the situation of deceived souls, tugged at my heart, and captured my thoughts. I looked at David and his countenance, as well as that of Goodness and Mercy. They were sober. All three were passionately concerned like Jesus. Finally, I turned and looked up at Holy Spirit. He turned and looked down at me. I could even see great sadness in His eyes such as I had never seen before.

Turning back, I said, "Ok Jesus, how can I help? Where do I need to go? Is there any hope at all for all those people in Decision Ville?"

There was a time before my journey began that I would never think to ask those type of questions. Even if I had, I would never have spoken them out. My fears would have abducted and imprisoned me. But now I was almost free. I could feel the difference inside. I was determined and impassioned to take away His sorrow, even a little, if I could. I could now feel His passion for these people rising in me and I wanted to make a difference somehow, someway.

"I want to send you to Decision Ville to help those who are on the brink of making their last decision. A decision that will seal their eternal destiny. They are like Esau. They are about to sell their birthright for temporal and pleasurable things, rather than for their eternal future. David and the others will help you. Will you go for Me? I'll tell you the truth up front. Few will heed your words. But I need you to try."

"I will go, Jesus! I must go! I must do what I can for You and the Father. I don't want them to miss having the relationship that I have with You. They must reach the *City* and be a part of the marriage feast and celebration. They must be reminded once again of Your love for them and how wonderful it will be in Your Presence for all eternity."

Jesus hugged me tight then pulled back and spoke. "I'm full of hope that you will lead some to leave Decision Ville and come to their real home in the *City*. You will need to encourage yourself, because the task is difficult. Tragically, many you encounter have already sold their birthright. They've sold their betrothal ring for pleasures or power offered in Decision Ville. Turn your inner eyes upon your Words from your tablet. Remember what was written. You will hear the words resonate in you. They have power from the hand of the Father to strengthen and encourage. You will be led to where you need to go in the city to reach those yet reachable."

"Now, let's eat, fellowship and rest. For soon you need to be on your way to this task on your journey to the *City*. I will leave you soon, but David, Goodness, Mercy and Holy Spirit will travel on with you to Decision Ville and help you."

"But, Jesus! Why are you not coming? If they could see your face like I see you now, I'm positive they would all leave Decision Ville and come to the *City*."

"Your hope springs eternal and that's a good thing. But everyone that you will encounter has already seen me many times along their journey. I have reasoned with each of them many times, like I have come to you on your journey. But by their will they have chosen their own pathways. Seeing Me would not make a difference right now. They need to hear your words, the words of a fellow traveler on the journey."

"I'm going to meet with Father and together We will pray for you and for the people of Decision Ville. He is on His throne and I will be at His righthand. We will pray that your words will have power and might.

We will pray that some will see and hear what Holy Spirit is praying through you."

A thousand questions now rushed into my mind. A heavy weight came upon me. It wasn't something I could wrap my mind around or something that made it difficult for me to move or walk, but it was something invisible. It came upon me the moment Jesus said that He and the Father were going to pray for me. It had settled down upon me and felt like a heavy cloak had been placed upon my shoulders. I could feel its weight and its warmth. It wasn't restrictive, just new and different; yet it felt empowering at the same time. Jesus nodded toward someone on my right. I turned to see who, but whomever it had been, they were gone. Instead I saw a fire and food being prepared. It looked like a feast and in that moment, wonderful smells greeted me. I was hungry.

"Come!" Jesus said. "Let's eat".

We got up and David, Goodness and Mercy joined us. Holy Spirit made another of His eagle sounds from up on top of the rock as if to say, "I will take my place here and watch."

Jesus spoke again, "Let's enjoy this last meal together before you confront what is ahead."

We all ate and fellowshipped. Every bite was delicious. We didn't talk anymore about Decision Ville. Rather, the conversation was all about how I was going to love the *City* and how everything was almost finished for the feast and celebration. It was a time of joy and great satisfaction to hear from the others. Their description of the *City* was beyond the understanding of my imagination. Peace settled over me like a warm blanket. Sometime, while Goodness was describing the banquet preparations and Mercy told about the new garments being made for us, I drifted off to sleep.

I awakened to David squeezing my shoulder saying, "It's time." I sat up and rubbed my eyes. As I focused, I looked for Jesus.

"He has already gone to the Father. Now we head for Decision Ville." David spoke.

The fire was out. The food gone. He bent over and picked up the rod and staff by the loop and placed them on my shoulder. I stood up feeling their weight, but it wasn't as noticeable as it had been before saying yes to go to Decision Ville. I had grown accustomed to them. David handed me the bag.

Without a word, he stepped out quickly, heading around the rock and back toward Decision Ville. I stepped up my pace and kept up with David, just as the time long ago when I was learning to take in the mist. That seemed a lifetime ago. I breathed in and felt the mist, ever present yet unseen. It energized me and I quickly took in a few more breaths knowing that I may need their power soon. Matching David's strides, I looked behind me. Goodness and Mercy were keeping pace as well. I saw Holy Spirit lift off the rock where He had been standing watch the entire time. With strong wing strokes, He mounted up high, out of sight.

Turning to David I asked, "David, how do I do this? I mean I don't know who to approach. There must be millions in this city of suburbs as it goes up into the fingers of the mountains. How do I find them? When I do, what do I say? I don't have great wisdom or words like Jesus. I've never preached to people. I've never even had conversations with others about Jesus, except at church. I don't know that I can do this!" As I said these last words, the weighty feeling I had associated with an invisible cloak pressed on my shoulders again. The rod and staff went full size. It startled me, stopping my ramblings. David chuckled.

"Jesus is praying for you. The weight you feel upon you is His mantle as Shepherd of the World. He has passed a portion of that mantle to you and equipped you in this moment for such a time as this. It began with the commissioning of the rod and staff. They are His Authority and His Power transferred to you. Now you know the hope of His calling. It is to serve Him and help His people! Together these things are the exceeding greatness of His power toward you because you said yes to what He has asked of you. All of this infuses you with His power. The power of Jesus's victories; His choices, decisions and obedience even to death. It all flows directly to you from the *City* as Jesus sits at the Father's right hand. The fullness of everything you need in every circumstance flows from the position Jesus occupies."

I nodded my head that I understood and started to ask again about where to find the people when David continued.

"The Father knows those who have settled here in Decision Ville and retained their betrothal ring. That means they have not sold out totally to deception and still have a final decision to make. Will they give up their pleasures and choose their eternal home as the *City*? Or will the pleasures of their flesh cause them to stay. They are being wooed even now to come out of this place. They are being touched in their inner spirit and drawn to where we will encounter them. If they heed the call, they will be divinely led and directed to our location."

"But where do we go in the city and if someone shows up, what do I say?"

"When you see the people, you will be moved with His compassion. It will rise up within you. From His passion, you will know what to speak. Now prepare yourself for war. Lives hang in the balance. The power of the deceiver is strong in Decision Ville. Let's stop for a moment so you can focus on the tablet and recall its words. You'll need the strength that comes from knowing who you have been created to be. Knowing your destiny, empowers you to be strong and courageous."

We stopped and joined hands. "Take a deep breath," said Goodness.

"Let the power of life within those words on the tablet arise in you now" said Mercy.

I did. I focused my inner mind like a movie screen. I saw myself with Jesus, reading out every blazing word as they rose to life with the power of creation behind it. I could feel the surge of energy running through me, energizing every cell. I saw myself come to the last word. I knew my identity. I was totally His.

I inhaled deeply. As mist flowed into my nostrils, I could feel it fill my lungs and then permeate into my blood stream, traveling to all my cells. With every breath, I could feel its effects, until it made its way through my entire being. As it moved, it burned a passion for the people of Decision Ville into my heart. It filled me with a force I had never experienced before. It was electrifying and I almost fell down from the jolt of power that coursed through me.

"You are feeling God's heart for the world. Jesus felt it when He processed through Gethsemane and endured the cross." David's words brought me back.

Without another word or explanation, David continued, "First we will encounter the workers of iniquity and the wolves who prey on the deceived. They are always watching for travelers on their way to the *City*. Their goal is to allure travelers and seduce them to take up residence in Decision Ville, rather than go on to the *City*. Do not engage them in debate. Listen. You will begin to discern how they deceive many into selling their gifts from Jesus as well as their birthright. As you listen, wisdom will arise within you and you will know how to proceed."

Although I was still reeling from the powerful infusion, I pulled myself together at David's warning and the instruction of his words. We took off again at a quick pace.

It wasn't too long before we approached the bridge and this time, unlike before, several people saw us. They scurried over to greet us. Some hastened their pace to pass others in their bid to be first to connect. A tall, nice looking man was the first to greet us.

"Welcome pilgrims. I see that you have been traveling. I know you are tired of all the trials and tribulations of your journey. Surely you are in need of some things."

As he spoke the words, the others arrived, jockeying for a place to get close enough to speak.

"What do you need, travelers?" Another asked.

"Decision Ville has much to offer you." Someone else spoke loudly.

"Many have found that this city has all they are searching for. I bet you will too." Another promised.

"We have everything to fulfill your desires, needs and senses. Come, allow us to show you our merchandise. There must be something that you need." Yet another spoke up forcefully.

"You have things we want to trade for, like that staff and rod or the things hanging on the chain we see around your neck." A voice from the second row spoke in a tone that made me think of snakes hissing or vultures shrieking.

Since they were all speaking one after the other, there wasn't an opportunity to engage in conversation. I was forced to hear their words. But their words put me on edge, sick to my stomach, slimed. My inner man became agitated. As the last one spoke, two of them reached out to take hold of my free hand, while another one tried to take the staff and rod from me.

David's firm grip onto my shoulder stabilized me and helped me to pull back my hand and secure a firm hold on the staff and rod.

"No! Don't touch me!" It came out of my mouth with such force and authority that I shocked myself, as well as the people. They fell back a step like they had been hit by a shock wave.

"You're one of 'them', aren't you!" A new voice from a row back sneered out the allegation. "We won't bother you anymore." It was said with total disgust. "Come on, let's go. They are useless to us." All of them turned and walked back to the bridge.

I was stunned by this encounter. The words they had spoken, and the feel of their touch had unnerved me. Thankfully, wisdom and discernment were welling up within. However, a tiny thought from way deep inside, wanted me to call them back. I wanted them to like me and not be offended by my sharp response. *Didn't I need their help?* My mind was asking.

Holy Spirit sounded from high above. At His piercing call, I rejected the thoughts. Instantly the tiny seeds of worry and doubt wilted and died.

"Now you are free." David said.

"Free from what?" His word brought my focus back from my internal thoughts to the present.

"Free from the last vestiges of the need to please people and have them like you."

My mind instantly flashed memories from past struggles I had all my life, wanting to please people. I would routinely win such struggles and make right choices. But the hours of mental agony, sleepless nights spent analyzing how to keep people happy with me and not compromise my values, plagued me. In reality, I had never gotten free from the twinge of remorse of saying no when I knew it would not make them happy. Now I felt like Superman, taking off my glasses and changing into the powerful person I was becoming. Being set free of the need to please people was so liberating! I could feel the difference deep inside.

"What did they mean by 'one of them?'" I switched topics and questioned David.

"One of the sealed ones." David replied with awe in his voice.

Intrigued I continued. "Sealed ones? Why do I hear awe in your voice? What does sealed mean?"

"Sealed ones are firmly established in Jesus as their savior. They have been consecrated and anointed by the Father. They have yielded to Holy Spirit's call and direction. Sealed ones have chosen to not grieve God and to take up their cross daily. They have decreased so God could increase in them. You are a sealed one. You have chosen to take up everything Jesus and the Father set before you. Obedience on your journey has changed you. The woman I met on the train is not the woman that stands before me now. The workers of iniquity we encountered, they understood that, when you told them "No!". The travelers who arrive and are under deception to their flesh cannot endure the pressures you just encountered and they will say yes."

"And yes, the angels are in awe. We desire to understand God's grace to you, our fellow creation. We lean over the balconies of heaven and observe it in action, astonished at the lengths the Father and Jesus go to for mankind's salvation."

"The word that "sealed ones" have arrived in Decision Ville will spread and any other workers of iniquity will not bother us again. In fact, you will be avoided."

"But how will I be able to speak to anyone if they all avoid me?" I felt a moment of panic.

"Not everyone will avoid you. You could say that the knowledge of our presence will separate the sheep from the goats. Those who still have another chance to hear, will come to the trade areas. You will find them there. Those who still hear the soft quiet voice of the Father will be called one last time. They will have to choose: Decision Ville and its pleasures or the *City* and the Father."

"Sold out? Trade areas? I don't understand, David." I wasn't clear on all the dynamics taking place.

"It's possible to trade away your gifts and inheritance. The blood of Jesus paid the price for your dowry, out of the world's family and into the family of God the Father. When you said "Yes" to Jesus, because you said you wanted Him to be your Lord, your birthright became legal and you became betrothed to Him. The ring was placed on your finger that day. Do you remember when you said "Yes" to Jesus years ago? You were in that church meeting, listening to a traveling evangelist preaching salvation, all because you couldn't say no to a friend who asked you to go with her."

David laughed at the irony of how God had used a past tactic of the enemy – not being able to say no–to hook me. "Because you couldn't say no back then, God used it for His plans and purposes. This demonstrates that God works all things for His good." He chuckled again.

David continued. "If the devil only knew how many times God uses what was meant for evil and by His supernatural power turns it to advancement for the Kingdom, the devil would cringe. Anyway, I digress."

"Yes, I remember." The memories and emotions were as fresh now as they had been so long ago. "But, I never got a ring! I only got salvation." I blurted out.

"You received many things that night. Nevertheless, you didn't know then everything you had access to. You couldn't see the ring or the gifts, but the ring placed on your finger that night was as real as it is now."

"People may say yes to Jesus as Savior, but because there is so much going on inside of them, as well as the baggage of their past, they are not able to receive the full intimacy Jesus offers. They have to come to trust Him and believe in His perfect love for them before they will let Him be their Lord. It takes time. Jesus patiently waits. He pursues them relentlessly. It can take years of wooing and courting them before they feel what you felt the moment Jesus had your ring appear. Over time, they can forget about Him as their Lord and become enslaved to another."

"On your journey, you began to desire, trust and believe in His love for you. With each encounter and each revelation of His love, your intimacy grew. He became your Lord as was intended. Now you pursue Him at every opportunity. But make no mistake. Jesus will pursue everyone passionately until they desire this intimacy or make their final decision to turn away."

"But why am I feeling so many mixed emotions?" They were churning like chaotic leaves in a whirlwind.

"You are desiring for other's hearts to be ignited with that same passion. Because you feel His passion, He is sending you to Decision Ville. He hopes that some will choose to return like the prodigal. It is His heart to see others come into the same place of intimacy you now know."

The insights from David continued. "Those we hope to reach this last time in Decision Ville avoided intimacy. When the workers for the evil one discerned their lack of intimacy and decrease, then they knew the traveler's flesh could easily be manipulated. All it took was to offer them something that they couldn't refuse. Just as Satan tried to get Jesus to trade for things in the wilderness, the travelers are tempted to trade their gifts and ring for the pleasures found in Decision Ville. Their hearts will justify their trades. Once they yield to the temptation it is a simple task to lead the people off to the trade areas which are full of carnal substitutes and temporary pleasures. Trades take place. Choices are made. As a result, they became enslaved here in Decision Ville."

Quickly jumping in I asked, "But what do we have to trade? I only have the staff, rod, food and torch. What value are they?" I was unclear with all that I had heard about trades.

"The rod and the staff are valuable because they represent levels of power and authority given by Jesus. The enemy always strives to usurp and steal the place of authority and power from Jesus. Because His power and authority flow from Him to you through the rod and staff, they would have a high trade value. But there are even more precious things. Around your neck is a gold chain with several unique gifts from Jesus.

They are precious because they are one of a kind and were personally made and given by Jesus. They will pass the test of fire. They are valuable to the traders here. You could trade them for land, a beautiful dwelling, food, materials or high standing positions for your remaining days in Decision Ville. With all that you have, their value would set you up for every pleasurable thing imaginable. But don't forget about the invitation. It is especially valuable to the evil one. To trade your invitation, means one less person comes to the marriage celebration because they sold their birthright and ring. That makes the Father and Jesus very sad."

In disbelief I exclaimed. "But if people trade it all away, they would never get to be in His Presence or dwell in His *City* with Him. Why would they do that?"

David replied, with profound sadness in his voice. "Because they have chosen to serve self. They believe they can go to the *City* when they choose. They think because it is so close, why hurry. There is always tomorrow. But it is pure deception. Time is not theirs to control. The Father's hands control each individual's time."

I couldn't emotionally process what I was hearing anymore. The weight upon my shoulders for the people and the gravity of what was happening with all those in Decision Ville, was too much. I broke down and wept, sobbing until my body was wracked with uncontrollable shaking.

David came close. Holy Spirit swooped down and hopped up to me until His beak was almost touching my stomach. Goodness and Mercy flanked me. No one touched me, but I felt their grief at the sadness of it all. Profound grief radiated from them, mixing with mine. Time stood still. At some point the grief and sadness emptied out. I had no more ability to mourn. I took a long deep breath. I breathed in the mist for strength and looked into Holy Spirit's piercing eyes. Comfort poured from His eyes and filled me. It literally felt like His beak was a finger piercing into my soul and filling me with comfort and compassion. I felt like a balloon filling with helium, enlarging and rising. The comfort transformed into a greater measure of compassion along with resolve. My thoughts turned to those who had not yet sold their birthright and still had a choice and a decision to make.

"We must go! Time is running out. Any minute someone else might trade away their birthright. We have to get as many people as possible to make the right choice. They simply must choose the Father and Jesus over Decision Ville. Now is the time. We must go and tell them. I must go and tell them now!"

Chapter 10

Word of the Testimony
He who has and ear, let him hear.

"He who has an ear, let him hear... To him who over- comes ..." Revelation 2-3

"I'm going to need your help finding the trading centers and the people Jesus and the Father are praying for," I entreated of David, Holy Spirit and the two other helpers assigned to me.

Holy Spirit made a series of deep throated sounds that my inner spirit understood. "I will show you where to go. There is only one trading area. It is on the bridge and you will find those you seek in the large agora area. All the trading for the seven suburbs takes place there."

David added, "That is where Jesus and the Father will call them. They're providing the people one last opportunity to choose their inheritance and the Eternal Presence of the Father."

I turned toward the bridge, inhaling three more deep breaths of the mist. Then I squared my shoulders to go. I untied the rod from the staff then used the free rope to tie my bag of food to the torch placing them across my shoulder and chest. I wanted them secure from theft. My hands freed, I took the rod in my left hand and the staff in my right hand.

"Let's go!"

With steely determination I set off toward the bridge. David had to keep up with me this time. A smile came across my face and I turned to look at David. The irony wasn't lost on him. I was setting the pace now and in a few minutes, we were on the bridge. It was packed, and everyone seemed to avoid us by moving out of our way. In a few more minutes we reached the agora and came into the trading area. It appeared to be one massive market. The tents, booths and open stalls were all crowded together, making it impossible to gather a large group where we could speak. The randomness of how the buildings and tents were set up left no orderly way to navigate through the market.

"Jesus, I need wisdom. How do I connect with those that You are calling and leading here? Help me, Lord!" I cried out in an overwhelmed plea.

"Wait upon Holy Spirit. He will help you." The clear words of Jesus welled up in my heart. The touchstone warmed on my neck. As I reached up and touched it, scriptures flooded my mind, scriptures I never knew I had memorized. Yet they came clear and strong. 'Get behind me, Satan! For it is written, you shall worship the Lord your God, and you shall serve Him only.' (25)

I had learned on my journey, that nothing happens by coincidence or chance. This was a clear direction from Holy Spirit. With my loudest and strongest voice, I shouted out the words, "GET BEHIND ME, SATAN!" The words projected across the air like the voice of the head referee at the Super Bowl. They reverberated off of every person, every dwelling, and echoed into the mountains. Even the River canyon echoed it down and back up. People fell over in every direction. It was like I had hit the people with the full force of a water cannon. They got back up quickly and scurried away. As they left, I wondered what had taken place. Holy Spirit let out a piercing shrill sound. Those trying to close down their shops and tents scattered as if a gun had been aimed at them. They left everything behind. I know my eyes were big as saucers as I slowly rotated 360 degrees to see what remained from this vocal tsunami.

"Oh, this is very, very good!" David said with great joy in his voice.

"Good? What took place scared everyone away. How will I ever get them back to tell them about the *City?*"

"Peace, be still and wait on the Lord." David looked me directly in the eyes as he said the words.

So, I took in another deep breath of the mist and felt its strengthening power. I was at peace inside as I centered my concentration on the inner flow of what Holy Spirit might show me. A chorus popped into my head–"There is none like You" (2). I had never sung out loud by myself before and I didn't have a solo voice. But the words of the chorus were strong in my inner spirit and so I began to sing them. "I worship You, Almighty God, there is none like You." My voice was strong with conviction and each word pleasing to the ear. "I worship You, Oh Prince of Peace, that is all I long to do." David, Goodness and Mercy flowed along with me and the rest of the lyrics came forth. The sound was incredible! The song was reverberating again from everywhere, making it sound like the choir of Heaven had joined in. With each line, the power of the words became almost a tangible force changing the atmosphere. It even enhanced the brilliance of the *City* and the painted surfaces of Decision Ville began going dim. As we finished with "There is none like You", I said, "We have to do this again." And so, we sang it again and again. By the fourth time, I noticed people from all directions coming closer and closer. They were crying and weeping.

"Oh, David look! People are coming back."

"Yes, when you took authority over Satan, it temporarily pushed back the ruling spiritual power and removed the veils of deception over some of the people's hearts. They are drawn to the freedom flowing through the atmosphere with the acknowledgement of the Lord."

"Tell me David who are these people." I looked at those close to us and saw their rings. I looked at their faces, filled with emotions. They were weeping and crying. I knew Jesus was praying for all of this.

David replied. "These are people who were deceived by Satan, God's enemy. He enticed them to trade their chain and any gifts on it for pleasures to satisfy the lust of their flesh, the lust of their eyes and their pride. Their lack of intimacy because they had not decreased, kept Jesus from increasing to the position of Lord over their life, They became the perfect target for enslavement to their flesh, in subjection to Satan and the pleasures of Decision Ville. They had no power to break free and leave. Your words opened up their prison doors and broke the bondages, allowing them to once again be free and choose."

As David spoke, I was listening, turning full circle and watching the faces of so many people. "Sing it again, Goodness and Mercy!" They did, and their two voices filled the agora with the presence of Heaven. The people began to respond more and more. They lifted their arms toward the *City* or knelt with eyes closed, praying out in every language.

"Jesus, what do I do now?" More scripture came back to mind. I declared it out, never questioning.

"For it is written, 'You shall worship the Lord your God, and you shall serve Him only.'" (25)

The words rang with the force of creation as Holy Spirit's call pierced the air. I could see transformation; clarity of mind and softness of hearts begin to spread over the throng of people.

"It is happening, David! It is happening! They are making the decision to leave. They are remembering what it was like to have Him as their first love and to be strong in the power of His might." I looked on with awe in seeing this transformation take place. "Now what?"

"They need to repent and turn and leave this place." David directed.

Yes! Encouraged with David's words, I cried out. "Repent! 'The time is fulfilled, and God's Kingdom is at hand! Repent, and believe in the Good News' (26). Believe in Jesus once again. Believe in His love and provision for you. Even now He is praying for you and making preparations for you at the feast and celebration. Come with us and leave this place. We will all go to the *City* together."

Holy Spirit calls were heard again and again above us. His sounds pierced their hearts. Some moaned in anguish and said, "But we have also sold our invitation, what will we do? We still have our ring, but our invitation is gone! We shall be forbidden to enter without it!" They wailed in abject sorrow.

Others moaned, "We still have our invitation, but no food for our journey." I also heard, "Who will protect us? We don't have a protector from the evil ones." Still others cried out, "How do we go over the cold high mountains with no light or any way to warm ourselves?"

In that moment, I felt their despair. Here were people ready to repent and move out to the *City*, but their new fears were like shackles, keeping them bound in this place.

"What am I to do now Jesus?" I cried out.

"Remember the bible story about the loaves and the fish!" His voice rang strong in my inner spirit.

Instantly it was clear and direct, and I knew what to do. *My food multiplies. I still have my invitation, my rod and staff, and a torch to light the way.* I possessed everything the people needed to help them feel secure in leaving this place. I also had the help and protection of David, Goodness, Mercy and Holy Spirit.

"'With God, all things are possible'. (31) Peace! Peace, be still!" I spoke the words that had been spoken to me so many times on my journey.

I spoke, sharing with these people, the power and truth of what I had learned on my journey.

"'Don't be anxious for your life, what you will eat, or what you will drink; nor about your body and how you will stay warm'. (27) Jesus has given me provisions to share with you along the way. I will give you a piece of my invitation to show at the gates and I know Jesus will honor it. He sent me here to rescue you from this place. Come, do not be frightened or worried. God will not abandon you."

With these words, people began to clap, cheer and shout. Those who had knelt down stood up and they all began to push in closer. They held their hands out for their piece of the invitation or what else they needed for personal provisions. They pressed in so franticly, I thought I might be crushed by their desire for what I was offering.

"I think this is where you need our help", David laughed, turning quickly to the people. "Ok everyone, take a seat. If you need an invitation, raise your hand and we will get you a piece of the invitation." The people were quick to obey David, and sat down on the pavement, their faces, like children at Christmas were full of expectation.

I reached into the bag past the food, flask and torch, to find the scrolled invitation. I pulled it out and I could hear people gasp with joy. The faint responses of "I had forgotten what it looked like", "It is glorious", "God must love us so much to come to our rescue", could be heard. Cries of "How could I have been so deceived", came like sweet music to my ears.

On and on each person was praising God and speaking out their thoughts of wonder and thanksgiving.

"David, there are so many people, I think I will have to tear the pieces so tiny to make sure they each get a piece! I am afraid they will lose them on the rest of their journey."

"Remember, 'The liberal soul will be made fat', (5) David recited. This is what Jesus practiced with the loaves and fishes. He tore that first loaf into the portions that a person would need to sustain himself and dropped them into the basket. He did the same with the fish. With every tear making a serving, the loaves and fishes multiplied back in their entirety, and the baskets became full. Each disciple was given some and told to pass them out. As they modeled tearing their own generous portions, the loaves and fishes continued to multiply. Everyone was provided for, and there were leftovers to share with others. So, I suggest you tear your invitation in half. Watch and see the Lord multiply and provide whole invitations for the people."

The thought seemed entirely plausible, so I opened the invitation and tore it in half. Right before my eyes, the two halves each made a whole invitation, including the red ribbon to tie it shut. I handed a whole invitation to David. I tore mine again and now David tore his. Both multiplied like before making four whole invitations. "See what a generous spirit will do!" David laughed out.

I passed a whole invitation to Goodness and David passed one to Mercy. Now each of us had a full invitation to tear and multiply. We began to walk through the crowds of people tearing and passing out full invitations. Although it took some time, everybody who needed one, received one. Everyone waited patiently. As David, Goodness, Mercy and I met back in the center of the people, David spoke out.

"Does everybody now have an invitation? Raise your hand if we missed you."

No one raised a hand. In that moment, Holy Spirit swooped down and landed. The people all fell over as dead.

"Oh my gosh! What happened?" I asked as I gazed incredulously at the crowds now slumped over on the pavement.

"They are being touched once again with the Presence of Holy Spirit, so they will have strength for the rest of their journey." David answered. "Soon they will awaken, new, refreshed, and delivered of all deception and fears. Then Goodness and Mercy will lead them to the touchstone rock across the valley where we all met up before. They will be safe there, waiting for the others. Goodness and Mercy will take the bag of food and the torch. They will be warm and fed until those who may still leave Decision Ville have been called out."

"Others?" I queried.

"Yes, Father and Jesus are still calling out one last time to one last group who remain, offering them their final opportunity to leave this place."

"Still to leave Decision Ville" grabbed my attention. I was about to ask David what he was talking about and how that would happen, when I caught a bit of motion out of the corner of my eye. I saw that some people were beginning to awaken and stand up. With that, Holy Spirit took off. Goodness took the bag and torch and started walking back across the bridge toward the valley and the rock. Mercy directed the people to follow Goodness. Soon there was a steady stream of people awakening and leaving. The procession looked like a long, long exodus.

"Now is the time for the last call." David said with a serious tone. "I know you are wondering what I am talking about and how that will take place."

"There is yet one more group being wooed, even now, to become the final group to leave Decision Ville. But this group will be harder to convince because they dined with the devil himself and did not even perceive the enemy of their soul. They listened to the workers of iniquity, and believed the lies of demons. This group has hardened their hearts to needing anything from Jesus. Unlike those making the exodus, this group has never even considered needing Jesus to be their Lord or their savior. They have made their journey on their own terms and in their own efforts. They are friends with the workers of iniquity and the wolves. They have been given many opportunities to come to the salvation that Jesus offered, but they have always rejected Him. God the Father in His justice to all mankind will give them one last opportunity to say yes to Jesus."

The seriousness of David's words stunned me. My joy switched from the exodus, and I became sad, grievously sad, thinking about the remaining people David had just identified. It almost brought me to my knees. Holy Spirit's sorrowful call from above echoed my feelings of the weightiness of this moment. *What if they refused?* Immediately David recognized my emotional distress.

"Do not think this is your cross to carry. Jesus carried it for them long ago. He is interceding for them even in this moment! He will be the one to personally reach out to each one of them, one last time. Those who say no this time, do so to Him personally. So there will be no excuses, thus settling their fate. All you need concern yourself with is tuning in to His voice and allowing His Spirit to guide you. Remember that Jesus only mirrored what He saw and heard from His Father. That is your mode of operation to always follow as well."

In that instant, I remembered my recent dream, seeing Jesus ministering to people. It was now clear that He had already shown me this last call.

But what was to be my part in this last call? I closed my eyes and tuned my inner screen to the Spirit and let the visions of the dream replay.

On my mind's inner screen, I saw Jesus go throughout every suburb of Decision Ville. He searched out those who were hiding from Him and the confrontation of this last call, to come out and leave. He let no one escape His searching. He would plead with them, reason with them and even tell them of their fate if they stayed in Decision Ville. Few responded. Those who did would be led from Decision Ville by Goodness and Mercy, to the Rock where the others waited.

"David, I was given a dream."

"Yes, I know. You saw Jesus making the last appeal to the people to come to the *City* and to be with the Father forever. They were not at the agora when the others responded to your call, because they did not recognize the voice of the Father and Jesus. As a result, they fled when you changed the atmosphere. Now, they have retreated to hide in shame. But Jesus will come as He showed you in the dream to woo them one last time."

"Jesus is coming?"

"I'm already here." His voice, strong and sure, was like fresh water to a weary soul. I ran the short distance to Him and gave Him an extra tight hug. He laughed that laugh that says, "I love you and I am happy to see you too."

"Jesus, what are we going to do? What suburb do we head to first?"

"In this I must go alone. I need you to wait and pray until it is finished. Pray what you see in the Spirit. The Father will give you insights for prayer from what He is praying. He will show you what I need, then pray for that. He will show what the people need to repent from or what spirit is keeping them deceived. Pray for those things. Pray fervently, but only what is revealed by Holy Spirit."

Jesus continued. "Now take your rod and staff and go back to the touch rock in the valley where Goodness and Mercy are waiting with the first group of people. Go back and pray out what you are shown. Those who repented when you spoke, need you to shepherd them. They have been without guidance and leadership far too long. I'll meet you with those who will come out with Me from the city. Then you and all the people will head for the *City*. Take courage. Your journey is to lead them to the *City* and to the Father. Now go. David will stay here with me."

I turned to leave, saddened by not being allowed to help Him, but also realizing He knew best. If praying produced the most success, then that's what I would do. If the people waiting at the rock needed my presence and to see the rod and staff to stay the course, that's where I needed to be. Life on this journey with Jesus was all about obedience and yielding to His ways. I would watch over them with His strength.

"When we next meet at the rock, I will have something for you."

I stopped and turned back to look at Him.

"Something for me? What?" His look said, "wait and see". I responded with a contented smile, because He never ceased to delight me. So I headed toward the rock as asked, with the rod and staff and the mission that awaited.

"Righteousness is near, salvation has gone out, My arms will judge the peoples" Isaiah 51:5

Approaching the rock, you would never know how many people sheltered on the grassy area behind it. I realized now the massiveness of the "bowl" shaped geologic depression that held the rock. Clearly many more people could wait here, securely out of sight of Decision Ville.

This knowledge brought assurance. Holy Spirit gave out a single call and I turned my gaze upward to find Him high and circling over us. His presence brought comfort, yet I knew I didn't want to stay here too long. I felt the pressing need to move on toward the *City*, but Jesus had said wait on Him and pray.

I stopped beside the rock, looking intently for Goodness and Mercy among the mass of people before me. The people were in groups, sitting around fires, eating, laughing, relaxing or sleeping. Their countenance was vastly different from before. They looked vibrant and joyful. No longer did they look like the walking dead with depressed, fearful and empty eyes. A miraculous transformation had taken place.

"It's the life and love of Father now flowing freely and fully through them that makes the difference." Goodness's voice from right beside me caused me to jump.

Mercy laughed. "I see our sudden appearance took you by surprise again."

"I should be used to it by now, but it seems I'm not." I laughed.

"Your senses are acutely attuned to watching over the people. Jesus commissioned you to watch over them and with that assignment comes the equipping of oversight, like the shepherd who watches over his sheep attentive and vigilant for the wolves."

As Goodness said "wolves", a switch flipped inside of me and I had an "eyes opened to truth" moment. I was His representative to these people while He was away. I felt that responsibility settle into my whole being. It was weighty like other times, yet more so. I felt the weight on my shoulders, but now it traveled down my whole being. In a moment or a flash, many thoughts came to mind. *Did the people have enough to eat? Did they feel safe and content? I would need to let them know I was here and that all was well as we waited for His return.* I was inundated with thoughts of how to help them as we prepared to go to the *City*.

"Sheep among wolves" Matthew 10:16

"Wolves" came fluttering into the periphery of my mind, like ghostly grey specters hovering close, waiting for their opportunity to strike and destroy the people.

Mercy spoke, "You are discerning correctly. Do you recall being told before about wolves being present around Decision Ville? They are not literal wolves, but spiritual. They are spirits that operate within the workers of iniquity. They lust for the souls of men and they are stirred up because they have lost all of the people that came out with you."

Mercy pointed to the people who were enjoying life once again and who were waiting for their final walk to the *City*. "They were and are still unaware that wolves lurk."

Mercy continued. "When the wolves see Jesus leading away the last souls to be saved, they will be furious and want revenge. They will come. They will want to steal, kill and destroy whoever they can. It's still their primal mission."

I was gripped with the realization that before me waited many people with no clue of what might be headed their way. They were not equipped for battle, neither was I. I felt inadequate to lead them or battle for them. The cold boney fingers of fear and death began reaching in, grabbing my heart. Holy Spirit's call was ear-piercing. He landed right behind me on the rock. The intensity of His sound instantly caused the heart-stopping image to vanish.

"Peace!" His words filled me, then flowed like the warmth of a hot shower when you are cold to the bone. "You must contend for the things you have learned and experienced from the journey; never forget them. That is where Wisdom will spring forth." The words flowed into my spirit as Holy Spirit let out a series of throaty sounds.

I took in a deep breath. The mist swiftly filled me, bringing comfort and strength to my spirit. I closed my eyes. My inner screen tuned to the memory of my time in the wilderness with the beasts and Satan. It played back in slow motion. I heard my tone of authority. I heard the words of my declarations and truth. I saw the power of the *City* light as it was refracted by the sphere on the chain. I saw the power of wielding the rod and staff. With each flash of memory, resolve grew, and I knew I could make a stand in defense of these people, if needed. I wasn't alone either. I was sure I would have the help of Jesus Himself. I knew David, Goodness and Mercy would play a role too. Hope billowed like fluffy clouds inside me, leaving no doubt we would all arrive at the *City*.

"Thank You, Holy Spirit, for reminding me." *Why do I forget so many things I have experienced along this journey?*

His "you are welcome" and "that is part of my job helping you" came clearly to my mind; as my ears heard the soft throat sound of the eagle from the rock.

"What do we do now?" I asked in general to the three of them.

"We wait on the Lord. We renew our strength with the food and thank Him for this warm, safe place. We set our minds on the *City* and we rest". The words were from Holy Spirit but there were no eagle sounds this time. His internal words resonated in my spirit.

Goodness pointed, drawing my attention to the alcove in the rock and the three of us made our way there as Holy Spirit kept watch up top. I sat down, expecting the rod and staff to go small, but they did not. I was about to lay them on the ground beside me when Mercy took them.

"They need to lean against the rock, so everyone can see them as they wait. The presence of the rod and staff brings the people comfort. I will make sure nothing happens to them."

I was glad because I didn't realize that I was tired until I sat down. Goodness put some meat, fruit and bread on a platter and handed it to me. The smell of the food was wonderful! My stomach growled and we all laughed. Even Holy Spirit made a cheeping sound that resembled a laugh. I poured myself a cup of the sweet red nectar from the flask and started to eat, but paused to bless the food.

"It's already been blessed," Goodness said even as I started to speak. With that, I ate and enjoyed every bite. The food made me content and satiated, causing my eyes to became heavy.

"Go ahead and rest. You're going to need it for what lies ahead. Mercy, Holy Spirit and I will keep watch."

"But I can't go to sleep, no matter how tired I am. Jesus needs me to keep watch. I must pray!" Goodness and Mercy each touched one of my arms.

"Trust us. You will pray." Goodness's words drifted through the fog of weariness.

"Prayer is supernatural. Let the supernatural be at work in you now."

I gave in and closed my eyes. Sleep came, and I began to dream. As I fell deep into sleep, the dream of Jesus in Decision Ville moving through the city, began to take shape. I was positioned behind Him watching and observing. The scenes did not change from before, but they became even more vivid. I noted that He had the staff and rod. I watched as He used them to herd people this way or that and isolate a few to His side who would cooperate with His leading. The first insight for how to pray, came to me then, clear and concise.

"Pray that those who still are open to His offer of salvation, will yield to His direction and come to His side."

I prayed that out. As I did, I was shown something new.

People that I had not noticed before, were yielding. The group that Jesus was able to separate out from the others, grew. It wasn't hundreds, but it was sizeable. I couldn't hear what He was saying, but His body language was earnest and insistent. Most of them acted like they were responsive. They appeared to say, "Yes". But here is where the dream changed from before. I saw the group that Jesus pulled aside divided into two groups. I could see all of their faces and I knew their hearts as well. In the first group who said "Yes", peace and relief came to their hearts transforming their faces. They watched closely what their fellow city dwellers in the other group were saying. In the other group who said "Yes", the people said "Yes, I'll get to it sometime," or "Yes in little bit, I'll think about it." Others said, "Yes thanks, but I'm good."

Again, I discerned what to pray. "Pray those who are double-minded can't sway those who are fragile in their faith. Those who are fragile have become people pleasers. Pray they gain strength to stand and come out from among them."

I prayed. Then I saw David take those who were fragile and weak in faith and turn them away from the others, walking them out of the city. I knew instantly, that David's assistance was connected to my prayer for the people to have strength to leave.

Jesus proceeded on and on, until He visited every single section of Decision Ville. When people responded to His message, the change in their countenance was always the same–transformed. As I watched the dream, I would catch or discern something in each section of the city and pray it out. Prayer made a difference in the numbers who choose to linger, listen and respond. David was always available to take the next transformed group out of the city to the rock. They would walk together through the city's gates onto the bridge and head to the growing numbers at the rock.

I awakened to Jesus calling my name and saying it was time to go. The workers of iniquity were coming, along with the wolves. I woke up, sat up, yet not fully awake. The emotions of the dream, the intercession, victories of right decisions, and transformations filled me, keeping consciousness at a distance.

"What did you say, Jesus?" As I said the name "Jesus", I was at full attention, realizing He was back.

"We must gather the people together now and leave. The workers of iniquity and the wolves will soon be here."

As He spoke, I looked at the people and pondered how to get them up and moving toward the *City*. As I surveyed the vast numbers now present out on the grasslands, I was awestruck. The number of people had doubled, at least. The reality of the power through prayer, even in my sleep, astounded me.

"No one can snatch my people from my hand. In the end, only they can decide where their future home will be."

"Jesus, there are so many! It will not be quick or easy to get them up and moving."

"Yes, but each one has renewed their connection to My voice, and they will hear My directions. Holy Spirit will fly throughout the camp and everyone will know what to do and when to do it."

"But Jesus, how can we outpace the wolves and the workers of iniquity that are coming? These people are not ready to fight, and they don't have much to make a fighting stand with. What are You going to do?"

As I spoke, Holy Spirit flew into the encampment. Goodness brought me the rod and staff, and without a word, turned to meet David and Mercy. I watched Goodness and Mercy walk off together toward the encampment carrying the bag of food and torch, but David remained.

"Goodness, Mercy and Holy Spirit will lead the people toward the mountain and the *City*. We take our stand elsewhere."

Although I knew He was going to say something like that, I felt a twinge of trepidation in my spirit. As I pushed out doubt and fear, my anticipation grew. With my confidence firmly in Jesus, I could stand and do my part in this confrontation with evil.

"Before we go to take our stand, I have a gift for you, remember?"

I nodded my head, still processing the "taking our stand" part.

"Here." Jesus held out His hand. His open palm held three different pieces of polished stones that I knew were for the chain.

"What are they?"

As Jesus walked closer. I stood up and instinctively removed the chain from my neck. As I did, the touchstone warmed my hand and the crystal sphere refracted a beam of rainbows upon His face. I placed the chain into His palm, and He began to place the new stones on the chain.

"This piece completes this stone." He pointed to the log shaped piece that I thought had been representative of the "dive rock", where I had stepped off the waterfall. He took the new piece and laid it on the horizontal log piece. As He did, the two pieces fused together forming a cross.

"This cross is to reward you for all the times you practiced self-discipline and self-denial. In Decision Ville, you willingly shared your provisions in the bag. You willingly shared pieces from your invitation. You never once thought there might not be enough for you. This represents 'Victory' over all things of the flesh."

"Now this," He picked up what looked like a miniature replica of the rod, "this, is for walking in your authority, as you led many people out from Decision Ville! I am proud of you."

"And finally, this one is very special." It looked like a miniature of the staff in every detail. "It represents the special glory you have brought to the Father and to Me by accepting the commissioning to be a faithful shepherd and lead these people to their final destination at the *City*."

After each piece was attached to the chain, Jesus handed it back to me. I put it back on my neck, heavy from the pieces spread from one side to the other.

"Your chain is now complete." Jesus said with great joy in His tone.

I didn't know what to say or do. I was full of His love and felt His Presence in every cell of my being. I couldn't comprehend all that I was feeling. It was overwhelming, and I was faint with the myriad of emotions. Jesus took my hand with a firm grip allowing His strength to fill me immediately.

"It is time to go and take our stand." His words projected strength and power.

**"With His mighty angels in flaming fire,
punishing those who don't obey the Good News"
2 Thessalonians 1:7-10**

I looked back at the people, amazingly they'd already gone a great distance maintaining their orderly ranks. Jesus continued to hold my hand and grabbed the rod. I took hold of the staff and we walked around the rock and headed toward Decision Ville.

"Jesus?"

"Yes?"

"How will we take our stand? What should I do? What is the strategy for fighting so many, when we are only three?" As hard as I tried to mask my apprehension, I'm sure He could hear the quiver in my voice.

"You will know." He looked lovingly into my eyes and continued. "Let My peace reign inside of you. Out of that peace, you will know how to engage the enemy."

We walked on in silence, holding hands till we reached the main street that lead to the bridge connecting the access points for all of Decision Ville. Our walk was easy because of the grassy highway that had been trodden down by those leaving the darkness and deception of Decision Ville. I looked up and watched the dark hordes moving in our direction. David took his position on my left side.

"We have taken the offensive by coming here. They will be caught off guard to see us and that we are only three. Now take your staff firmly in your right hand. Breathe in the mist and let My peace fill your entire being. We take our stand here."

I did just that. I let go of Jesus's hand and held my staff firmly. I breathed in the mist. With a couple of breaths, my inner spirit was at full attention, yet fully at rest. We waited in silence as the hordes approached and made a semicircle around us. They were on both of our flanks but stayed at some distance. Three evil-looking spokesmen, with beastly countenances, approached and stood before us.

The middle one moved a step closer and with a half hiss and growl spoke, "Do you think that you can stop us from taking those people back? They are ours," he seethed, and "we will stop at nothing to get them back. What right do you think you have to come here and take them from us? They chose to stay in Decision Ville and not go to the *City*." He said 'the *City*' with a slow, disdainful snarl.

"'The people who sat in darkness, saw a great light, to those who sat in the region and shadow of your deceptive death, to them Light has dawned.'" (3) David projected with power and authority.

"And where is this light? Here we reflect our light as we choose! We do not need such Light," spoke a second.

"'I am the Light of the world. He who follows Me will not walk in the darkness but have the Light of life.'" (4) Jesus spoke softly, but with such power, all three fell to their knees. Many rows of this evil mob fell with them. The three leaders were absolutely incensed, having fallen in front of their legion. Their visage became even more beastly as they struggled to stand up. Hate filled their devilish glare. I tightened my grip on the staff.

All three turned their attention from Jesus and glared at me with contempt. Nodding at David and Jesus they continued, "We may have to work a little harder to take those two out, but you, you scrawny imposter, you won't last a minute."

I would have run in fear before my journey from such a threat. But I was not that person any longer. Their words struck something in me. It was like a trumpet blast signaling my "call to arms". Indignation began to arise from deep inside of me like molten lava slowly making its way to the surface.

I squared my shoulders and declared with righteous indignation. "Who do you think you are dealing with?" The words flew across my mind and out of my mouth, exclaiming, "I have earned my place here!"

I pulled out the gold chain, as I voiced these words out loud. The crystal caught the rays of the *City* and flashed a laser of light temporarily blinding the three leaders and several rows of evil cohorts behind them.

Jesus laughed. "I wouldn't mess with her, she means what she says."

The three snarled with rage and violence toward us. They pulled out their swords and lifted their clubs; as they did, their standing ranks followed suit. They bellowed out a war cry that shook the ground. The three leaders turned to their hordes and signaled to attack.

In the breath of a moment, my mind flooded with words that I could not recall ever reading. Without thinking, I acted out what welled up within me. I took my staff, raised it up, and then slammed it down onto the ground, shouting with authority and proclaimed, "'The unclean shall not pass over! A highway has been made and a road for God's people and it will be called the Holy Way.'" (5)

I continued declaring, "'It is for those that walk in the Way. Wicked fools cannot go there, but the redeemed will walk there. The ransomed ones will return and come with singing to Zion; and everlasting joy will be on their heads. They will obtain gladness and joy, and sorrow and sighing will flee away.'" (6)

As the last syllable jetted from my lips, David began to spin. As I watched him turn ever faster and faster, he began to glow, his garments broke into flames swirling up all around him. His fiery form grew in stature, taller and taller as the swirling flames encompassed him. Round and round he spun until he was transformed into a colossal pillar of fire that began advancing toward the massive hordes. I watched as the devilish army expressed unfettered panic and sprinted toward the city. David's pillar of fire moved, pursuing them as they fled. David continued his quest until the army was contained on the bridge cowering in fear and rage; unable to move.

"Come, let's go to the people waiting for us at the base of the mountains. They need a way to escape through them." As Jesus finished speaking, He took off briskly toward the mountains in the distance while I stood staring at David. I was mesmerized by his flaming appearance and dismayed that I'd spoken to him with sarcasm and dishonor. It gripped my heart that his power could have torched me where I stood, and I rejoiced in the goodness of the Father.

Transfixed in thought, I heard the voice of Jesus calling. "Are you coming?" I turned to see Him in the distance and knew I'd need to run like Elijah to catch up.

"Lord give me special strength!" I ran like the wind to catch up just as He approached the people waiting at the base of the mountains.

"He reveals the deep and hidden things"
Daniel 2:22

As I slowed, I glanced ahead expecting to see some pathway or opening in the base of the mountains to pass through. I didn't see anything. As we approached, the people made way for us till we stood at the mountain's base. As I looked for the passage or pathway, reality hit me; there was no way forward.

"Jesus?"

"Yes?"

My thoughts jumbled into words. "I don't see a passage through; they are too steep to climb. David is stilling holding back the evil hordes. but how do we take these people through?"

"I always make a way or a path to escape when it is needed. It is no different here. In fact, the way has already been provided. It was provided when the mountains were created at the foundation of the world. It's one of the finishing touches from the Father, preparing the way for all weary pilgrims on their journey. He knew they would need a way to reach the River on their journey to the *City*. Come, I will show you."

I followed as He walked off to the right. We had not gone far when I saw a huge boulder that had fallen down from the pinnacle of this spectacular mountain. It was at least three stories tall and nearly as wide. Jesus walked by it and made His way to the far side where it touched against the mountain. As we got there, He stopped and asked, "Do you recall the beginning of your mountain trip and the cave that led you into the belly of the mountain?"

My mind flashed to that moment in memory. I remembered that I had been amazed that on the back side of a boulder I discovered a path on which I could continue. With memory as my guide, I rushed ahead of Jesus. Sure enough, this boulder although immense, only touched the mountain above my head. Below that point, was a gap wide enough to squeeze past the boulder. I pressed by the obstacle to discover a large pathway curving ahead through the heart of the mountain. It was wide enough for a dozen people to walk side by side and continue on. A memory of a TV show about Petra, in southern Jordan, flashed through my mind. I knew this was a Siq (32) like the one leading to Petra. This pathway through the mountain's heart truly was the way Jesus had spoken of, which would lead us to the waiting River.

"Come!" Jesus called me. "It's time for you to take this people through to the River and the *City*." I returned and found Jesus, smiling His warm and wonderful smile. "Let's go tell the people."

We walked back to the people who had been watching and waiting. Jesus spoke out with authority. "The path through has been found. My servant and friend will lead you through. I have commissioned her to take you quickly and safely to the River and on to the *City*. I will go ahead to finish the last arrangements for your arrival. Goodness, Mercy and Holy Spirit will stay with you." At His last words, Holy Spirit swooped down, crying out commands. Goodness and Mercy walked over and stood on each side of the entrance.

"Jesus?"

"Yes?"

"What about David? Will he ever join us again?"

"Yes. When all are safely through, David will fire out a lightning bolt bright enough to blind evil from ever seeing this opening or the trodden pathway leading here. You will see him later. Now it's time for you to lead the people through. Here is the rod. Take it."

When my hand touched it, both rod and staff shrank. That sign made me feel like victory was assured. I walked over to Goodness and Mercy where Goodness took the rope, rod and staff and tied them together, hanging them over my shoulder. Mercy started to hand me the bag with the multiplied provisions and the torch.

"Please, keep them Mercy." I said. "The people will need one more piece of food to strengthen them for their last part of their journey to the *City*. Please distribute it as they pass through the opening. The torch will be the light that follows them now."

I turned and look at Jesus. He nodded His head to me in what felt like His approval for providing the food to the people. Then I realized we would not see each other for some time and I never wanted to be out of His sight. My heart was sad.

"My heart feels the same, but I will see you soon at the *City*." His words were soft and full of love. "You have all you need to lead these people home. Walk in the power and authority I have given you, it is strong and growing." With that, He turned and was gone.

I turned to the people and joyfully called out, "Let's head for the River and the *City*!" The people cheered, and we began the exodus through the mountain.

Chapter 11

The Glorious Ones

"They go from strength to strength. Every one of
them appears before God in Zion." Psalm 84:7

I squeezed through the opening between the rock and the mountain's base and quickly realized that it would take forever for all the people to cram through one at a time. This problem needed His power. I decided to appropriate the power that Jesus had said was strong and growing in me. So, I laid my hands on the rock and the mountain's base and commanded the space between them to widen. In that moment I heard a crack and a rumble followed by ground shaking that caused me to lose my balance. Right before my eyes, the mountain's base widened creating a large gap. The people on the other side shouted and began rapidly pouring through. I saw them eating food given by Goodness and Mercy. The people flowed through, reminding me of sand quickly flowing through an hour glass, filling up the Siq. I advanced into the Siq's passageway and became aware of its extreme descent. I turned to get a good look at the passageway and saw that it continued to run steeply downhill in a series of switchbacks. The people pressed through and kept advancing into the Siq, undaunted by the passageway's steep grade. I kept backing down the pathway, watching as the people continued to press in and follow.

Before I had given any thought to what was next, I was outside of the Siq. The light from the City was blinding, illuminating everything. The light allowed me to see just how steep the exit through the mountain had been. People were pressing in behind me and spilling out onto the grassland. I fixed my gaze on the horizon; we were closing the distance to the *City*. It appeared so close now, looming into the clouds and sending light beams in every direction.

I scanned to the left for the River and I was not disappointed. In the distance, I could see something that looked man made, lying at the base of some trees. I was wondering what I saw, when Holy Spirit swooped down and called out to me. "Lead them to the River. Now! Do not linger, the people will follow." I was still amazed at how I understood what He was saying.

I visually followed Him as He flew toward the stand of trees and the structures. The River was closer than I originally thought. It apparently curved sharply after cutting its way through the mountain's base in the deep gorge. In that moment, I wondered if the rapids and gorge were going to stand in the way of easy access, becoming another barrier to overcome.

Glancing back, the people continued in a wide procession; a solid stream of humanity coming out from the Siq. They were happily making their way steadily behind me. Where once they had been foolish, now they were redeemed and full of joy. As I drew near to the trees, I could now discern piles of large boats stacked and waiting for anyone to take them onto the River. Each boat was exceptionally large with at least six oars to a side, with capacity to hold many people. A group of them walked to a pile, picked up a boat and awaited instructions.

"Let's see what our access is to the River," I said to those with the boat in hand as we walked down to the River's edge.

I rejoiced to see the River was not in a deep gorge anymore. Here the River was calm, wide and easily accessible from a sandy beach that was only a few feet below the grassland. As others arrived, they picked up boats and moved toward the River. A gentle slope greeted them, making access easy to launch the flotilla.

"Let's take our journey, and let's go" Genesis 33:12

Holy Spirit spoke from a tall tree on the other side of the River. "Tell the people to continue launching the boats into the River and fill them, but to wait for you. You need to be in the first boat, so you can lead them. The journey will be quick and easy. But first, appoint twelve people to stay on shore and direct the launch. Goodness and Mercy will be last to make sure everyone gets down the River to the *City*. But you must lead the way."

I told those with the first boat in the water, to hold their position on the River so I could give Holy Spirit's directions to the twelve leaders. I walked up the slight incline to the grassland to identify potential leaders. I saw immediately that there were several, at least eight people already helping take charge by directing those still coming from the Siq. I walked over to them and as I did, the rod and staff immediately went to full length. That not only got my attention, but those around me. Instinctively, I knew what to do.

"I need you and you. Yes, you, and also all of you over there. I confirmed with the pointing of my staff. I need you and yes, I need you and you also."

I counted, and I had my twelve people. My heart was thrilled.

"Holy Spirit has directed that we are to move out to the *City*. I am putting you twelve in charge to make sure everyone gets into a boat and oversee their launch down the River to the *City*. Goodness and Mercy will bring up the rear and that is how you will know that all the people are through the Siq and accounted for. I'm launching out now on the first boat. Launch the boats as they are filled; until everyone is on the River and heading for the *City*."

Looking at the steady human stream still coming, I took the staff and held it up and called out to those still making their way, speaking loud and clearly.

"Listen! Look around at all the people. You are all brothers and sisters in the Lord. You have come out in strength and you will go forth in strength to reach the *City*. You have chosen to see your Father and to be part of the celebration. Nothing will stop you again. Follow us and together we will fill the *City* with His praises."

My words reverberated throughout the grassland and I could hear them echo off the mountains. People still making their way, lifted up a cheer so thunderous, it shook the ground. Chills ran through me. With that, I turned and made my way to the first boat. I knew I needed help climbing in, because the rod and staff were still at full size.

As I climbed in, Holy Spirit's voice filled my mind. "Make your way to the front, and you will find a place to securely mount your staff at the bow of the boat. It will point the way."

Knowing to obey in all things, I made my way forward over all those packed in. I found one bench, a single seat, at the bow of the boat. There was enough space to wedge the staff and rod between it and the bulkhead in front. Resting on the boat's bow, they pitched forward leaning out over the water, pointing the way. As I took my seat, everyone was looking, waiting on my directions.

"Head for the *City*! Let's finish our journey!" My voice came out strong with purpose and joy!

Everyone gave another resounding shout and we pushed off, out onto the River. People took to the oars and we moved forward with great speed. Because I was facing the back of the boat, I saw the boats launching from shore, following close behind. Looking toward the mountains and grassland, I could see a growing gap between the exiting mass and the Siq. In my natural mind I couldn't comprehend how so many had come through so quickly. I was astonished.

As rapidly as they were progressing toward the River, this people would soon become a massive flotilla making its way to the *City*. Relaxed by our progress, peace overshadowed me. I was ready for a nap, when a flash of brilliant light, shot across the sky like lightening. It came from the backside of the mountains. David had finished his job. We were safe! No hordes could ever follow us. How I looked forward to seeing David, Goodness and Mercy at the *City*. I leaned my back against the rod and staff which made a perfect back rest and closed my eyes.

"How precious to me are your thoughts,
God! When I wake up, I am still with You."
Psalm 139:17-18

I was awakened by a pressure on my lap. As I opened my eyes, the first thing I saw was David sitting on the bench facing me. He and Jesus always had such a radiant smile that filled me with joy and peace. David's smile beamed into my soul!

"David! I didn't think I would see you until the *City*! I'm so glad you are here."

As I spoke, the weight upon my lap drew my attention. I looked down and saw a tablet like the one I had read with Jesus. That one had contained such wonderful and powerful words about who I was and how the Father saw me. Then I remembered that Jesus said there would be more tablets.

"This is what you need to hear next about your destiny. Go ahead and read it." David encouraged.

I looked down. The words on the tablet glowed red. As before, they were in a beautiful yet unrecognizable flowing script.

"But Jesus isn't here to help me read it." I whined briefly.

266

"He doesn't need to hold your hand, because you are strong with the power of His might. You will be able to read it on your own, this time." David answered assuredly.

"I will? I want to read the words. I long to know what the Father's thoughts concerning me are and how He sees me."

Encouraged by David, I placed my hand on top of the tablet, I shut my eyes and took a deep breath of the mist. My fingertips lingered on the first word, letting its warmth and energy come through my fingertips into my spirit. The longer I lingered and breathed in deeply, the more the fire and energy of the words increased. Would I be able to do this? Suddenly I knew the first word.

"It says 'time'. David, the first word is time!" I was so excited that I had understood what the word was.

"Yes, the word is 'time'. See, you are able to read what is written. Now go ahead and see what the Father has to say. I'll wait while you read it out loud. Then Holy Spirit will come and take the tablet back to the *City*. The Father keeps every tablet and every book that is written for each person. They are kept in the library at the *City* for all time. This one will be placed back with the others that bear your name."

"Others?"

"Yes, there are other books and tablets. They will be brought forth when you need to hear the Father's thoughts and plans for you." (49)

The marvel of the Father having books and tablets exclusively for me, filled me with wonder. The thought of His love humbled me, yet permeated me with confidence and connection to Him. I wanted to delve into and devour every word written on this tablet that God had for me!

David chuckled, "Don't let me stop you."

Closing my eyes again, I took a deep breath, then began with the first word, "Time".

"Time is of the essence, yet it isn't. A paradox for sure, but one you do not have to worry about. For time and times are in My hands to move and expand. I expand time or compress time, as I deem right. I play time as an accordion, making the melody of My song spring to life. Sometimes the tempo increases with wild and frenzied abandonment. At other times, I make it slow, methodical and orderly. I even have periods of rest when all of creation waits in expectation for what will come next."

"This is where you are now in your symphony of destiny. You are in a holding place, a place of rest, waiting for what comes next. This is a time when others need to play in order to move My symphony forward. This is not punishment for you. This is My commissioning you into a new movement of the symphony. It is a time for your rest, so when We move forward to the grand finale, you will be forceful, confident, loud; heard clearly to the very end."

"I am conducting others now to come in and carry the lines of this musical score. They are busy in this movement while you are at rest. There remain many that have not yet been heard nor have they been given a part to play to this moment. Now is the time for them to be mixed into the score. It is their time to shine. Every instrument is needed to carry forth the sound that was created to be My audible utterance across the whole earth. My symphony needs to fill the airways and resonate throughout every nation across the earth. My sound will bring fear into the hearts and the camps of My enemies. They have not heard the full score, nor have they heard all the instruments before this time. They always assumed it was a score of lesser intensity and composition!

But, when the full body of instruments come together and play their distinct notes, the enemy will shudder with unrelenting terror. It will bring confusion and fear into their camps."

"Think it not strange that you are on this journey at this time. For I have called you to be a part of the full symphony as I begin to put My sound out into the air. You are no longer the same person as you were before the journey began. No longer are you hiding behind the security of others. No longer are you hanging back and avoiding risks. No longer are you aware of only yourself. Now you see all of My people and you passionately desire to see that each and every one of My people make it to the *City*."

"But there are still many out there who have yet to begin their journey. Some do not even know there is a journey waiting for them. I am calling you to make this truth known to others, so they can begin; knowing My Son, knowing My Spirit and knowing My Presence. It is My desire for all peoples to come to know Me and My love for them. You've come to know the joy and the love We have for you. Now you have begun to flow with the symphony. It is time for you to help others, those who have not yet taken their place as My instruments."

"A new season is about to come. You can't see it yet, you can't sense it yet. The things around you do not reveal what it could be. But My times are My times and this next season is even now moving forward. Each day the light changes. My light is growing brighter, and the darkness continues to grow darker. People are asleep, people are unaware of the consequences of this change. That's why the enemy's camps are seducing, enslaving people with their deceptions and the tickling sounds in their ears. The people are being drawn into the false light and into real darkness. As the light goes dim, everything and everyone cools. Without the warmth of 'The Light', people will become frozen and dead. It's the gradual cooling that deceives them, until it's too late. When the light is dim, people cannot see the safe path to take".

"It is critical that people comprehend the necessity of moving toward the true light and the true safe path. You saw what happened in Decision Ville. Even the elect can fall victim to this deception. It won't be long now till you come into the *City*. There you will know what eternal joy will be like. You will see what it means to be with Me eternally in the light. Rest in what you see and experience in the *City*. My Son is preparing a special place for you and you will dwell in the house of the Lord, forever. But know that outside of the *City*, winds of adversity are blowing. The enemy is moving, trying to stop the full expression of My symphony. There is more for you to do My daughter. Take rest in the *City*, but do not forget about those whom darkness is even now causing their hearts to grow cold toward Me."

The words ended and I was filled with mixed emotions. A part of me was happy with the words about how the Father saw me and was planning to use me. But I was sad that others had not yet experienced the opportunities of this amazing, formidable, and fulfilling journey. I was confused a little with what exactly He was saying about rest before more of the symphony continued. He hinted that more was coming, but what? When I reached the *City*, my journey would be complete. My travels would be over. *Or, would they? Why did I just think that?*

In the midst of my pondering, David spoke up.

"Do not fret! Jesus will make all things known to you in His time. As for now, the *City* is waiting for you. We need to make our way to one of the twelve gates and enter."

With that, I turned my attention to where David was looking, but my gaze was interrupted by a swooshing sound as Holy Spirit flew in and landed on the seat next to him. The movement of Holy Spirit's large wing span blew my hair back as He flapped His wings backwards, sticking a perfect landing on the seat.

"He has come for the tablet." David's words snapped me back from Holy Spirit's amazing arrival.

I carefully picked it up from my lap. It was heavy. I handed it toward David, but Holy Spirit snatched it with His beak and took off flying in the direction where David had originally been looking. I turned and saw the *City*. My eyes became riveted by what I was seeing.

I saw movement in my peripheral vision, noting that people were rapidly disembarking and moving up the large ramp toward the *City*. I could actually feel the joyous response in their hearts and noticed the atmosphere was suddenly charged with great excitement. Then I felt a release as tension flowed out of me. It was tension apparently, I was not aware I had held within me. My body relaxed, and David spoke, but I could not look away from the *City*.

"You are feeling the release of the commission you had been given to assist these people to their destiny. It is only part of the mantle that rests upon you. It comes and goes with each task given to you, as one commissioned to shepherd His people. For now, you can rest in the completion of your assigned task. You have been faithful to bring the people to the *City*. Each person is released to their own place of intimacy with the Father and Jesus. For now, you are one of many glorious ones, reaching the *City*."

I heard his words. I processed his words, but my eyes could not take in what I was seeing. The *City* was nothing like any city in my comprehension. Yes, there were attributes that I could relate to. There were towers and structures like high rise buildings, but that is where similarities ended. The things I saw went beyond my comprehension. I had nothing on earth to compare to what I was seeing. There were things my eyes told my mind were not possible, yet obviously were. John's description in "The Revelation" of the *City* was amazingly accurate for his time in history. I marveled how he had even found the descriptors he used. Even with my modern-day experiences, I couldn't have described it any better.

As I tried to wrap my mind around the incredible things I was seeing, my attention was pulled away from the *City*. It was directed back to the shore where the people were disembarking from the boats. Shouts of joy and alleluias filled the air.

The *City* sat upon a very high hill which added to its towering height. Where the boats pulled up on the shore line, there were steps and ramps to take the people up toward the gates. The pathways were large, smooth but they also glistened. People from the *City* were on the shore waiting for the next incoming boats so they could help the people out and direct them to the *City* gates. Their next actions caused me to ponder more about this supernatural place. The people helping, would place the oars back into the boats securely and then push them out onto the River. The boats would move toward the opposite bank, slowly turn all on their own, and drift toward the beach where we found the boats originally. How strange! Having had some knowledge of rivers, currents and bodies of water, my natural mind tried to figure out how it was possible for the current's flow that moved us in one direction toward the *City* could also move in the opposite direction, all in the same river channel. The River was flat and calm with no signs of competing, underlying currents. A force was moving these boats away and I didn't know how. I began to ruminate over this strange force at work.

"There are forces at work that defy your understanding. You should know this by now." There was laughter in David's words.

"I am going to assume they will end up back were we got them, and somehow, they will be neatly stacked for others to use if needed?"

"You got it!"

"Fantastic!"

There wasn't anything more I could say. I turned toward the *City* with a curious thought about the River and how it was connected or flowed in relationship to the *City*. I noticed that the River ended at this side of the *City* near a corner. Or, I should say disappeared into the foundation of the *City*'s wall. Here at the River's end, I could clearly see the large foundation of the wall of the *City*. The foundation had twelve layers of massive stones which appeared to be brilliant gemstones. Each layer was a different color and I assumed it was a different type of stone. There were random letters creating words, but in a language, I didn't recognize. These words were carved into the stones in different locations on the various rows. The script appeared written in gold, resembling the script on my tablets.

The River's elevation came to the lower level of the foundation stones. There I discovered a large tunnel, channeling the River as it disappeared under the *City*. The tunnel had a portcullis that came down from an upper row of the foundation stones and appeared as if it extended down into the River bed rock. It allowed the River to enter but blocked all human access. I took a closer look. The River was so sparkling clear, I could see the grate's metal fingers plunged into the stones creating the River bed. It was obviously designed to allow only water to pass.

"David why does the River terminate here going into the foundation of the *City*? And why is it blocked off with that grate?"

I pondered as I looked at the grate, my mind went back to the basement of the cathedral and the stream. The look and the feel were the same except here, access was denied. Only the gates permitted entrance to the *City*.

"All things begin and end with the Father. The River begins here and ends here. It brings the traveler on their journey home. It flows out of the *City* on the other side into the earth, so others can start their journey."

Now I knew why the stream pulled at me to travel on it, back in the basement of the cathedral. The River was the source of that stream I had embarked on seemingly a life time ago. The Father had provided me a way to start my journey.

"Everyone who comes to the *City* must pass through a gate holding their invitation in hand. There is a narrow way to receive an invitation. Neither a thief nor someone bypassing the way will receive an invitation. The foundation depth and a wall over 200 feet high, prevent anyone from climbing over or digging under."

I gazed along the high wall that surrounded the *City*. I could see a large entrance gate a few strides up from the top of the ramp. Looking the opposite direction from my corner location, I could see another gate. Where were the other 10 gates? The walls were so long they disappeared into the horizon in both directions. Comprehending the size of the *City* was beyond my natural ability to process, I was in awe!

David spoke out what I was processing.

"There are three gates on each side of the *City*. As you can see, the *City* is very large, and the gates are spaced evenly around the four walls."

"Large doesn't begin to describe it! It is incredible! I can't image walking around it or even getting around inside it. It would surely take weeks!" I exclaimed.

As the words left my lips, I was spellbound and in awe at the height of the wall; then the height of the *City,* inside the walls. The *City* was made up of towers and various other structures. What I could see of the *City* structures, literally rose into the clouds, out of sight and into the blue heavens above. It was such an architectural and engineering marvel! The levels of the structures were too numerous to count. But beyond the overwhelming height of what I was seeing, structures would canti-lever out at incredible angles and join themselves to other structures, creating snowflake-like designs. Everywhere I looked the design was dif-ferent. Some structures were small yet held up another that was incred-ibly much larger. The structures defied gravity and all logic. The overall effect looked like star shaped edifices intersecting, linking and building up and up into the heavens. Each projection glistened and radiated bril-liant light. Some actually projected that light out in every direction. It was incredible to behold.

David understood my need to make sense of what I was seeing and spoke up.

"The top reaches into the heavens as you know of them. It would require walking at a leisurely pace over 200 days, just to walk from one side to the other. Its base would fill most of what you call the United States."

The immensity of this information took my breath away. I had to sit down because my knees went weak at the thought of such wonders. As I sat there trying to take in all that my natural eyes were beholding, boat after boat of people landed and unloaded. All were rejoicing at having reached the *City.* The boats would be turned around and then sent back down the River. People poured in from the boats in droves. Multitudes were making their way toward the gates. So many people!

I looked again and again at the structure thinking about the millions upon millions over the ages who had come to love the Father and His Son. The structure was beyond massive; still I was only beginning to realize the possibilities of every follower, in one place, at one time worshipping and being in Their Presence. Overcome, I started weeping. David hugged me close with a comforting embrace.

"It is overwhelming. The Father has left nothing to chance. No one will ever feel left out or alone again. Here completeness of all things is reality. Untold numbers of people will fill this place, yet each will feel like they are the only one with the Father and have Jesus' full attention. It definitely demonstrates the greatness of our creator and the immensity of the love He has for each individual person."

It took me awhile to process the magnitude of the *City* and the things I was learning. I sat briefly just gazing at the *City*. My eyes beheld colors and beauty on such a scale, I had no context to hang them on. I began to understand how the *City* had sent out the light into all the land. Everything my eyes beheld reflected and refracted the light that radiated from a source within the *City*. There was so much gold, all transparent. Amazingly my eyes were now accustomed to the brilliance of the light. That was a source of wonder in its self; in my world before the journey, I would have needed the darkest of sunglasses on bright sunny days. Every part of me was changed.

"Yes, the wonders here go beyond all comprehension. The light comes from the Lamb and is called unapproachable light. But here, those redeemed by His blood have new bodies, new spirits and new eyes! It is with your new spiritual eyes that you can behold His Glory. Are you ready to go up and into the *City*?"

Part of me was ready and excited. A part of me felt like I wasn't able to process anything more and would crumble to the ground, weep, tremble or just fall apart.

"Are you going with me, David?" I needed his strength right now.

"Yes, I will be with you for a bit."

I caught the 'for a bit' part and wanted to cling to him until I got to see Jesus again.

"It's all so magnificent, isn't it? Angels stand in awe of everything the Father does for His creation and His children. Even though we've had a few years to get accustomed to it we're still amazed." I heard amusement in his voice.

I laughed with him. "Thanks David, you always help me get things in perspective."

I stood, getting ready to step out of the boat when David cleared his throat, getting my attention.

"Forgetting something?"

I didn't have a clue. My mind was focused on the *City*, the Presence, Father and Jesus.

"The rod and staff?"

Yes! How quickly I had forgotten. I clenched firmly to pull them from where they were stowed. At my touch, they went small, making it easy to pick them up. I was about to put them on my shoulder when David reached and took them.

277

"I'll give them back to Jesus. You won't need them in the *City*. Now, your entire focus can be on the *City* and coming into the Presence. Everything else you bring will have a use."

"What do I have to bring into the *City*? I don't have the rod, staff, torch or the bag."

"You have yourself, your chain, your gifts and the weight of the mantle upon you. You also have your invitation."

"Invitation!" Shocked revelation flooded through me like being hit in the face with an unexpected bucket of cold water.

"David, I don't have the bag anymore and my invitation is in the bag! Remember Goodness and Mercy took it to pass out the food at the Siq entrance. I haven't seen them and now all the boats have come and gone. I can't believe I forgot! What should I do?"

Fear, then panic gripped me. The thought of finally arriving without my invitation was staggering. I almost collapsed from shock, as it hit me.

"Peace!" David spoke with authority.

That powerful spoken word of truth brought peace to my chaotic thoughts. It extinguished my fear and panic like a heavy, wet blanket does a fire.

"I know you were consumed by all your commissioned tasks and care for the people's welfare. So, I retrieved your invitation for you."

Then he pulled my invitation from a hidden pocket. It looked like new, showing no signs of wear or tear. I latched on and held it close to my heart.

"Oh, David! How can I ever thank you? You never fail me. I couldn't have done anything without you."

"That is my service. I am His ministering servant and His messenger-helper. My service to Him includes my service to you."

There were no more words. In that moment, overwhelming praise to the Father and Jesus rose up within us. We were both aware of how great is our God!

David took my arm and we climbed out of the boat together. Halfway up the ascending ramp leading to the gate, I turned to glance back at our boat. It had already turned and was heading down stream like all the others. We walked to the gate in silence.

Pearls, Gold Streets, Trees of Life and the River

The gate was massive. It appeared made from one solid pearl with an opening carved through the middle. I couldn't imagine the magnitude of an oyster which could produce this massive pearl let alone the production of eleven more just like this around the wall of the *City*. Only a creator such as the Father could create them! The light of the *City* made the opalescence of the pearl's finish sparkle and reflect the light magnificently.

Throngs of people were entering, and everyone held out their invitation for entry. The angels assigned to guard the entrance to the *City* were attentive and continuously observant. They would nod, acknowledging the raised invitation and motion the people to come in. We were about to enter into the *City* through a pearl. A pearl of great price obviously from its size. I had a memory flash instantly from a scripture, telling of a merchant who discovered a pearl of great price, then sold everything he had to possess the pearl. (8) Jesus had spoken about Himself as the pearl. When we find Him, we would give all we had to possess Him. Now here I was, standing outside of a pearl of great price, because I had chosen Jesus above everything else. I was now going to enter in to the *City* and have my home with Him forever. Nothing was lost or unconnected in God. I too held up my scroll and received my nod of approval.

The hollowed-out pearl had a tunnel effect. It echoed and intensified the excited voices of those coming through into the *City*. I glanced down to put my scroll into a pocket, when my eyes caught a glimpse of the pavement that we were walking on. It was gold! I could tell by its appearance but, as with so many things I had observed on the journey, it was different. The gold was so transparent, that I could see through and view the same foundation stones below the golden street. Apparently, the solid foundation stones extended from the perimeter wall into the *City,* supporting the clear golden streets as well as the massive *City* structures. I was stunned. I had never seen transparent gold nor such clarity or brilliance in gemstones.

Looking all around as we came out on the other side of the pearl gate, I saw the gargantuan *City* above us. It was supported by gigantic golden pillars and occasional walls that were at least two stories tall. That was the first level! It also had a maze effect and my mind immediately thought about the need for a GPS to even find my way around this place. The *City* was more than I could comprehened.

"It is grand beyond all things imaginable." David, aware of my thoughts continued. "But you do not have to fear getting lost. Remember, you can close your eyes and your inner spirit will see and take you to wherever you want to go. Soon, you will be able to think of where you need to go, and you will be translated there in the spirit, just like Philip. One moment he was in the wilderness and suddenly found himself in a city far away." (9)

I couldn't imagine how to do that, but since I had already experienced other times of walking by spiritual sight, I knew I could. As we walked on, I looked about contemplating everything inside the *City*. I watched the comings and goings of angels, people, spirits like Goodness and Mercy and other created beings that were beautiful and strange; talking, carrying strange items, pushing carts full of beautiful fruit and bread. It was a hive of activity. But nothing appeared unusual to me now.

"David? Where are Goodness and Mercy?"

"They are handling other business for the Father right now."

We walked on in silence for some time. I walked in wonder of what I was seeing, trying to take it all in; just people and supernatural beings, walking and talking. They chatted and interacted with great enthusiasm, no harried rushing, everyone in harmony and peace. Some sat together on beautiful benches. No one seemed alone. It was like everyone was on "holiday" and enjoying life together.

Eventually we came to a shop where many people were coming and going. Those leaving were carrying bags, so I glanced up to see if the shop had a name. It did. Two words. "Gifts Exchanged". As I processed the shop name, the touchstone warmed on my chain, which drew my attention to the "gifts" attached.

"Do you want to go in and look around," David asked.

"Yes, sure."

As we entered the shop door, I saw a massive store layout. Everywhere I looked were shelves laden with crowns of many types and sizes. People were trying them on, some were stacking, putting on several at the same time. I was confused by what I saw. We wandered around and then I approached a counter where people were laying down a crown or several crowns, picked from the displays. I watched as they pulled out their chains that looked like mine. Some had several gifts attached, others only one. But their enthusiasm was the same. The people behind the counter would remove a gift or gifts from the chain and drop them into a large urn. It appeared that gifts were removed based on the number of crowns selected. One crown for one gift. The chain was returned to the person and their crowns placed in a bag. They left rejoicing!

"I know you by now. You want to know what's going on." David had humor in his voice as he spoke.

"Yes! I don't get it! Why would anyone want to trade their personal gifts from Jesus, for crowns? My gifts mean so much and each one came from passing a test or from making hard die-to-self choices."

David took hold of my arm and led me over to a side wall where hung a huge portrait of Jesus. It was breathtaking in the majesty, might and power being portrayed. At the bottom of the painting was the title – "Faithful and True". (10) Jesus was sitting upon a magnificent white horse. The depiction of the horse was powerful, commanding respect by its very appearance. The eyes of Jesus were not the eyes I had come to know. Rather these eyes were full of power, authority, determination and fury. His hair was white, yet His face looked young and eternal. He wore a white robe that shimmered in the light. His pure white robe held many crimson stains that resembled blood spatters. They started at His chest and heart area and flowed increasingly down the robe pooling around the hem resembling a blood red border. On His head were many crowns identical to the ones in this shop.

"Do you understand now?"

"No, David, I'm sorry, but I don't."

"Jesus received many gifts from the Father for His obedience and service. Some of those gifts are the crowns you see Him wearing in this portrait. Jesus received crowns for the same things for which you received your gifts. Jesus overcame the lust of the flesh, the lust of the eyes, and the pride of life."

"He had to step out of His supernatural abilities to step into human flesh with all of its frailties, limitations and consequences of the Garden Fall. He had to walk out His life on earth totally human, having set aside His supernatural power and authority. He had to be tempted in every way, as humanity would be. Yet, He overcame the temptations and was rewarded. Jesus copied what His Father did for Him. Now Jesus rewards all who follow Him and overcome their flesh. He will speak these words to all who have overcome, 'Well done good and faithful servant.'" (33)

David continued explaining. "On your journey, you wouldn't have been able to carry or wear multiple crowns. Instead, Jesus gave you gifts, symbolic of the things He was rewarding you for. Now you are in the *City*. That means you have been transformed on the journey! You are ready to receive the final transformation of your appearance. That transformation will fashion you into a child of royalty. You are the heir of a King. Taking on a crown is one of the final steps of transformation. Since you will one day reign as a king, you are destined to wear a crown."

"As the people enter the *City*, they exchange their gifts for crowns. In Decision Ville, the people were deceived to trade their gifts, invitation etc. for temporary pleasures. But here, there is a divine exchange. It will soon be the time for the wedding feast. The Bride, these transformed people you see, are getting ready for the marriage feast and celebration. As the Bride beholds the Father and His Son, Jesus the Bridegroom, all who make up the Bride will fall down in worship. The Bride, will worship in adoration and in gratitude. We angels and the elders will also fall down and worship, and the elders will cast their crowns at the feet of Jesus."

"As an angel, we wish we could add to our worship as you have the chance to do, by exchanging your gifts for crowns to throw at the feet of Jesus." Why would anyone withhold anything they could present joyously, just like the elders? Everyone who has finished their journey to the *City*, understands His incredible and extraordinary sacrifice, that transformed and redeemed their lives."

As my touchstone warmed, I finally understood. I fingered my gifts, pondering how special each one was. How would I part with them? How could I, since each one was uniquely made for me? Yet the exchanged crowns gave me something much more visible and glorious to present in worship. How could I not make this final divine exchange? Looking at the crowns again, I saw them with new eyes and new insight. There were five different crowns but I had been given seven gifts, allowing me to keep the two most special. I was overwhelmed at the fullness of all I was experiencing.

"You do not need to exchange them now, you have plenty of time." David said encouragingly.

"But I thought everything was all going to happen soon!"

With more emphasis in his words, David answered. "Remember your tablet words? 'Time is of the essence, yet it isn't. A paradox for sure, but one you do not have to worry about. For time and times are in My hands to move and expand.'"

"How can you remember my words?"

"The angels who minister, are told everything that has been written about the person we attend. I know all of your destiny words. That is how we can have the wisdom to choose how we interact, when we interact or if we interact at all."

He continued. "There are still so many more who need to come on their own journey. The Father and Jesus are controlling times and seasons so that all people have the opportunity to decide to begin their own personal journey."

"So, we are waiting for more people to come?" I asked.

"Yes."

"Good, that means that I have plenty of time to explore."

David didn't comment, which I found a little odd. I looked quizzically at his face, but he smiled one of his teasing smiles. The kind that meant, "Oh you have no idea what lies ahead." Now that thought, brought me new wonderings.

"Since there is time, come with me. I want to show you some other things." David's words erased my wonderings. Instead I was excited to explore this infinite and magnificent place.

We walked out of the shop and back into the open area. David took my hand and said. "Close your eyes and say, 'Great Hall.'"

Holding onto his hand I said, "Great Hall". An immediate rush of sensation created a slight flutter in my inner being. It was over in an instant. David let go of my hand and I opened my eyes. I was standing in the midst of a great hall. I saw a few people passing through, but some were so far away they looked like ants. The hall was enormous. The best descriptor that I had to frame it with were photos I'd seen of a huge, empty exposition center in Hanover, Germany. It was about the same size as a 125-acre farm.

"How did we get here? What happens here in this place?" My stunned questions poured out.

"This is where everyone will one day gather for the feast and celebration. Now we go to the thrones. Close your eyes and say 'thrones.'" David didn't even give me time to ask more about the Great Hall.

The same unique instant feeling in my belly came and went in a second. This time, I didn't need David to hold my hand. I opened my eyes and David was smiling at me, knowing that I had recognized the advancement of getting around without holding his hand. I saw twenty-four thrones placed in a semi-circle. The thrones were facing away from us and toward an intense, brilliant sphere of light some distance from the thrones. The sphere of light pulsated with flashes, reminding me of lightning. I saw vague outlines of rapidly moving images darting in and out of the sphere of light. An emerald rainbow crested the brilliant pulsating light.

David explained. "You're looking at the Father of Lights. He is waiting for Jesus, His son, the Lamb, who is the Light of the World, to bring more people home to the *City*. Soon when the time of times have come, Jesus will take His place upon His own rightful throne. This Throne Room which is a continuation of the Great Hall, will be filled with all who will worship at the coming festal celebration. There will be an innumerable company of angels, along with the Bride of Christ. Now look at where we stand."

I looked all around and finally down. The pillars and structures around me were made of the same translucent gold. The transparent pavement revealed the solid jeweled foundation here, like I first saw at the gate. But my eyes caught movement between the transparent pavement and the foundation stones. Clear water was running under it, in a large stream.

"Where is the water coming from?" I asked.

"It flows from the throne. The River as you saw when we landed, flows into the foundation on the corner of the *City*. It goes into the tunnel and is absorbed and dispersed into the foundation stones and all the structures that surround us. But it has its creation and beginning in the throne of the Father. 'For all things are for Him, through Him and to Him'. (11) All of creation and life, everything that was ever made or will be made, originates from the Father of Creation. What you are seeing is the beginning flow of the River of Life. It springs up from the Fountain of Life within the Father. It flows out from His throne and under the *City*. Come, I need to show you where it goes out."

"This time you do not need to speak the words out loud, think of them in your mind. Think of desiring to see 'The Tree of Life'."

I closed my eyes and immediately pictured a large, in fact an enormous tree. The instant flutter happened again. I opened my eyes and we were standing at the edge of the structure. My eyes beheld one of the most beautiful vistas ever. The structure was open to the outdoors; no walls, the occasional double gold translucent pillars stood on the transparent floor and the open expansion to the outside. The transparent floor stopped, and the gold pavement started sloping downward, away from the structure, following the topography of the hill. It reminded me of the ramp and steps which we had walked up, from the River to the Pearl gate. The hill and pavement were terraced. I heard the sound of rushing water and turned slightly toward the sound. I saw the River emerge from the transparent gold floor in a golden channel. The water was shallow, ankle deep. It fell downward in the channel like a mini waterfall to the next terrace, creating a stream. At each terrace, the channel became wider and the stream grew deeper, continually falling until the stream became a large, clear River boulevard.

On either side of the water boulevard, the golden pavement continued in tiered steps and landings. This allowed anyone to easily make their way down as they followed the flow of the River. Every terraced landing held several benches over shadowed by large flowering trees. As I looked at the two trees nearest me, I noticed a variety of blooms, different in shape and color, yet the trees looked identical. Mixed in with the leaves and unusual blooms, were different varieties of ripe fruit. Every tree lining the long length of the River boulevard had the same appearance. One side of the River mirrored the other. On and on it went until the River finally went through the *City's* wall far in the distance. Because the land sloped downhill as it did, I could see over the tall wall and all the way to the horizon. On the other side of the great wall, lay a lush and beautiful valley. I saw grand, wide-open vistas, scattered with clusters of forests. I noticed a complete absence of buildings; simply beautiful rolling land, going all the way to the horizon.

The lilting song of a bird that I had never heard before, broke through my gaze and I turned toward the sound. The bird was sitting in a massive towering tree, resembling the giant Sequoias of the Pacific Northwest where I had visited years ago. They were so large you could drive trucks through the base of their behemoth trunks. Yet, this tree was even bigger; its base would encompass a very large home. The limbs were thick and full of green leaves with various flowers and fruits, just like on the boulevard. They spread upward and outward, reaching toward the heavens. The scents of many different flowers suddenly filled the atmosphere with the sweetest of fragrances. They were all distinct, yet they blended together like the many notes of an expensive perfume. The tree's monumental trunk was full of many knotted areas showing evidence of the times when branches had been pruned away. In that moment, I wondered why so many had been removed. David always sensing the right time to speak, replied to my questioning thought.

"You are looking at the Tree of Life from the Garden of Eden. It was moved here after the banishment of man from the Garden. Every tree you see down the hill and lining each side of the River were propagated from this tree. They are rooted and then transplanted along the River's boulevard. Everything about this tree and its transplants are important. Do you see how the roots of this tree grow?"

I looked down and saw the strangest thing. The roots went through the transparent gold pavement and into the River that was flowing from the throne, between the floor and the underlying foundation stones. They somehow assimilated through the glass, down into the water almost like a form of osmosis. Because of the transparent pavement, I could see the roots spreading out, reaching into the water and then burying themselves into the foundation stones. Once David knew I understood the root system, he continued.

"All the trees you see grow this way. Their roots get their life from the River. They transfer that life to every part of the tree. The roots secure themselves into the foundation for support and strength. The leaves have healing properties and each tree bears fruit continually. The fruits are all different. On any tree, at any time, twelve different ripe fruits are always available. For those who take a hold of wisdom, they embrace The Tree of Life. (34) To eat from its fruit brings life. Come on, let's walk down the terraces to one of the boulevard levels and rest. Jesus is coming to meet you."

"Jesus is coming?" My joy surged the instant I heard He was coming.

"Yes, He is coming for fellowship and to tell you some more things. Things that are on His heart."

We walked down the terraces, finally coming to where the boulevard was level. David motioned to a bench and we sat under the bough of one of the propagated Trees of Life. Its fragrance was intoxicating, and I imaged that the fruit must taste amazing. We didn't talk, but it was not strange or awkward. The serenity here with its sounds and smells kept my mind engaged in wonder. I couldn't say how long we sat. But time, as I had learned on the journey, was not "Chronos" time or "clock time" as in my world. Rather it was "Kairos" time, the "time of the divine moments".

"I see that you are enjoying the serenity and beauty of the *City*."

The voice of Jesus behind me, reeled me back from my contemplations about the twelve different fruits on the trees and whether they would be served at the marriage feast. Excitedly, I shot up off the bench and maneuvered to His side. He put His arms around me in a long bear hug that filled me with peace and contentment.

"Thank you, David, you can go now." Jesus said as he let go of me.

As I pulled back, I saw David nod at Jesus, smile at me and walk back up the terrace steps, toward the structure.

"Let's walk. I want to take you farther down the River and share some things with you." Jesus spoke with such love in His voice.

We walked in silence for a little while and stopped at another bench. It was then that I noticed a small row boat tied up at a landing on the River. It looked like the one I had climbed into so long ago in the basement of the cathedral.

"I see you recognized the boat." Jesus said. "Yes, it looks like your boat because it is your boat. The very one that we left so long ago when we started off across the land for Crown Derby. I have it here for a purpose."

"Purpose? Whatever would you need my boat for, here in the *City*?" I was confused. "I don't need it anymore. I've finished my journey and have arrived at my final home to be with You forever! Haven't I?"

"Yes and no." Jesus spoke each of the three words slowly, separately and distinctly. He accentuated each word with a slight head tilt to each side as He spoke them.

His response felt strange and my face must have shown it. Jesus smiled and took my hand in His.

"You know that I love you and I will never leave you, right?" I shook my head in quick agreement with His words.

"And you know that no man can take you out of my hand." I nodded my head again. With each question, I felt internal pressure building.

"I need you to go."

There was no smile on His face, He had a solemn and serious expression. Each spoken word reverberated off of the trees and every surface of the boulevard and came back to hit me in the face. I looked into His intense gaze for some clue behind the words, I saw purposeful earnestness in His eyes as He spoke the words again.

"I need you to go."

I didn't need for Him to say the words again because I had heard them the first time. What I needed in this moment, was to know why He would say those words to me. I thought I had completed my journey.

In that moment, it was like stepping off one of those high cliffs all over again! Everything solid was gone. How could this be? Astonished and dumbfounded, I couldn't even begin to process His words. It was not what I was expecting Him to say at all! I felt my inner self begin to fall in slow motion, head over heels, as I spiraled into nothingness.

Go! Why would He want me to go away when the journey had brought us together? I was wearing His ring. I had come to the City with His invitation to the wedding feast and celebration. He had even told me that I was His intended and beloved Bride. Why had David taken me to the center where I could trade the gifts for the crowns? These thoughts didn't add up to "I need you to go." I was heartbroken. The ghost of my safe twin wanted to resurrect itself. I'm sure all joy of life had drained from my expression and He could see my bewildered rejection.

"Peace, My Beloved, Peace!" His words, of course, instantly brought my inner being to rest.

As peace came into my spirit, the spiraling stopped. Then the words "I need you to go", began to recede into the recesses of my mind. Just when I was beginning to think I had learned how to always maintain peace, an experience would come my way, trying to steal peace from me. My head was filled with so many questions.

"Let me tell you a story." His words and His gaze told me He was waiting for me to say "Ok", I was willing to listen to Him. So, I nodded in affirmation. Somehow, I really needed His help to make sense of all of this.

"A certain man made a great supper, and he invited many people. He sent out his servant at supper time to tell those who were invited, 'Come, for everything is ready now.' But, they all began to make excuses. The first said to him, 'I have bought a field, and I must go and see it. Please have me excused.' Another said, 'I have bought five yokes of oxen, and I must go try them out. Please have me excused.' Another said, 'I have married a wife, and therefore I can't come.' The servant came back and told his lord these things. Then the master of the house, being angry, said to his servant, 'Go out quickly into the streets and lanes of the city, and bring in the poor, maimed, blind, and lame.' The servant said, 'Lord, knowing you would want a full house, I have already done this, and there is still room.' The lord said to the servant, 'Go out into the highways and hedges, and compel them to come in, that my house may be filled.'" (7)

As I looked into the face of Jesus, the call of Holy Spirit high above reached my ears.

In that instant, I had a flashback of how my awakened passion for Him had transformed into intense yearning for others to know of His love. I recalled how I wanted as many people as possible to experience the transformation of loving and being loved by Jesus and the Father. I could feel the same passion even now rising in me, as it did before, for the people of Decision Ville. I wanted His house to be full for the marriage supper. Many people's faces came flooding into my mind. In my own world before I had started on my journey, I knew many who lived in their own Crown Derby or Decision Ville every day. I had been one of them. So many souls were still in the valley of decision. So many souls needed to know the love of the Father and His Son, Jesus.

I understood. Yet, I was sure I had not grasped the full depth of it, because Jesus had been so intense in telling the story. This time David, Goodness and Mercy were not around to confirm what I was feeling and no Holy Spirit calls sounded to bring me clarity of action. I knew what He was asking. *Would I go and tell others of this place, of my journey and of His great love for the whole world. Could I leave this place for the sake of others who needed to know and experience what I now knew and experienced? Could I give up all of this now that I was here?* At the same time, I also felt the urgency to repeat words from so long ago, *Ok Jesus, what do you need me to do? Where do I need to go? How can I help?* So, with all my strength, knowingly giving up what I was seeing, experiencing and yet to experience, I allowed those words to re-emerge. I spoke them without hesitation before I could reconsider.

"Ok Jesus, what do you need me to do? Where do I need to go? How can I help?"

As I heard my spoken words resonate in my ears, I sensed a change in my inner being. I was now at peace. There was no fear this time. There was no doubt nor any hesitation. I knew staying here was not an option for me. I felt compelling love rise up within me for all those who did not know what I now knew. There were people out there who needed to come to know and feel, what I had come to know and feel. I had felt the transformation for some time now. The difference was at work, deep down inside my being, changing me, refining me, strengthening me. It was who I was becoming, because of the journey. I could feel His passion for people surging within me even more.

Without hesitation, I responded more forcefully, "Yes, I will go!"

I didn't question how it would happen, I didn't question when it would happen, I didn't need to question any longer. Those type of questions came from uncertainty and insecurity; two attributes of my old safe self. Now my only questions would be, "Where next, Jesus? Who next, Jesus?" Looking deeply with eyes reaching down into my soul, Jesus hugged me fiercely. I held on tight, drinking in all of His love and empowerment.

I knew that it might be awhile before I would be back here in the *City*. I smiled to myself at the thought of time. I smiled brighter knowing that I would be able to lead others on their journey to Jesus, the Father, and the *City*. I never doubted I could do it, because He is always Faithful and True. Jesus slowly let go of me and kissed my forehead.

"Thank you, dear beloved friend. I know that your passion and love will compel many to come and join us for the feast and celebration. Come, your time of rest is about finished here."

I knew what He meant. He was referring to the last tablet and its words about the symphony, where I was at rest while others were playing. But now my time to join in for the great finale, was about to begin. I still yearned to stay a little longer with Jesus.

"Come." He took my hand and led me to the small boat. Actually, I felt mixed emotions of sadness and joy. I wouldn't let myself dwell there, so I climbed into the familiar boat and sat down. As I looked up to Jesus on the edge of the pavement, I saw David standing behind Him, grinning big like he had gotten his heart's desire.

David handed the rod and staff in its small form back to Jesus.

"Here, Jesus, is her rod and staff."

They were still linked together with the rope, so they could be carried over my shoulder. Jesus took them and handed them down to me.

"You will need these as you go to bring others in." Jesus said with a proud look on His face.

I took them from His outstretched hands. As I took hold of them, I felt the familiar weight of the mantle rest upon my shoulders once again. I laid the rod and staff securely in the bottom of the boat. Then I saw that David pick a big piece of fully ripe fruit. David handed it to Jesus who passed it to me.

"Take and eat." Jesus said.

"Now?"

"Yes. It will last you until you return to the *City*."

I took a huge bite of the shiny, firm fruit. Juice ran down from my mouth onto my chin and dripped on my shirt. I laughed, wiping my face with the back of the other hand. This fruit could become my favorite food from now on. I took another bite with the same effects of juice, drips and wiping.

"What is this fruit called?" I asked Jesus, swallowing and taking another bite.

"Love".

I immediately choked with the thought that love could be tasted as well as touched and viewed. It hit me all at once. A warm wonderful feeling filled my spirit, as the bites were settling into my stomach. I sat amazed, in awe.

Jesus continued. "It's the most wonderful of all the fruits grown on the Trees and that makes it the greatest to have. Now you know its taste and fullness. You can share its fruit with all those that you are going to meet on your new journey."

Jesus intently studied my face. "I do understand the sacrifice you are making!" He said it with a serious tone. Our eyes locked and His love poured into my soul. Then Jesus said quietly, "It's time. It's your time to play Our love song for others to hear. Now go. I will see you soon."

With that, Jesus and David pushed the boat out into the middle of the River. Like many other travels on the River, the current was deep and slowly began to move me down stream; away from Jesus, David and into my destiny. As I watched, David and Jesus got further and further away. I looked away from them for a quick moment to capture the *City's* greatness and glory into my mind's eye. I turned back with tears. David waved and turned back, walking toward the structure. Jesus continued to stand and look at me. He got smaller as I moved down stream, but I could still feel the immense love of His gaze across the distance, as I drew near the wall.

WALL! A moment of panic hit me as I remembered that the River flowed through a huge grate on the other side of the *City*. How would I get through? Certainly, there was a gate or grate here too. I turned to look at what was ahead. I saw I was quickly approaching a gate, but it was going up in a timely manner so that I could safely exit. I passed through and lost sight of Jesus as the River took a slight turn. I watched the gate lower, preventing anyone gaining entry. No one was going to enter as a thief.

The River picked up speed and I passed quickly through the area I had seen while gazing from the open wall of the *City* structure. I was in new territory. I got comfortable since I didn't have to row because of the speed of the current. The current kept the boat right in the middle of the River, so I decided to sit back, relax and finish the piece of love fruit. I was amazed that although it was sweet, my hands and face were not sticky from the juice. I started to put the core in my pocket and felt something. I pulled it out and found my invitation, all rolled up in perfect condition. I smiled and put it back. I knew I could share it with those starting their own journey with Jesus. I put the core in the opposite pocket and settled in for my new journey. I was warm and full. The light from the *City* was still brilliant and I was at peace. I knew that the River would bring me to where I needed to go next. I had no worries or fears, only the sense that an adventure with Jesus awaited me. Holy Spirit's piecing sound caused me to glance up, I saw Him circling, looking down at me. I waved, and we connected in the Spirit. I knew then that He was going with me and was comforted with that thought. Now it was time for a good nap because I would need my strength soon enough. A symphony was about to begin.

Chapter 12

Full Circle

"The old things have passed away. Behold, all things have become new." 2 Corinthians 5:17

It was the hard thump, that caused the hand cradling my head to fall away and make sudden hard contact with the bench. As I got my bearings, the first thing I noticed was it was shadowy. The absence of any brilliant light brought me quickly upright and alert. Shadows always meant that darkness could be near. Experience with shadows on my journey had taught me to be cautious and aware. It also meant I was not near the *City* anymore. Something was blocking the light. As my eyes adjusted to the shadows, damp smells caught my attention. I looked around and saw that my boat was resting against stone steps and a short stone wall that channeled the water. I knew instantly where I was. I had come full circle on the River. I was back in the cathedral basement where my inconceivable journey had begun.

How long had I been away? I couldn't say for sure ... days ... weeks ... years? What about Jenny? Would she have reported me missing? Oh my gosh! What about my family? Had they been trying to reach me since I had been gone?

All I knew was that my journey had returned me to my world. Realizing this, I wondered if my old safe, negative twin came back too. It all seemed such a lifetime ago that I first stepped into this boat to begin a journey full of wonder, intrigue, trepidation and joy. I waited for the old safe twin's negative words to swirl within me, instead laughter bubbled up and out. My laughter echoed down the cathedral hallways. In that moment, I knew I was not the same person that had left this cathedral. I was so different. I was transformed and I was thankful.

The events, struggles, and encounters of my journey were real, in ways I didn't fully understand; they had changed me from the inside out. I closed my eyes and I could see the *City* with its shining brilliance as if I were standing right there. I could see Jesus standing as He watched me float down the River and even David's smile and wave. I waited to hear Holy Spirit's call but nothing came. I was disappointed. I had grown so accustomed to Holy Spirit's piercing call as He communicated to me. I guess He would show up when I needed Him.

As the boat jostled against the steps, I refocused. I knew I needed to get up, move out, and step into a brand-new life adventure. "Adventure", it was David's word. Now it was mine. So, I bent over and picked up the rod and staff. As I did, they disappeared from sight. They hadn't gone away because I could still feel their weight and substance in my hand and on my shoulder. The familiar weight of the mantle still rested on my shoulders. Everything was tangibly present, only invisible. I looked down at my betrothal ring and saw it fading. I could feel its firmness and substance, but like the rod and staff, it too had become invisible. Reaching up to my neck, I felt the gold chain with all the gifts. Yes, they were still present, and the touchstone warmed to my fingers. But I knew they would become invisible, until I returned to the other dimension where the *City* awaited me. I reached into each pocket and pulled out the fruit core and the scrolled invitation, both were visible. The core of fruit began to manifest into a full ripe piece. I watched in fascination as the fruit took its fully ripened shape. I was tempted to take a bite because it had tasted so good, when I noticed that it began fading. The fruit and the scroll slowly faded from view, although, I held them in my grasp.

I rejoiced at the thought that the supernatural world was now forever with me; at work in my world. I was back in my world, yes and no. I'm still Melissa, but not the Melissa that cringed at the word adventure. My life would now be my adventure, only without fear.

"It was never your world, it's always been Mine, and I've just been waiting for the real Melissa to appear." The voice of Jesus sounded as if He was standing right in front of me.

His words told me, I have access to the supernatural. I could share the invitation to the feast and celebration freely. I could share the fruit of love fully with those He would direct me to, confident, His love would never run out. It also meant, that everything I had seen, learned and experienced, will always be useful on my new journey. One final check was needed. I breathed in deeply. The familiar mist filled my lungs, giving me energy and life as it had done so many times before.

Putting the invisible fruit and scroll back into my pockets, I climbed out onto the steps. As soon as my feet left the boat, it quickly drifted away and headed to the archway where my River journey had begun. Part of me wanted to jump in, grab hold, and go back. Another part of me was looking forward to what the Father and Jesus had in store for me. I looked for my watch which I had not seen or even thought about for so long. I rubbed my eyes and looked again. *How? No way!* The invisible now visible watch, said I still had about twenty minutes to go before I was to meet Jenny. *How could that be correct?* The date and time were clear, yet somehow, a lifetime of events had transpired in only a few moments of time. Again, I laughed. I was liking this new me and the ability to flow with the supernatural. I pondered again, how the tablet spoke of time being manipulated by its Creator. Time could be stretched out and time could be compressed. I was thankful that the fullness of my journey had taken the time necessary to transform me. I remembered everything and would cherish each moment forever.

I made my way through the basement hallway with a slight angst of finding my way back up to the entrance. I wasn't exactly sure how to get back upstairs because of the round-a-bout way I had ended up down here to begin with. But in a few short strides, I found some large broad stairs and a sign indicating they led to the main floor and exit. Like many things on this pilgrimage, I knew they had been hidden from me, waiting for this moment. I had no regrets. I knew that my steps had been directed for my destiny. I quickly ascended to the main floor and found the exit. The same guard was standing at the door as when I went in. He acknowledged me and so I went over to verify the date and time on my watch. Sure enough, it was accurate.

As I started out the door, the guard said, "Hey, you should come again and spend more time here since you haven't been here long. There's a lot here to see and explore. I hear they have opened up the basement area too, but it might be boring, because I hear there isn't anything down there but some water or stream or something like that."

I chuckled to myself and smiled. "Oh, you would be surprised at all I have seen while visiting. I wouldn't say the basement is boring at all." The guard returned a puzzled look at my remark and shook his head.

My feet skipped down the outside steps and I headed across the street, making my way back to the terminal station. As I did, I glanced back, for one last look at the cathedral. It was grand and stately but, oh, what secrets it held! Looking back toward the station, to my surprise, I spotted him. David was across the street, leaning with his back against the building. One leg was bent, his foot resting on the building, all casual. He was dressed as he had been on the train. Looking at him, no one would have ever guessed he was an angel, but I knew. He smiled his familiar dear smile as I waved to Him. He waved back. I quickened my pace to reach him and hugged him fiercely.

He laughed saying, "What was that for?"

"I never thought I'd see you again."

"Oh, I'll be around." He said. "Sometimes you'll see me and sometimes you will simply know I'm near."

As he said that, I heard the piercing call of Holy Spirit high above me. We both looked up, He was circling and hovering. I connected with Him immediately.

"I am always with you, hovering and brooding, even when you do not see me. Just connect and I will be there." His words were affirming and strengthening.

"He's here! I can see and hear Him, just like I see and hear you!" David laughed and shook his head in agreement. Holy Spirit made one of His endearing sounds as He descended closer.

David explained. "You see Him now to validate the reality of His Presence and know that He is always with you no matter where you are. After this, He will be invisible like the spiritual gifts, fruit, invitation, rod and staff. You will always hear His voice because Jesus has you covered." David's spoke with delight. "In fact, you may see Jesus sometimes down the road on your new journey."

Jesus! Here! The thought of getting a Jesus hug, made me giddy with joy.

"Let's head to the station. You have luggage to reclaim, remember?" David's words brought me back.

With the thought of luggage, I remembered the locker retrieval bracelet from checking my bags. Sure enough, just like my watch, the bracelet was now visible. I couldn't remember seeing either of them on the journey. Yet now, they were visible and things from my other world were not. Lessons kept coming to me and I took note to remember. I smiled that I still had things to learn about life's journey with God.

We retrieved my luggage, ready to exit the station. As I grabbed my backpack purse, my phone chimed a text. I had forgotten about my cell phone. Pulling it out, a text from Jenny popped up saying she would be there in a few minutes.

"She is right on time," David said with laughter in his voice. "It took creative maneuvering by some unfettered sheep, blocking the roadway to coordinate her arrival. You know, she does like to speed at times."

I shook my head and laughed a deep contented laugh. All things were in the Father's control. In quiet meditation, we headed outside to meet Jenny. David helped with the bags as we made our way to the street side loading zone where Jenny would pull in to meet me. I looked at my watch. It was just now the designated time to meet. God was never too early or too late, He was always right on time.

"Here, you're going to need this too. Put it in your carry-on."

David pulled the torch from his jacket and handed it to me. For a brief moment, I could see its brilliant light, but quickly in the hand-off, it became invisible. I unzipped my bag and placed it securely inside.

"You will need light here in your world too! There are many places where He will lead you on your journey, places where the light has grown dim and deception has brought its shadows; cooling passions and numbing hearts. The light and its warmth are desperately needed to change the atmosphere for Holy Spirit to work on hearts."

I wanted to hear more, but Jenny was pulling into the loading zone. As she got out, David and I made our way over to the trunk of her car. I hugged Jenny. After a moment, she pulled back and looked intently at my face.

"Ok, so what's going on with you? You're radiant and there is definitely something else different. You seem at peace and relaxed, yet your eyes are intensely alive. I thought surely you would be stressed to the max from travel and every other thing outside of your comfort zone." Jenny stared at me like I had two heads or an alien body.

I laughed. "Well it's a long story, which I'll share on our drive. You are one of the few people I know, who would believe the strange turn of events that I've had."

"Really? Oh, do tell! I can't wait! You know how I love a good adventure. At least I assume it was a good adventure since you look calm and radiant."

"Yes, it was the best time of my life!"

"Now, I am dying to know! Let's get loaded up, so you can fill me in!"

As Jenny turned to help put the bags into the trunk, David stepped out from behind, drawing her attention. "Oh, who is this?", she said, a little shocked by his appearing. I wondered if David had been invisible and then suddenly appeared. Undaunted by his abrupt appearance, her face was smiling, like he might be a romantic cause for the change she saw in me.

"Oh no!" I laughed, hearing her inquisitive tone of question. "This is not my boyfriend. But he is a great friend and helper that I met on the train." I wanted to blurt out that he was an angel and to tell her everything, but I reeled myself in and said, "Jenny, meet David. David, my best friend", I paused to word the rest of my statement cryptically, "here in my world. Meet Jenny."

David's eyes sparkled at my cryptic meaning and put out his hand to shake Jenny's. As he did, a brief look of recognition flashed across Jenny's face.

"I've met you before, haven't I? You were working with another man that had come to help me on a mission trip one time. Is that right?"

"Yes, absolutely! His name was Micah." David confirmed her question. My head started to jerk around at the surprise of hearing that I too had met Micah in Crown Derby but caught myself. I just smiled.

"You worked for a large business, specializing in resources and management. Right?"

"You have a good memory." David smiled.

In that moment, I knew. David and Micah had been tasked to help Jenny. She probably didn't know that they were angels sent to help her. I suddenly thought, *Had I ever encountered the help of angels before and didn't have a clue?* David looked at me and winked! *Now did that mean I had, or was he acknowledging I was becoming more aware of life in the supernatural?* I would definitely have that conversation with him another time.

I knew then, I was going to be able to open Jenny up to a new adventure and understanding of the supernatural. She had always been the one to open my eyes to deep and hidden truths of scriptures. Now it was my turn. Oh, I couldn't wait for the drive. It was going to blow her mind.

Turning to David, I hugged him again. "I'm sure I'll see you around. Let's keep in touch. Maybe you, Goodness and Mercy could come my way sometime. I'd love it, if we could talk more about those atmospheric changes." David shook with laughter.

"Yes, that's a great idea." He could hardly get the words out.

"Tell them, I said hi."

"Oh, I'm sure we'll see each other soon."

"Ready?" Jenny asked.

"Oh, I am so ready to see what God does on this trip. It's going to be an adventure, I know."

Jenny shot a quizzical look my way. That was not the response that the old me would have ever given. As I opened the passenger door, Jenny walked around and got in to drive. I turned and waved to David, standing much like Jesus had done as I floated down the River. I turned and secretly wiped away a tear that Jenny didn't see.

"Hey, who are Goodness and Mercy? Did you meet them on the train too?" Jenny asked as she pulled out to head home. I didn't think she had picked up on that.

"Oh, where do I begin?" I took a deep breath of the mist, as I gathered the energy and wisdom to tell her about my journey.

"Ok, I'll start with David and his advice to fill my time while I waited for you. He suggested exploring the old cathedral. By the way, did you know that a river runs through the basement of that place?" Not giving her time to answer, I quickly continued.

"Well, let me tell you of my little adventure while waiting. It has been the most incredible and transforming journey! Oh, the things I have to tell!"

Cited Scriptures and References

1. All Scriptures are taken from the World English Bible (WEB)
2. I Worship You, Almighty God by Don Moen, album Worship with Don Moen, 1992
3. Matthew 4:16
4. John 8:12
5. Isaiah 35:8
6. Isaiah 35:8-10
7. Matthew 13:45-46
8. Acts 8:39-40
9. Revelation 19:11
10. Romans 11:36
11. Luke 14:15-23
12. Romans 8;1
13. Hebrews 13:5
14. John 14:6
15. Psalm 85:8
16. John 12:35-36
17. Numbers 22:26-27
18. Hebrews 2:14-16
19. John 8:12
20. Philippians 4:13
21. John 16:33
22. Song of Solomon 2:10
23. Matthew 13:11-12,15
24. Matthew 13:16
25. Matthew 4:10

26. Mark 1:15
27. Matthew 6:25
28. Psalm 46:1-2
29. Psalm 103:20
30. Isaiah 30:21
31. Mark 10:27
32. Petra Siq: Bourbon, Fabio (1999). *Petra: Jordan's Extraordinary Ancient City*. New York: Barnes & Noble Books. ISBN 0-7607-2022-3.The Siq is the main entrance to the ancient Nabatean city of Petra in southern Jordan. Also known as Siqit. Unlike slot canyons such as Antelope Canyon in the American Southwest, which are directly shaped by water, the Siq is a natural geological fault split apart by tectonic forces; only later was it worn smooth by water. The walls that enclose the Siq stand between 91–182 meters (299–597 ft) in height.
33. Matthew 25:21
34. Proverbs 3:18
35. Hebrews 11:1
36. Luke 10:19
37. John1:1
38. Psalm 93:4
39. John 4:32
40. 2 Peter 3:8
41. Matthew 8:23-27, Matthew 14:22-33
42. Hymn by Horatio Spatford
43. Psalm 23:4
44. Deuteronomy 31:8
45. 1 John 2:16
46. Trust and Obey by John Sammia
47. Psalm 34:8
48. Graham Cooke
49. Psalm 139:16-17

About the Author

Betty A. Rodgers-Kulich
Contact: contact@transformed-image.com
Website: transformed-image.com

Betty is an ordained pastor and serves as an Associate Pastor along with her husband Rick of 47 years, at the Redeemer's Church in Columbus, Ohio, teaching and preaching since 2003. Betty is a minister who believes in the power of the Holy Spirit to enable her messages to become rhema words for the listener, opening doors that they may be transformed into the image of Christ.

She ministers with the power of the Holy Spirit for healing, transformation and release from the past. Over the years she has gained much wisdom about "taking up our personal cross".

Betty also serves as a Women's Conference Director for Harvest Preparation International Ministries (HPIM), a non-profit Biblical ministry, that trains and impacts leaders globally. She travels internationally doing women's conferences, teaching, developing and mentoring other women. Betty's passion is to see individuals come to know Jesus intimately as their personal savior, develop a deep relationship with Him, become transformed into His image and grow into a leader that builds His Kingdom!

CPSIA information can be obtained
at www.ICGtesting.com
Printed in the USA
BVHW082143020622
638529BV00003B/4

9 781630 505387